ABSOLUTION
SAVAGE DUET PART TWO

RUSSO SAGA
BOOK FIVE

NICOLINA MARTIN

nicolina martin

Editing by Sandra Havro

Cover Design by Deranged Doctor

For my love of enemies to lovers.

PART ONE
SACRIFICE

ONE

Christian

Finding Kerry and Cecilia again is a lot more complicated than I'd have ever thought.

Have I changed?

Or do I just keep destroying?

I struggle against the wind next to her, slipping in the mud, trembling from the cold, and the shock of waking up only a few moments ago to find the front door slammed open, ice cold gusts of wind whirling through the room. Far off in the darkness I see the little light in the kitchen window. Too far. I can't believe she took the risk of taking Cecilia out in this weather. In the middle of the fucking night! I should've just kept her tied up and saved myself the trouble. She's so fucking stubborn. I have to admire her incredible strength, and I must admit my defeat, at the very least to myself. I've underestimated her.

Again.

History repeats itself.

When we're finally inside, I slam the door closed behind us, drowning us in darkness. Kerry stumbles and falls to her knees. At this very moment I don't give a shit about how she feels, but I do care about the little life next to her

"Let her go now, Kerry."

She's too weak to protest and, freeing Cecilia from Kerry's clutch, I unwrap the blanket and assess her status. Her cheeks are rosy and she's fast asleep, only stirring slightly when I push a tendril of dark hair off her cheek. She smells outdoorsy, fresh. I don't want to wake her, so I only take off the thickest clothes and then carefully place her back in her crib. I study the little person, something warm flaring in my chest, warmth that turns to black heat as I think about Kerry endangering her out there. I stalk back out to her mother who is still sitting on her knees on the cold floor, wet, with twigs, leaves and some mud on her jacket and in her hair, tears streaming down her face.

"What the fuck were you thinking?"

She answers with a sob.

I sway. As the adrenaline slips away, I realize how foggy my mind is. I don't recognize myself, and that I'd sleep through her leaving the house is extremely unlikely. My heart speeds up as fury fills me. The coffee. The overly sweetened coffee.

"Did you drug me?" I grab her hard by her nape, forcing her to look at me. "Answer me!"

All she does is wail and I let her go with a push that sends her tumbling to the floor. I have to occupy myself with something or I'll hurt her, so I go to the only person in this house who doesn't hate me. My little miracle of a daughter.

She's breathing regularly, her skin is warm and has good color. She seems all right. When I turn, I almost bump into Ker who's standing in the doorway, hunched, swaying.

"How is she?" Her voice quavers.

"What do you care?" I growl and push at her chest to get her out of my way. I flinch when she grabs my arm.

"It's a prescription, Christian. For her. From when she was a baby. It isn't dangerous. I'm sorry." Her voice trails off.

I swallow and my dry throat rasps. I have slept too little in the last few days, but I feel dizzy in an uncomfortable way that I can't seem to get rid of. I grab her wrist hard and twist it, backing her out into the main room. She winces but doesn't try to free herself.

"What the *fuck* do I do with you?" I snarl, forcing her down on her knees before me. I want to shake her, slap her, but I fight it. I don't want to hurt Kerry again.

Kerry

"I hoped you'd sleep. That it'd make you sleep deeper... that's all... I didn't try to kill you, Christian," I sob.

He's silent and then he barks out a laugh. "Did you try to drug a full-grown man with stuff prescribed for a baby?"

"Why didn't you just sleep?" I cry.

"It's fucking hard, sweetheart, with the front door wide open to a storm. You should've done a better job closing it. Why the hell did you try to go out there? It's insane."

"W—why?" I look up at him, sitting back on my heels. "*Why?* I only did what every sane person would do in my place!"

"What? Go out into a storm with a baby in the middle of the night? In a car that's not going anywhere?"

"I couldn't have known it wouldn't start!"

"What the hell were you thinking?"

"We're *hostages*, Christian! You're keeping us hostage! You're dangerous, unpredictable, a known killer, a... a murderer. You've hurt me..." I swallow hard. "God only knows what you'll do to us if we don't get away from you. I had to try and save my baby."

"You—What the *fuck!* I've *told* you I'm not here to hurt you!"

I glance at him. His face is a mask of deadly anger.

I scoff. "Everything you've done so far has proven otherwise." I rub the back of my head. It hurts where he pulled my hair in the fight.

"And I'm not a 'known' killer!" he sneers.

"You're known to me," I mutter.

He regards me but doesn't answer. Instead he starts pacing the floor. "She's my kid too, Kerry."

His? Who the hell does he think he is?

A shudder wracks my body. I'm so cold and wet. I don't think there's a dry thread left on me and the room's cold, the floor's even colder. I jerk when he grabs my arm and pulls me back up, pushing me in the direction of the couch.

"Sit!"

I fall onto the cushions. Swaying with defeat and bottomless exhaustion, I pull the throw blanket off the armrest and wrap it tightly around me. A sob escapes me. Then another. And another. "Why did you come here?" My breath hitches as I stutter out the words. Warm tears make their way over my cold cheeks, pooling under my chin. "Why did you have to destroy everything I've built up? Again." I pull the blanket even tighter, still shivering violently.

He paces the floor in front of me and when he stops, I expect anything but what he says.

"I want you, Kerry. I couldn't stop thinking about you, and about her. And then you had to go and fuckin' disappear on me!"

For a moment I'm stunned by his honesty, then a red haze of fury washes over me. "Well, you can't *have* me," I scream. "You blew that, *Chris!* I'm never forgiving what you've done to me! How can you even *think* that I— that *we...* You're so pathetic!" I stare up at him in defiance.

His jaw clenches and he's a frightening vision with the growing rage flaring as an aura around him. It electrifies the air between us and wraps me in the storm that suddenly boils inside my living room and not only outside. He takes a step closer, his moves measured, unnaturally calm, controlled, showing no emotion. I cringe, closing my eyes to block out the sight of him as he grips my chin and squeezes it, tilting my head.

"You really don't know when to stop, do you?" he rasps, his breath hot on my face.

When he removes his hand, it leaves a cold patch on my skin. He sighs heavily and I open my eyes again to peer at him. His eyes are closed. He's still bent over me and with his nostrils flaring, it looks as if he's inhaling my scent.

"I'm trying, Kerry, I'm trying so fucking hard." His eyes are pitch black when he opens them, soulless, and my gut clenches.

"Well, that's the thing, isn't it? It's not there. You have to try. There's no compassion, no humanity—"

I scream when he slams his palm to the wall behind me, an inch from my head, and my heart darts up to my throat. "You don't get to talk about compassion!" he growls. "You risked her *life!* If I hadn't woken up— What the *fuck* did you think you were doing? You're just as much of a monster as I am, reckless and stupid. I should fucking take her. She'd be better off."

New tears well up in my eyes and I swallow hard against the panic that threatens to cloud my mind, forcing myself to meet his dark gaze. His words hit home. I don't want to admit it, but they hurt, because they carry some truth. Did I still really think he was going to hurt us when I left, or am I just so stuck in old tracks that I'd rather risk Cecilia's well-being than actually stop and think?

Guilt consumes me, tearing through my chest as if I have eaten barbed wire. "Please," I whisper, "please, don't take her from me. I'll do anything. I can change."

His eyes are cold as he glares down at me. "Anything? Is that so?"

I realize my mistake too late. That's not something you offer a man like him. "I..."

I don't know what to say, and from the glint in his eyes it's obvious he sees my inner conflict, the turmoil that makes my head spin. His hands come up to my cheeks, cupping them, rubbing away the tears with the pads of his thumbs.

"You're dancing on razor blades, Kerry. Push and pull. All the fucking time. I know you think you know me, but it's nothing but your own made-up stuff. You don't know shit about who I am and the things I've done."

But I do. I know him so terrifyingly well. With his hands on me again, his skin on mine once more, I remember it all. The pain, the violence, and the hurt. He's just... incapacitated. This is all he knows. The cruelty, the force, the power games.

I'm not excusing him, but I get it.

This is not what he wants, the threats, the rage. I know it. I cup my hands over his. His skin is so cold. Mine is just as cold.

"I won't run again. I promise."

"I'm not sure I believe a word you say." He pulls his hands out of mine and straightens, magnificent, terrifying, where he stands, towering over me.

I scoff. "That's rich, coming from you."

He frowns as his eyes dart to mine, then he shakes his head and drops onto the couch next to me. Lifting the blanket, he stares at my soaked clothes.

"What the fuck, Kerry? Go and change or you'll catch a cold."

"I'm too tired." And I am. I have no energy left whatsoever; our last fight took the very last ounce I had, and I just want to sit here. I just want to sleep.

"That's not good enough."

"Since when do you worry 'bout my health?" I slur. "That's just so... not you."

"Since now. Raise your arms."

I obey and he yanks off my wet pullover and my thicker sweater in one move. My two T-shirts cling to my body and I have goosebumps all over as I hug myself, shaking violently.

"You have two choices. Either I undress you, or you do it yourself, either way you're getting in the shower."

His suggestion shoots heat straight between my legs. I want his touch. But I can't have it. How can I let him close again? I can't. Yet again it washes over me. I could have been dead, murdered by these hands, the hands that rest hot on my cold arms, making me tingle in all the wrong places.

Then the moment passes, and the choice is taken away from me.

"Arms up, Ker."

Our eyes meet. He doesn't let go and I'm sucked into the depths of that dark gaze that is filled with too many emotions for one human to carry alone. I inhale erratically as I obediently raise my arms. Christian grabs the hems of my T-shirts and pulls them up and over my head. I have no bra and my hands fly down to cover my breasts as I stare at him.

Christian shakes his head, and puts a large palm against my cheek. "Sweetheart, relax. You're frozen blue. No matter how hot I normally find you, you look like a wet puppy right now, and that's not a great turn-on."

I scoff. My arms remain where they are.

"Stand up, hon."

I dart up. "I can take it from here." I am *so* not getting naked in front of him. That's... No way. "I'll go shower."

He smiles, and it's the most beautiful sight ever. "Good girl. Hop into the bathroom. I'll bring you a bunch of dry clothes."

"You've sure made yourself comfortable here."

"Had to. Had to look for anything you could use as a weapon."

I snort. "And here I was thinking you'd turned domestic."

"Nah. It's me 'needing' to be nice."

I shake my head and stumble into the bathroom, locking the door behind me.

"And Ker!" he shouts.

"Yeah?"

"I really am sorry."

Sure. Okay. I know *he* thinks he means it. I fall back against the door once I'm alone and exhale. I tremble hard as I pull off my pants and underwear, and it's not only from the cold. The rollercoaster that is being around this man makes my head spin.

"I want you, Kerry."

Good God! How do I get out of this?

Two

Christian

It's one a.m. and I'm fighting sleep while I listen to the clattering sound of her showering. I shiver inside a damp blanket, the same one Kerry had on a few moments ago. Trying to make myself useful, and to get a little less cold, I get up and grab a couple of towels from a shelf in her cupboard and wipe the puddles of water and the mud off the floor. Then I sit and listen again. It's quiet from inside the bathroom and I wish I knew what she is doing. I wish even more I knew what she's thinking. I see her before me. The way she looked long ago, before I killed the light in her eyes. I wonder what it'll take to get it back.

If anything ever will.

Trying to keep my teeth from chattering, I huddle in the blanket. I should light a fire, but I'm too drowsy. Running through the woods, fighting her, and the arguing took my last energy reserves. My knee screams at me whenever I move and my shoulder pounds ominously. I just don't have the will to examine it closer.

I jerk awake when the bathroom door opens, and a cloud of warm-wet, soap-scented air fills the living room. My heart already pounds hard and, a few moments later, when she materializes through the mist, it feels like it's gonna beat its way out of my chest. She's dressed in flannel pajamas, covered from top to toe in pink roses. The one I found and put in a neatly folded pile right outside the bathroom door. On her feet, fluffy white fleece socks. Her face looks naked, new somehow. Her short black hair is still wet, unbrushed, and lies in unruly tresses around her head. Like a dark halo. She's so fucking beautiful.

"Cute." I nod toward the outfit.

"It was a gift." She fiddles with the collar and adjusts the top button. "Christian..." She walks up to me, hesitantly. "Oh my God, you're soaked. *You* have to get out of *your* clothes. Now."

I grin. "Are you offering?"

She raises an eyebrow as her face stiffens.

I backpedal. That wasn't clever. "Sorry. I haven't got any other clothes."

"I've got some that should fit. You get out of that now."

She disappears into the little hallway on the opposite side of the room, the one with the jammed backdoor. I start fighting my shirt but my left shoulder refuses to let me raise my arm enough and I have to give up. I yank and pull to get out of my pants instead. When I look up, my soggy pants clutched in my hands, she's standing in front of me, her eyes wide. She's holding a pile of clothes and hands them to me with trembling arms. Her eyes dart between my naked legs and my face.

"Here," she says. "I... You..."

I take the clothes and look through the pile. There's a pair of green cargo pants, a thick checkered flannel shirt, thick fleece socks, a couple of T-shirts. I look back up. She appears calmer again, chewing on her lip as she studies me.

"Where've you been hiding these gems?"

"In the back. They were my dad's. I—I couldn't throw them away."

I take in her solemn features. She still mourns her old man. "I heard. I'm sorry."

"Thank you," she says quietly.

"He went way too young."

"Dad had a massive heart attack. He died instantly. We had no idea he was ill. He rode his bike to work every day, seemed healthy as a horse."

I reach out with my good arm and lay a hand on her shoulder. "You were close?"

Kerry looks down at her feet, not pulling away, almost leaning into my touch as if I'm really comforting her. "Yes," she whispers. She sighs and closes her eyes and I don't know how to interpret the look on her face. "Where do we go from here, Christian?"

I study her, letting my eyes roam over her straight little nose, the plump – very kissable – lips, the damp dark tresses of hair. Clenching my hand into a fist, I have to fight the urge to pull her to me. "Ker. None of us are going anywhere the way it looks outside. When that day comes... we'll just take it from there. Okay?"

She bites her bottom lip and nods as she looks up at me, her dark green eyes flooring me with the depth of emotions in there. Very much like the first time I saw her. Flashes of a tipsy, over-confident redhead in a bar shoot through my mind. So much has happened between then and now. Not only years, but hurt, betrayal, Cecilia. Her eyes are the same, and yet, with the underlying solemnity that permeates her whole being, they aren't.

"Okay." Turning on her heel, she leaves for the bedroom and pulls the door closed behind her.

I remain standing, looking at the closed door. My chest tightens. I wish I could have helped her get warm, hold her tight, take some of her pain away. Her lips were still bluish and her skin so pale. Myself, I feel hotter than hell right now. It must be all the fighting, all the adrenaline. Sorting through the pile of clothes, I then put on stuff I'd normally never wear. Cargo pants that hang loose on my hips, a thick gray flannel shirt that I pull on over my own shirt. I don't have the energy to take it off when it should dry up soon enough anyway. I look like a new man. A new man I right now wish I was. For her. Them.

It's hard to find a comfortable position on the narrow couch. My shoulder hurts worse than ever. I'm too tired to look at it now. I'll do it tomorrow. I toss and turn. I'm so drained I could throw up, but I can't sleep. My shirt is wet from sweat and I shiver constantly even though my cheeks burn. And the damn shoulder throbs.

I dart up, pull off the flannel shirt and again try to wriggle out of the still soaked one, but it clings to my body and it's impossible. I try ripping it to pieces with my good arm, but it doesn't budge over my shoulders where the seams are stronger, and I end up with shreds. Why do I have to buy such fuckin' high quality clothes? Tiptoeing to her bedroom door, I listen for sounds of breathing. I hear Cecilia's light snoring and an occasional snivel, but nothing else. I push the crack wider and enter. Spotting the contour of Kerry in the bed, I bend over her and intend to whisper in her ear.

"What do you want?" she whispers tersely before I have a chance to say anything.

"I need help."

"With what?"

My cheeks heat up even more, and I suddenly feel as if I'm intruding. "It's nothing. Go back to sleep." I turn to leave.

I jerk when she grabs my wrist. "With what?"

"I need help getting my shirt off."

Her silence is deafening, and I'm surprised when she gets up. "Sure."

I stumble to the table by the couch and sit on it. I'm dizzy and nauseous. She could overpower me easily right now because I'm a wreck. I can only hope she won't notice. I look up at the woman before me. She is pale but looks calm and as spent as I feel.

"My shoulder hurts... it's stiff and swollen and I can't get this shirt off. It's wet still and—"

"I see you've tried. You've ruined it completely." She plucks at the strips that hang over my chest.

I nod. "It wouldn't budge. I can't get my arm up in the right angle to get it off. It's too strained. It's ridiculous."

"It's okay. I got it." She pulls the right shirt arm off behind my back, yanking at the material that almost sits like one with my skin. Then she carefully peels off the left one the same way.

I shiver when her fingertips touch my skin as she works the shirt.

"My God, Christian. You're burning hot."

"I'm cold as hell, Ker."

"Yeah, your arms are, but up here you're so warm." She touches my left shoulder, and her fingers leave traces that burn hotter than any fever. "Your dragon is scorching," she says with a short laugh, her fingertips resting on my tattoo.

"Thanks," I growl and suddenly need to pull away. There's clearly one part of me that isn't tired. At all. I want to pull her to me and...

Do what? She'd scream and beat me.

"How does your wound look?" To my great surprise her voice is suddenly laced with worry.

"It's fine," I snap. I don't need her hands on me again.

"Let me have a look."

"What for? It's fine."

"Christian! You stubborn cretin. Let me."

"All right. Whatever." I shrug, feigning indifference, the indifference I should be feeling.

She pulls at the makeshift bandage that has covered the wound since yesterday. "Why did you let your hair grow so long?" she asks as she works the strips, her eyes darting up to meet mine, then back to focus on her task.

Layer after layer comes off.

"Why did you cut yours short?" I reply. "I don't like the black. It's not you."

She pulls at one of her short choppy tresses, twisting it around her index finger. "I didn't want to be me anymore."

I nod. It stings, because I think I understand why. "I stopped caring. It grew."

She stops and regards me. "Hmm. I'd have figured you as vain."

I scoff. "Vain?"

"Definitely. Pretty boy-vain."

"And you haven't been 'pretty girl-vain', then?"

That was a long time ago," she says quietly and looks away.

Her last words wrap us in an uncomfortable silence. I clear my throat to say I can take it from here, wanting to get her out of the room. It's as much for her sake as for mine. But what comes out sounds a lot harsher than intended.

"Leave. Go the fuck back to sleep, Ker."

She lets go of my shoulder and takes a step back.

"You're such a dick, Christian. You know that, right?" Her lips tighten and her nostrils flare, then she turns on her heel and leaves. I have no words. No words of comfort. No clever replies.

Fucking. Nothing.

THREE

Kerry

Cece sleeps until nine. Had I been awake I would have worried and wondered. But I slept like the dead. My first real sleep since *he* came here. I wonder if he has slept too. I let her down on the floor. Slipping my feet into a pair of thick socks, I tiptoe out into the main room. Cece isn't as subtle and barges out, her feet pattering against the floorboards.

"Bwekfaa!" she squeals, making me smile and ruffle her silky dark hair. It's short. I've cut it, but now I can't help thinking she'd be cute in braids.

In the living room the air is stale and used. Outside it's darker than it was yesterday, and the wind howls.

He lies on his back, completely still under a thick blanket. He's taller than the couch is long, and his legs are curled awkwardly. I stiffen and stop for a moment to look at him. His eyes are closed. Does he move at all? But when we walk past him, he lifts his head.

"Is it morning?" His voice is rough and raspy and there's something in it that sends shivers down my spine.

"Yeah. Nine."

"I think I need more sleep. Is it okay if I lie here a little longer?"

My mouth falls open. Since when does he ask for anything? "Of course."

"Are you leaving?" he asks, his voice faint.

I frown. "Are you hallucinating?" I walk to the front door, open it and look out into the maelstrom that is the outside world before I pull it closed again. It feels as if a large hand is trying to keep it open. "No car, still windy... No. I don't think so."

"Thank you," he says. Then his head falls back onto the pillow and he closes his eyes.

Thank you?

Preparing breakfast for us, I make an extra cup of coffee and put a couple of extra pieces of bread in the oven. He can slice them himself, though. I don't have a single knife left.

He turns his head toward me as I walk up to him.

"Hey. Breakfast."

His eyes are dark and hollow, his face pale and a little pasty.

"Good for you."

"I made you some."

That wakes him up. "You—"

He sits up, swaying. "You made some for *me*? I must be Alice."

"What?"

"In Wonderland."

He's hung the flannel shirt over his shoulders and I suddenly wonder what his wound looks like. Then I remember his harsh words, how he chased me off. He can go fuck himself!

"Just shut up and eat it." I spin on my heels and stalk back toward the kitchen. His sudden change in demeanor makes me uncomfortable. I don't like that he says please, that he asks before he takes. I don't recognize him, and I don't like it. I don't trust it to last. With him everything is an act, and I have to remember that.

"I'll be back in a minute." I look at his back as he heaves himself up off the couch and leaves for the bathroom, swaying a little. He looks different. Calmer. Weaker. I frown as a twinge of unexpected worry nips at my heart.

We eat in silence. Christian has fetched the bread knife and everything seems oddly normal. Except 'normal' never used to be with *him* at the breakfast table. I steal a glance at him and blush as he catches my gaze. His cheeks are a little flushed and his forehead is sweaty.

"Did you spike my coffee again?"

I almost choke on my tea. "*No.*"

He takes a sip. "Good. It's less sugary that way."

My face burns and I look down. "So... what now?" I don't even know what I mean myself or what kind of answer I expect. I busy myself with spreading butter on a piece of bread.

"I don't know anymore, Ker. Does it matter, though? At this point?" He glances at Cece's jam-covered cheeks and grabs a paper tissue, wiping some of it off.

I frown as I look at their interaction. "What do you mean?"

He shrugs. "Is it important to know everything, to have everything plotted out?" He drops the now-crumpled tissue on his plate and leans back.

Cecilia waves a spoon in front of her and yogurt splatters in a wide circle around her. I reach for a new tissue and wipe it off, as I study him. I don't get it and I don't know how to answer. I'm beginning to think he's hallucinating because he doesn't sound like himself anymore. I wonder when I started to believe I knew anything about him at all.

He clears his throat. "Is it that important... to be in control?"

I stare at him as I ruffle my daughter's hair. "Spoon belongs in your mouth, love," I tell her before I turn to Christian. "Yes. Of course it is. Don't you think so?"

He takes a bite out of a piece of bread and chews it annoyingly slowly, shrugging. "I'm used to plans changing, to needing to adapt."

"But you try to control it, don't you? I doubt you're that much of a hippie inside that sharp suit."

He looks down at his flannel shirt and wrinkly oversized pants and grins. "Not very sharp at the moment."

I follow his gaze, swallowing against the bolt that shoots through me, seeing his caramel-colored skin in the gap in the shirt. "You know what I mean," I say faintly.

"Yeah." He sighs and rakes his fingers through his hair. "I'm probably not much of a hippie, no."

I frown. He's acting strange.

The conversation dies. I help Cece finish up her breakfast and then I run a bath for the two of us. When we emerge from the bathroom in a cloud of strawberry-scented steam, fresh and sated, Christian stands by the window, his right hand clutching his left shoulder. Cecilia runs through the room, dressed in thick socks and a yellow bathrobe. She takes a lap around Christian's legs and then crawls to her doll that lies under the living room table. I smile at her, then I follow his gaze. The day seems just a nuance less dark than the night.

"You've raised her beautifully," he says softly as he turns to me.

That wasn't what I expected. I'd have thought he'd crack more 'wise words from the life of an assassin'. "She's a very easy child. Maybe you've noticed." I avoid his gaze.

"Yes, and no. I... don't have much experience with kids."

Something in his voice makes me glance at him, trying to catch his eyes. He sounds so desolate. I swallow hard. Not human. He's *not* human. I can't fall for this again!

"I figured as much."

He gives me a half-smile, his eyes dull.

Damn you! Don't be human.

I dress my daughter as I keep glancing at him. She trots off to the fireplace and starts piling some of the lighter logs. There's a peacefully crackling fire burning behind the thick glass doors.

"Thank you for the fire."

"Yeah. It was cold."

The morning passes agonizingly slowly. Cecilia sleeps when we should have eaten lunch and I fall into a coma next to her. I wake, sweaty, full of worry. *Where is he?* I need to see what he's doing. More hours have passed than I would have thought.

Yes. I need the control.

Christian is lying on the couch with his back to me. I immediately realize three things, all washing over me at once. He's exposing his back and I have access to a knife again, there's not a fiber in me that wants to hurt him anymore, and I don't think he's well. I bend over him and his eyelids flutter, but he doesn't wake. That's strange. His forehead is sweaty, and his face is flushed. Putting my palm against his cheek, I gasp when his hand suddenly strikes out and grabs mine. But I felt it.

"You're burning up, Christian. You have a fever."

"Yeah, I know," he mumbles and releases his hold on my hand. He rises with a grimace and remains sitting, swaying. "I think I need to look at my shoulder."

Guilt suddenly stabs me. "I can help you with that."

He chased me off last night, but I still feel the urge to help him with what he obviously can't handle himself. And in a way it's my fault, but I silence that thought, because mainly it's his own fault and I need to stop taking the blame. But I can't let him die.

"No, don't. It's all right."

He protests, but this time I'm not letting him. My stomach clenches with worry, and I've already pushed that side of his shirt off his shoulder.

Warm air rises from his skin mixed with a scent I recognize all too well, a scent that used to make me implode with need. His skin is too hot. I continue with his bandage where I left off last night, and sure enough, the shoulder is swollen, the wound has glaring red edges and there's white-gray goo between them. I press at his skin where there's an angry red swelling and it seems to fluctuate.

"This doesn't look good."

"That should please you." His voice is raspy, tired, sounding as if he's given up all of a sudden.

It suddenly worries me that he's ill, and that he's so indifferent about it. It worries me that I'm concerned. I shouldn't be. "Hey," I say, putting on a cheery tone, "not as much as it pleases me that I get to cut into you with a knife. Again." I grin and pat his arm.

He glances at his shoulder. "You're probably right."

"We're gonna need to open that. It's filled with pus." I press carefully at the red area and he groans.

"Fucking brilliant."

"Don't be such a wuss. I got a nail through my finger the second week we lived here. We were fixing the porch. It looked like this after a few days and I had to go see a doctor. He cut it open and gave me antibiotics for it. It could have destroyed the joint, he said. This—" I poke the swelling again, "this is just flesh."

I leave out the part about how I forgot to take the pills after a couple of days and had to have the procedure done all over again and with a new prescription.

He makes a face as he glares at his shoulder again, a shudder rippling through him. "If you leave it, I might die. I thought you'd like that."

"I wouldn't know what to do with your corpse, now can you please turn around and give me your damn knife. It's probably the sharpest thing in here." A brief shiver runs through me as I think about where that knife has been.

He sways and lies back down. "Can't it wait?" Closing his eyes, he turns his back to me again.

"Christian! Get a grip! Come on! Don't leave me alone with a child in this weather and with a broken car, you piece of shit!" It comes out even more desperate than intended. He's really freaking worrying me right now.

"Okay," he grumbles and sits back up. "You'll probably need to sterilize the knife first." Even weak and tired he's suddenly all business.

"With alcohol?"

"That'll do if you have something strong enough."

I probably don't. I only drink an occasional glass of wine. I shake my head. "In a flame?"

He nods.

"Where's the knife?"

"In my pocket." His voice is so damn faint. I hate that there's a flutter of worry in my chest when I should rejoice.

I open the leg pocket with trembling hands and haul out the knife. I look at its matte black blade. I've never seen anything like it. As I flick it before me, a shudder ripples through my chest.

"How many people have you killed with this?"

He gives me a glare through heavily lidded eyes that, despite his weakened state, is so filled with danger it makes me shiver. *That* is obviously a line I'm not supposed to cross.

I march off to the fireplace, opening one of the thick glass doors and sticking the blade in the fire for a few seconds. Then I walk back to the couch and sit down next to him. As I hold the tip to the wound, the blade is still smoking hot. Christian glances at what I'm doing and jerks away.

"For fuck's sake! Let it cool first!"

"Oh. Sorry."

"Are you sure you don't want me to—"

"*No!* I can take it." I blush and wait. After a while I let the side of the blade rest against the back of my hand. It has cooled off.

It's time.

Christian

Her hand trembles and her face is pale. She lifts the knife and aims its tip at the wound's entrance. Then she lowers it again. The surge of adrenaline when I thought she was going to fucking cauterize my shoulder woke me up pretty good and I'm a lot less tired than I've been these last hours.

"Ker, sweetheart, are you sure you're up to this? It's not as easy as you think, to cut someone."

She waves the knife in front of my face and I can't help a tiny flinch. I don't think she has the slightest idea just how sharp that thing is!

"I'm *not* your sweetheart, Christian! How *dare* you when I'm sitting here with a knife? Besides, I have cut you before. And shot you."

I purse my lips as I regard her. My little tigress. Closing my eyes, I lean my head back. I can't help but smile ever so little. She's coming back to herself. "Go ahead, then, tough girl."

When still nothing happens, I open my eyes again and peek at her. The tip of the knife hovers by the wound.

"Don't think. Just do. And you'll see that afterward you'll have that tingling feeling in the pit of your belly, like when you come so hard that you almost lose it." I shoot her a leery grin to piss her off enough to get her to just do it.

It works like a fucking charm.

Her gaze darkens. Biting her lip, she pushes the tip into the wound, pressing it deeper and deeper. I grit my teeth and squeeze my eyes shut, it feels as if she holds a torch to my skin and I can't help the shudder that wracks my body. When I look again, the knife is out and my shoulder feels a little less strained already. A stream of grayish, dirty-looking pus is seeping from where she punctured me. It's not as much as I'd have thought, but it seems to make the difference.

"You're such a piece of shit," she exclaims and gets up. The knife clatters as she drops it on the table.

I cock my head and look at her. She is so sexy when her eyes flare. I smirk as I get up off the couch, grabbing the strips of sheet, pushing them to the leaking wound. When she sees me standing, she takes a couple of steps back, her eyes darting between mine, my naked chest, and then back up. I know I scare her, and I know that's not the only thing she's feeling when she gives me that look. She wants me too, but she's gonna keep denying that to her last breath.

I start toward the bathroom and Kerry steps to the side. I saw a pack of antibiotics there when I rummaged through her cabinet before. Is it already a couple of days ago? Whatever they were prescribed for, it can't be wrong to try them.

Before I pull open the door I stop and look at her. "Was it as good as I said it would be?"

The slap is hard, unexpected, and probably well-earned.

I touch my burning cheek as I lick my lower lip. It tastes salty from her palm.

"*That* felt good," she snarls.

I pull the door open. "I'm sure it did, Ker." I flash her a grin and wink.

She puts her hands on her hips and glares back at me. "You're such a prick!"

I raise an eyebrow, holding her gaze. "I know." Leaving the flushed little woman behind me, I lock the door and exhale on a shudder. All this touching, and all this unexpected closeness, has made me itch. My groin aches and suddenly I'm anything but tired. I don't need her to see the thick bulge in my pants. I'm sure she'd freak out if she saw the urge to pull her to me and ravage her that I must radiate.

I need this woman so fucking much.

Four

Kerry

I don't know why he's being such an ass again. I was only trying to help. My stomach is in a tight knot from the tension of having to cut into his wound and then the charged afterplay. There was something in his gaze that I recognize all too well. I've seen it before. I've lived through the consequences. They were spectacular, and devastating.

Those nights when he came to me, the hunger, the possessive look in his eyes – the memory will never leave me. It still makes my gut clench with want.

I'm utterly thankful when Cece wakes up and gives me something to occupy my body and mind with. Except my mind isn't where my body is. I can't help thinking about his heated skin, the glint in his warm brown eyes, and about what the hell he's doing in my bathroom for so long.

I almost jump out of my skin when the door finally opens. I'm feeding Cecilia an apple I've cut into slices and I'm thankful to keep her between us.

There are new, clean strips covering the wound, and apart from that he's naked from the waist up. My eyes are inadvertently drawn to the thick string of dark hair that continues along his stomach and then disappears beneath the waistband of his pants. My dad's pants, but damn, they look good, hanging low on Christian's hips. He gives me an unreadable glance and slowly pulls the flannel shirt back on, leaving it unbuttoned. I avert my gaze. I do *not* want to look at this man's naked chest. It does things to me, makes me ache in all the wrong places. I have to remember what he is, what he's done. I fell for him once, so hard, but that was before I knew him.

Instead of coming to the couch where we sit, he walks to my bedroom and closes the door behind him.

I'm up and off of the couch the same moment the door clicks closed. *No way!* I grab the apple slices and put them on the counter, well out of her reach. Tossing Cecilia a doll, I then dash through the room and rip open the door.

"What do you think you're doing?" He's lying on my bed. He's lying on *my* bed! His shirt is still unbuttoned, and I stop flat. "Get out!"

He lies with his hand behind his head, glancing lazily at me, his cheeks slightly flushed. "I just had to get you alone for a second."

"W—why?"

"Come here." He crooks a finger and bids me closer. I take a hesitant step toward him.

"What?"

Gripping my wrist, he pulls me to him. His hand is warm, strong, and dry. "Please just sit."

Against my better judgement I hesitantly sit on the very edge of the bed.

"I *was* a prick. I admit. I just felt for a moment there was something there... Something more." His voice falters.

My heart makes an unhealthy jump. There was. There is. How can I ever get out of this spell?

"Look," I say and swallow hard, my thoughts a tangled mess. "I guess we can be moderately civilized as it is, being stuck under the same roof and all..." I squirm and adjust a little on the uncomfortable wooden edge of the bed. "But something more... I think you misunderstood, Christian."

He still holds my wrist, and I haven't pulled away. Why haven't I pulled away? I look him over, wishing things were different, wishing I could lay my head on his chest, listen to his heartbeat, his breathing, feel his warmth. I have missed him so much, despite everything. It's not rational, and I don't know if it will ever go away.

"I get that now," he says tiredly. "I know what you're about to say, but can I please sleep for an hour on your bed? I'm so, so tired."

Please again.

I exhale erratically, my skin scorched from his touch. "Fine. But in an hour, I'll throw you out."

He smiles, then pulls me toward him, lifts his head slightly and places a featherlight kiss on the back of my hand. "Thank you."

I jerk my hand out of his grip, jumping up from my sitting position.

He has closed his eyes. "Too much?" he mumbles.

I don't answer and slam the door shut behind me. Yes, too much. But it's not his fault. I'm the one who has lost their mind!

Cece has lost interest in the doll and is playing with a jigsaw puzzle on the floor, slamming the large pieces of wood against each other. Something is different. I rub the back of my hand again and look around me. I don't know wha—

It's quiet outside. The storm is over.

The symbolism doesn't pass me unnoticed. It's over outside. I believe it's over inside too.

Or did it just begin in earnest?

I NEED TO MAKE US DINNER, BUT I'M A MESS. I KEEP RUBBING at the spot where his lips touched my skin. It's like a twitch. I can't control it. My heart is still pounding. I'm in shreds. Like his damn shirt. Damn, damn, damn shirt! Unable to focus on anything, I finally manage to boil potatoes, mash them and cut some ham. I'm out of vegetables. I should make my way to the delivery box. *The box.* I realize I have no car. That's an hour's walk on a sprained ankle. And Ray? My heart drops. Did Ray get it? Did he call the police for me? Will cops come here now that the storm is over? Oh God, oh no. That can't happen.

I don't think that will go over well. For who, I don't know, but it *will* be a disaster! My knees fold and I slide to the floor, trembling and nauseous.

Numb, and with sluggish moves, I pull myself together, serve Cecilia and put some on a plate for me, but I can't eat. She tries her best to hit her mouth. I usually help her, but now I just sit and stare, fighting to not cry in front of her. I don't want to worry her.

"Mama?"

I jerk and look at my wonderful little child. She's holding out her fork for me, the piece of ham falling off it as I look. I smile and pick it up off the table, putting it in my mouth.

"Thank you, love." I caress her cheek and when I look up Christian is standing next to me. His face is a little less pale, and his eyes aren't as dull as they were a couple of hours ago. Something dark rises in me.

"What do you want?" I snarl and then the words just burst right out of my chest. "What do you mean when you say you want me? What do you mean 'want'? Do you want my... body? Do you want us to get married? What the hell do you mean?" Cecilia has stopped eating and stares at us, her eyes widening and filling with tears, but I can't comfort her right now. I'm frozen. I can barely breathe.

"Eat up!" I hiss at her. Her plump little lower lip juts out and begins to tremble.

Christian glares at me and then goes to sit next to her. Cooing, chasing a piece of ham on the plate with the fork and then feeding it to her, he makes her giggle.

I begin to cry again. "I hate you!" I bellow.

Christian throws me a dark gaze and then wipes some mashed potato off her cheek before he gives her another forkful of ham and potatoes.

I stand so abruptly the chair topples and falls to the floor behind me. "Stop feeding her! She's not your daughter! You have no right—"

"For fuck's sake, what's gotten into you? Get a grip!" He gives me a furious glare and helps Cece off the chair. "I'm gonna talk to Mommy a little, hon."

My heart rate picks up as he stands and walks over to me. He grips hard around my wrist. Too hard. "Come on, get it off your chest, whatever it is, but don't take it out on her." He pulls me with him and forces me to come closer.

"Wh—what are you doing?" I stutter, my heart leaping to my throat.

"Take it out on me, Kerry, on someone closer to your own size. I can take it. Not on her." He nods at our daughter and I have to swallow against the sudden lump in my throat.

"Mama?" she says, her little voice quavering.

"Do your job."

I stare at him, frowning, then back at her as I compose myself and smile through the tears. "Mommy'll be back in a second, honey. It's all right."

It's *not* all right! Nothing will be all right again!

Christian pulls at my arm and I stumble behind him until we're alone in my bedroom again. He shoves me inside and pulls the door almost closed, leaving a sliver open.

"What's with all these fuckin' questions all of a sudden? What's the matter with you?" His lips are a thin line and his eyes gleam in the dusky room.

"What do you want with me?" I snarl. "With everything you've done to me, what you've put me through, there's no way, never, I'm letting you 'have me'. You coming here and... It's too late for everything. You fucked it all up."

"And I've never done anything good for you? Never given you anything?" His voice is hard, his eyes charcoal black and lethal.

"*No!*" I scream.

"Keep your voice down! Not even *her*, then?"

For a moment, I can't say anything, a cloud of fury boiling up in my chest. "You didn't 'give' her to me," I snap. "She happened anyway. It's nothing you can take credit for!" I turn away from him with a sob. I don't want to cry in front of him, but there's nowhere I can go when the tears begin to fall again.

"Ker, I've told you already, in so many fucking ways, that I'm sorry. I don't know what else to do. And life is something to value a hell of a lot more than you do. Once it's gone it's just... gone."

"Why can't you leave me alone?" I sob. "Why did you have to be who you are?" I could bite off my tongue. Why did I have to say that? I sink down on the edge of the bed, hiding my face in my hands, completely drained, trembling with exhaustion.

He settles next to me. "I couldn't stop thinking about you. About Cecilia. I missed you so fucking much. It's killing me that I fucked everything up."

I let my hands fall into my lap and look up at him. Even sitting down, his hulking appearance towers over me. "I went to see your boss," I say.

"Oh, I know. That was fucking stupid."

"I *had* to. I carried your child. You showed up at my home. I thought you came to kill me. I needed to know. Then he said he couldn't control you, that you were going to do whatever you wanted anyway."

"He said that? The fucker!"

I don't answer. His presence makes my whole body tingle and I jerk when I feel his hand on my shoulder.

"Was there ever a time when things could have been different?" he asks quietly.

"A... what?"

"Was there a time when everything wasn't too late?"

I stare at him. "No, there wasn't," I snarl. "Even if you hadn't tried to *murder* me, you're still a monster I could never touch again once I learned who you really are."

"I don't believe you, Ker. I know you felt something too." His eyes darken again. "You're lying. To yourself. To everyone. That's how you're gonna raise my daughter?"

I open and close my mouth several times as I try to come up with a reply. Suddenly, he stands and opens the door. I look at his back as he leaves the room.

"Fucking fine parents she has, then!" I shout after him. "One murdering mafia goon, and one liar!" I dart up, slam the door shut and fall onto the bed, sobbing, my sorrow over what I am, what I've become, raw, eating at my heart, at my soul and my conscience. This is not who I want to be. I scream into my pillow, the sound hoarse and tearing at my throat.

I don't like who I am anymore.

Finally, when there are no more tears, I stop the sobbing and listen instead. What are they doing? I wonder what time it is. My stomach grumbles and reminds me I haven't eaten. A sudden panic makes my chest clench. It's too quiet. They've left! I've been bad and they've left me! I'm up and off of the bed in a fraction of a second, shoving the door open and bursting out into the living room

They're sitting next to each other on the couch, a little bowl of raisins in Cecilia's lap. A fire is crackling peacefully and he's reading to her. About Sammy the Fire truck. Her favorite book at the moment. Christian looks up and gives me a warning glare.

Cece doesn't look up at all, she points to the picture. "Sammy."

Christian looks back to our daughter, smiling at her. "And what did Sammy do?"

"Wouu faie."

"Yes, he did," he answers, without having a clue what she was saying.

My heart pounds so hard it hurts. He's taken her. Right before my eyes. He didn't even have to fight. I gave her to him. I'm a freak. I've turned into a monster. I've turned into everything I've ever accused *him* of being. With a sob, I turn on my heel and dart back into the bedroom. Slamming the door closed behind me, I fall onto the bed again.

The bed sinks as he sits down on the edge, making me jerk in surprise. I never heard the door open.

"Go away!" I rasp, my throat too clenched for proper words to pass.

"Ker." His voice is unexpectedly tender. "What's the matter with you? I honestly thought, earlier today, we had come farther than this. Suddenly, we're back on square one. What the fuck happened?"

"She hates me," I sob. "I hurt her and she hates me, and she prefers you over me."

He snorts. "That was nothing. She's already forgotten it ever happened."

"I've never—" My voice breaks. "I've never yelled at her. I hurt her!"

"So, she's a fuckin' lucky child, then, if that was her first yelling. It happened, suck it up."

I'm hugging the pillow, afraid of his closeness, and even more afraid of being left alone with myself. "When are you letting us go?"

"When you get over yourself and take your asses back to civilization."

"I— You—" Is he gonna let us go?

"Ker, you're not the only person in the world who's been hurt. You have to move on."

"That's rich, coming from *you!* When did *you* move on?"

He looks a little guilty, but then he shrugs. "Consider yourself stuck with me, then."

Anger wells up inside me, like a flood of dark poisonous mud. "No! No way!" I dart up from the bed and he follows suit. I push at his chest to get him away from me. He's too close and I can't breathe. "Get *out!*" I holler. "I hate you!" I push again and he catches my hands and shoves me backward until I hit the wall.

"Stop it, Ker! You're overreacting!"

He's holding both my arms, so I try to slam my head into his nose. Christian evades me and I cower as his expression changes into something less calm, something looking way too much like what I've seen before. In the harbor. Something dangerous. My heart speeds up as he grips my chin and presses my head back to the wall.

"Let me go," I gasp, terrified over what I've suddenly unleashed.

His lips thin into a straight line as he glares at me from under a curtain of dark hair. I squirm and try to get loose, but he presses harder against me, his whole body covering every inch of mine. "You have no idea—" he whispers. And suddenly he crashes his lips against mine. My whole mind, my whole world, is instantly filled with his scent, his being.

I moan loudly and try to get free. I can't do this! When I'm finally able to bend my head away, I pant and stare at him, shaking my head, my eyes locked with his.

Don't do this to me!

I know how this will go. He will take, and I will let him, and I've been down that road. It led to nothing but pain. He takes a sudden step back and lets me go. Shoving a hand through his long hair, he licks his lips, as if tasting me. I'm unable to look away from his hypnotizing darkness. I remember all too well how those eyes sucked me in from the very first glance.

I break the spell first. "Where's Cece?" She's my first priority. Now. Always.

"Gimme a sec." Christian peeks out into the main room and then comes back inside. "She's sleeping under the table, on the rug."

Okay... she's okay... and I... Oh God! I slide along the wall until I sit, my legs unable to support my weight anymore. Christian crouches before me. I sob and curl up, fresh tears spilling over the old, dried ones.

"I love her," I whisper, wiping my mouth repeatedly with the back of my hand, still feeling his lips, fighting the need for more.

"I know you do, Kerry." His voice is so filled with warmth it makes another set of sobs wrack my chest.

"I was so alone. I didn't have anyone to share it with. Not anyone. She is such a miracle and she filled me with so much life and— You should've seen her, smelled her when she was a newborn, they have a certain scent, powdery... have you—" I look up just in time to see him shake his head. "No, you haven't. Of course you haven't."

I hold his gaze. For a brief moment I ache for him and what he's missing in life by being who he is. I want him to know about her, and about what he's been losing out on. Maybe I want him to hurt a little, make him realize he's such a loser—doing what he does with his life.

I want him to get a glimpse of what he could have had.

What could have been.

"I have," he says quietly, "once. My little sis. I was fifteen when she came. Mom got a little preoccupied. She never even breastfed Angela.

Us brothers had to take turns with the bottle, and the diapers." He frowns and looks away, a look of pain passing his face.

I cock my head as I take him in. Something changes in his whole demeanor, his gaze turns distant, something about him looks softer than I have ever seen before and a sudden surge of jealousy shoots through me, shocking me. I shouldn't feel that way. Certainly not toward his *sister*. And why would I ever feel jealous about anything regarding him?

"What happened?"

Christian shakes his head, his eyes focusing on mine yet again. "It was bad times. We did what we could. Never mind. Tell me about Cecilia, please."

I study him a few moments more, fighting the urge to reach out, to put a hand over his.

"Her first sound that wasn't a hungry scream, or just sweet nonsense, wasn't 'mommy'." I smile through the tears at the memory. "It was 'amp', like 'lamp' you know."

I lace my fingers as I twist my hands nervously. My eyes can't seem to keep looking into his for too long. It reminds me of too much. Things I don't want to be reminded of. He chuckles, and when I glance at him again, he's got a smile on his face and my heart, my stupid, stupid female heart jolts at the sight. Because he is so heart-breakingly beautiful to look at when his features lighten, and all the cruelty disappears as if it was never there to begin with.

"Amp," he repeats. "That's cute. You'd think it'd be 'mommy'..." His voice falters. His gaze drifts toward the living room. "It should have been 'mommy'," he repeats, more to himself than to me.

FIVE

Christian

God, I want to take her in my arms as she sits in front of me, curled up by the wall, and whispers early memories of our daughter, her birth, her first words, when she crawled, walked. Her first wounds, her furious reaction when Kerry had to say no the first time. I smile then. I recognize myself. My distant memories of my baby sister come back to life. Losing Dad that very same day was such a trauma that we all went into survival mode. I became the man of the house, and with Mom plotting revenge even as she lay in the maternity ward, there was no one left to fend for the new little addition to the family. I *have* done this before. I had forgotten.

Finally Kerry is quiet. She fiddles with the hem of her pants and it's obvious she can't quite stand to meet my gaze. Her worry and discomfort around me makes me ache. I want to pull her into my embrace. I know I can coax a response out of her, give her warmth and pleasure. I know I can make her mine without much force. It's there. It's so close to the surface. Tension crackles between us, her breaths erratic, her eyes wide and filled with emotion. Her full lips... I want those lips on mine again so bad that it nearly chokes me.

It's time to back off or I won't be able to stop myself.

"I'm gonna check on Cecilia."

She looks up and then fights her way up to standing. My hand flies out and steadies her. She twitches at my touch and I pull back immediately, as if she had burnt me.

Moaning, she sags a little and grimaces.

"What?"

"My ankle."

I give out a short laugh. "We've beaten each other up pretty good, haven't we?"

She looks up at me, a hint of a smile pulling at her lips. "I guess we have."

Cecilia lies on the side with her little chubby hands tucked under her chin, and a drop of drool in the corner of her mouth. There are the prettiest little dimples where her knuckles should be. Her long dark eyelashes flutter as she seems to be dreaming something. I hope it's pleasant. I barely remember her from today. I barely remember today. I slept. I had a fever. Sitting down on the edge of the couch while Kerry carefully scoops up Cecilia and cradles her to her chest, I try to feel if I'm ill or not. I decide I feel better.

Kerry is making cooing sounds. "Oh, my poor baby, you had to fall asleep all alone out here and Mommy was so mean to you... oh my God." She puts her hand over her mouth and her lower eyelashes glisten wet yet again.

I refrain from rolling my eyes. She knows nothing about abusing children. What a blessing to be so unaware of how fucking ugly life can be for some. But I don't think that'd be an argument that would cheer her up.

"And we didn't get to brush your teeth," she continues.

I have to hide the smile with a yawn.

I remain on the couch as Kerry carries Cece into the bedroom. She takes her time, but finally she comes back out, her cheeks flushed, her eyes glazed. I believe she's been fucking crying again. What the hell? I can rough her up pretty badly, and she doesn't even make a face, and then she can sneer, once, to her offspring and it breaks her?

I don't get it. I don't get *her*. Sometimes I think the world that separates us is too big, even when we're stuck together in the middle of it.

She remains standing on the carpet in the center of the room. "The storm's over."

"So I noticed."

"How do you feel?"

I flex my arm. "Better."

"Oh."

"Disappointed?"

"No, I wouldn't have helped you if I didn't mean it."

I grin. "Perhaps. Or perhaps you're just a better person."

"Oh, I *know* I am." She flashes a brief smile and again I see a hint of that Kerry I met so long ago at the bar. An eternity ago.

I sit up, suddenly longing desperately to touch her, to reach for some of that soft and kind humanity in her. I'm so tired of fighting. "Come here."

She takes a hesitant step closer. "What?" Then she sits down on the edge of the table, just out of my immediate reach.

"Are you afraid of me? Still?" I frown. I don't want her to be. I understand if she is. I wish she knew me, that part of me deep inside that isn't a total fuck-up. The innocent I once was too. I have done bad, bad things, and she knows them all too well, but I am more. For her I want to be more, to find that again.

She regards me for a long time. "A little, yes."

My heart sinks, but I grasp at that she's just 'a little' afraid. "What are you afraid of?"

She swallows hard. "That you'll hurt me again, I think."

"Hurt? Or... touch?"

Her eyes widen. "Both," she answers with a small voice, almost as a question instead of a statement.

"Can I just hold your hands?"

Her fingers thread in and out of each other and she squirms. "Maybe," she whispers.

Victory. Small, but undeniable. I shuffle closer until I sit before her. Then I take her hands in mine and just hold them, my thumbs slowly stroking the sides of her thumbs. She gasps, and her mouth falls open, her eyes darting between our joined hands and my eyes.

"Tired?"

She nods. "You're still warm."

"You're cold."

She flinches when I lift my arm to push a tendril off her forehead. I stop mid-air before I make contact. When she starts breathing again, I carefully caress her hairline with the tips of my fingers. Her skin is so smooth. I remember that.

From before.

I lower my hand and let it rest on hers again. "You're beautiful, Kerry." My heart clenches. I doubt this woman would ever want to get to know the real me. As she wriggles her hand out from beneath mine and ties it into a fist in her lap, her knuckles whitening, I know she won't ever want to get to know me. Not after all I've done.

And yet, I can't leave her alone. Something in her calls for me, beckons me. I need her to become mine, I need to find our common ground.

I need her. I need Cecilia.

Or I'll drown.

Kerry

"You're beautiful," he says.

I ache so bad at his tender words. I want to believe him. I want him to be good, but those beautiful eyes can turn to death in a second. These warm, kind hands can remorselessly take another human's life. They came so close, so very close, to claiming mine.

His fingertips touch my cheek. His caress is lighter than a feather as he softly strokes along my jaw and then down my throat where I'm sure he must feel how hard my pulse beats. Goosebumps spread rapidly along the side of my neck, causing my whole spine to tingle and tense. I look into his eyes, barely able to keep my gaze locked with his. A soft smile plays at his slightly parted lips. It is as if he's directing a beam of light, want, need, and desire toward me, and me alone. It calls to me, pulls me closer, transfixes me. I want to stay in its center and remain there, safe, loved. I lean into his touch, I can't help myself, I'm pulled to the promise of closeness, the opposite of hurt. It stings somewhere deep inside as I remember Christian, before all the bad things happened, *this* is the man he was.

The man I *thought* he was.

He's pressing a rag over my mouth and nose, never letting go.

I stiffen, unable to defend myself from the onslaught of memories. They nag, burn holes in my soul, erode me and make me sway, tossing me violently between comfort and pain.

His fingers leave my cheek and grip carefully around my hands, pulling me closer, urging me to comply. I'm here, not there. It's now, not then! He's different, he's changed. His thumbs massage my knuckles, rubbing circles on them, making my skin burn.

He carries me in the darkness, toward my death, unaffected by my fear, by my screams, smells of rotten seaweed surrounding us.

Then, then, then!

Pulling me even closer, wedging his thighs between mine, his eyes roaming my face, he then smiles. Victoriously. Beautifully. I don't know if I'm strong enough to resist what's about to happen. He's given me the most, and he's taken the most. In my life. Ever. No one before I met him has meant more to me. How can I deny him? Maybe I do belong to him and have just never realized it until now?

"I want to kiss you, Ker." His voice is raspy and thick and it makes me shiver.

I don't say anything. But I don't back away either. Eyes, so familiar, and yet so foreign, dart between mine as he moves closer. Our gazes are still locked as his lips touch my mouth, softly, not intrusively. He feels the same... and still not.

A gun to my head. Cold, unyielding metal.

"Kiss me back... Please."

His face is a blur and my mind spins. The plea is such a soft whisper and his breath is warm on my mouth. The scent I know so well invades my every pore, fills my nostrils, and assaults my senses. He smells so good. Soapy. Musky. Familiar. I lick my lips and accidentally touch his. Jerking slightly when his hands leave mine and come to rest at the back of my head, I inhale, my heart stuttering. He pulls me to him more forcefully until there's no return, no backing away. Pressing his mouth to mine, he separates my lips with the tip of his tongue. I gasp and my mind spins faster and faster. He feels good. He is warm, tender, vulnerable, somehow safe, and yet so terrifyingly dangerous. How did we end up here? My brain refuses to stop the increasing whirl of panicked thoughts and memories. I see him now, I see him then, I see him as a twisted image from too many dreams.

"Oh my God, come, babe," he groans against my lips and puts his hands on my hips, pulling me to him until I straddle his lap. He cups my ass and pulls me even closer, chest to chest. He's getting hard, pushing against my sensitive core. I have only soft pants on and they feel like no material at all as he slowly rocks back and forth. His hands wander along my back, one hand finding my nape, tightening the grip, his other sliding along the gap between my shirt and the waistband of my pants.

"Kerry," he mumbles as he makes me breathless when his fingers meet the naked skin on my back, "I've missed you so fucking much."

I don't know what to do with my own hands, they lie passive on my thighs until I softly put them on his shoulders, careful to avoid his wound. The shudder that runs through him at my touch awakens something in me, a memory of when this felt real, when I thought he was someone not... him.

His hand wanders under my shirt, up to between my shoulder blades, then slowly slides to the side, his thumb brushing the side of my breast. I arch up in sudden, surprising need for him to really touch me.

Christian no doubt feels my sharp intake of air and how I squirm against his rock-hard bulge. Cupping my breast, he finds my nipple, pinching it, making me gasp as he keeps devouring my mouth, stealing every last bit of air along with my sanity.

He kneads my breast as his other hand travels along my back and slides inside my pants. I ache and tingle everywhere, swell, my pussy cries for his touch and it's insane, because it's not right. I try to remember who he is, what he's done, but when he finds my soaked slit my brain turns to mush. I bite down on his lip when he thrusts his fingers inside me, not gentle, nothing with this man is gentle.

A flash of a memory rips through me. Dark. Fear. Then he circles my clit, making me cry out. My thighs shake and I gasp when he suddenly twists us, pulling me under him, his fingers stabbing in and out, taking, taking, taking. It hurts a little, and at the same time it starts a furnace deep inside. He lodges himself between my thighs, pushing his thick bulge against my clit, rocking back and forth, teasing me, making me unable to breathe.

In a couple of desperate, jerky moves, he pulls up the front of my shirt, abandons my mouth and latches on to my nipple, licking, flicking, grazing it with his teeth.

"You're mine, Kerry," he growls. "You've always been mine. You said it once. You admitted it. I'm never letting you go now."

Salty air on my face. Deaf to my pleas for my life.

My heart speeds up almost impossibly. My body hums, responding to his touch, to the fear and the pleasure, to the beast who claims his woman.

Me.

I moan, I try to speak, but cry out when he bites down on my other nipple, as his thrusting increases.

My flesh screams that it's good, that it's right, while my mind tries to dig up my sanity from the depths of my soul.

"This has gotta go," he rumbles and starts pulling down my pants along my thighs.

He throws me to the ground. Rough hands around my throat.

When they're past my knees, he makes quick work, pulling up one of my legs as he sits up a little, looking me over. I stare at him, my insides ice cold and scorching hot at the same time. His dark hair partly covers his eyes. In the dim light there's something demon like over him, making my chest clench. I remember how he tied me up, spanked me until I cried.

"Say you want me, Kerry. Tell me you've longed for me as much as I've longed for you."

I have. I have longed for him and feared him more than death, and here we are again.

Death. He's death.

I see someone he's not. I see a man where there's nothing but a cruel monster.

With one hand he begins to pull down his zipper as he leans in and catches my lips again. My heart speeds up, slams in my chest, making me dizzy. I moan into his mouth and push at him until he lets me loose. He gasps, his lips full, newly kissed. I try to control my racing heart.

"I—I'm sorry," I hiccup, unable to meet his gaze. "I don't—I..."

I try to get up, but he grabs my wrists and keeps me down. It sends yet another surge of panic through me.

Pain. So much pain. His eyes cold and without mercy.

"Ker? Hey... look at me." Gripping my chin, he forces me to face him.

My eyes dart up to meet his and then I look away again. He radiates something I can't grasp. He wants something I can't give. Something he can take... I might even let him if it came to that... But I'm not sure I can give it.

Ever.

"Talk to me, hon."

I inhale deeply and let out a shaky breath. "I—I can't," I whimper.

His intake of air comes so abruptly it makes me jerk. "Ker! Fuck! I'm not gonna *hurt* you! Ever again! Do you hear me?" He suddenly lets go of me and climbs off the couch, stands. I slam my naked thighs together and cower, staring down at my knees. I don't know if he's angry or not, and what he's going to do now.

"Yes," I say unhappily. "I'm—I'm just... I'm letting you because I'm afraid of what you'll do if I refuse... I think." I swallow so hard it hurts, biting my lower lip, flinching when I feel his taste on it, familiar, unfamiliar.

Oh my God.

He breathes heavy, irregular. "Okay," he says then. "That's not good... Okay."

Backing up first one step, and then another, he rounds the table and starts pacing the room. I quickly pull up my pants and put my shirt back in place.

"We—" he begins.

It's not a scream. It's a whimper, and then a series of coughs, raspy, raw, sounding as if they hurt the little chest that has produced them.

I dart up, and he's already by the bedroom door in no time at all. Christian remains standing as I fall to my knees by her bed. She's sleeping, but there's a faint gurgling from deep inside her chest with every breath and then, as we watch, a new set of coughs wrack her little body. *Oh no, oh baby!* All my previous problems suddenly feel so insignificant. I caress her forehead and find to my shock it's sweaty and hot. Too hot.

"She's burning up!" I glance up at Christian in despair and he comes closer, settling himself at the edge of my bed.

"Is she ill?"

"I think she's sick, Christian! Oh my God, what do we do?"

He jolts. "Wait, I—" Digging in a side pocket in his pants, he pulls up a package of Advil.

"Thank you!" I grab it and go to fetch water, then a horrible thought strikes me. I hold it up between us. I don't even need to ask.

"I'm sorry. I needed it."

I shake my head slowly as I tighten my jaw. "So did I."

He winces and glances at my ankle before his eyes dart back up to meet mine. A new set of coughs startle us both and I spring into action, crushing a quarter of a pill in some strawberry jam, and fetching a bottle of water.

"You're unbelievable," I say as I brush past him.

"You stabbed me."

I pull a drowsy Cecilia to me and coax the jam into her mouth. She grimaces and then drinks greedily before she falls asleep again.

"You tried to murder me," I whisper and glance up at him.

He winces. "Yeah, can't argue that."

I shake my head, caressing Cecilia's soft dark hair. "That's not what hurts the most, Chris."

SIX

Christian

We take turns sitting by her crib, watching over our daughter as she tosses and turns in her sleep, her forehead sweaty, her silky, dark hair damp and curled at the temples. None of us have slept. It's Kerry's turn to try. I watch over my girls.

The kiss lingers still. I find myself tasting my lips time and time again. I was painfully hard for an embarrassingly long time after, and shame rolled through me at how I could think of nothing but fucking her when Cecilia is sick. The rejection struck harder than I'd have thought. And then her words, the words with no explanation, but I know what they mean. I've seen the agony in her eyes.

'That's not what hurts the most.'

Fuck!

It's too late. I realize I'm going to have to let it go. Let her go. I already feel the vastness of the empty life that lies ahead. It won't be very pretty, and I doubt I can take another shot at doing something else, being someone else, ever again.

It's just not worth all the pain.

Sitting on the edge of Kerry's bed, my gaze wanders from the little one to the adult and then back again. No matter what happens from here on, I feel blessed. Right now, in this moment, I have been touched by angels. People like these two don't happen to people like me.

But here we are.

Here I am.

At this moment in time we are like one, united in our concern. I wince, thinking about what I did to Kerry, but then there's Cecilia. There's beauty too, not only ugliness and cruelty.

I close my eyes for a moment, feeling a flutter in my chest. Examining it closer, I realize it's worry. I'm worrying. I never worry.

"Christian," she whispers and sits up, crossing her legs as she smoothes out the duvet over them.

I jolt. "Yeah."

"I'd never have pictured you—" She licks her lips and gives me a smile. Brief, but warm. "I'd never have thought you'd be sitting like this, you know... that you'd care."

I smile back. "Makes two of us."

Kerry's eyelids flutter and she yawns hugely.

"You should lie down. I'll be here."

She doesn't object and sighs as she falls back down, tossing and turning, trying to find the least uncomfortable position. The same does our daughter before yet another set of coughs pierce the night. The sound is harsh, raspy, as if something is tearing her little chest to pieces. When the cough finally subsides, a heavy snoring replaces the earlier noise.

"I'm so worried," she says, stroking a few stray strands of hair off Cecilia's cheek, looking up at me as if I could help.

"She's never been ill before?"

Kerry shakes her head. "No. Never like this."

"I'm sure it's nothing to worry about. Just a cold." I don't know if I believe it myself, but I have to say something.

"Oh, God!" Kerry clasps her hands over her mouth as a look of terror fills her eyes.

"What?"

"I let her play outside the other day, and she got wet and cold. We stayed out too long, she was so happy to play in the mud and with the fallen leaves and—"

"Ker. You've got to stop blaming yourself for everything. You're the most devoted mother I've ever met."

Her eyes narrow as she regards me, for a moment distracted from her concern. "And how many have you met?"

"Uhm..." *What the fuck?* I can't think of any. I think of Mama, my hardcore mob boss mom who took over the business when dad died way too young, a bunch of kids hanging on her skirts. She's not the snuggly type. She's cold, cruel and calculating.

"I figured," she says. Her tone has an edge to it. Not hostile, though... maybe slightly bitter.

I think again. No. No mothers. If they aren't targets, or related to targets. I think of Erica Davenport. Her motherly instincts, or lack thereof, pissed me off badly. Was it because I thought of my own child, somewhere out in the world? Here, as it turned out to be.

"Like I said. You're the most devoted mother I've ever met." I flash her a grin, trying to lighten the mood. It doesn't seem to work very well.

She sits up next to me, swinging her legs over the edge of the bed, letting them dangle next to mine. "I can't sleep. I'm too anxious."

"Aw, come on. She doesn't benefit from having an exhausted mother tomorrow," I say quietly.

"How much have you slept yourself?" she whispers.

Nothing. I don't answer.

"She doesn't benefit any more from having an exhausted father tomorrow either."

The world comes to an end.

Stops.

Then the wheels slowly start turning again. Slowly. Then faster. Faster. And we're back. She's there. I'm here. Things are as they were, except for one little thing that has changed. One word. Just one word. I'm stunned. I think it takes her a moment longer to realize what she just said.

You just called me her dad, Ker.

She suddenly stands, fiddling with the hem of her shirt. "I'm—I'm gonna go and make some tea. You want some?"

I take her hand and urge her to stay still. She's always running. Always escaping from something, or someone. Always on the move. "Let me. You stay here and watch over her."

She doesn't pull back her hand. Hers is so small in mine. We both look down at where our skin touches, where it burns hot with memories, and then our eyes meet.

"I'll..." she croaks out and tilts her head toward the bed.

I nod and let her go, feeling as if her hand is still in mine.

Weary-eyed, she makes herself more comfortable by the little bed, hanging her forearms over the edges of the crib, leaning close to our daughter.

Our.
Damn!
When the fuck did all of this happen to me?
How? How have I earned the presence of these two in my life?
My heart sinks heavily as I make my way to the kitchen.
I haven't.

Kerry

I called him her father. It just came out of my mouth without a thought, feeling like the most natural thing in the world. The change in him at my words, how his face fell, then lit up like I've never seen before, threw me.

He has shoved the couch all the way along the wall again until it covers the door to our bedroom. No one is locked inside the room, though. This time the door is wide open and Christian and I sit next to each other, wrapped in blankets, each sipping a cup of strong tea, staring at our daughter's restless form as she tosses and turns in her sleep. Sometimes she wakes with a hoarse cry that tears the heart right out of my body. We take turns calming her and I don't feel any jealousy when he holds her, and she calms in his embrace. Not anymore.

The night is slowly turning into early morning as we listen to Cece's snoring, to her sniveling and her uneven breaths and the cough that seems to thicken in a way I don't like at all. I suddenly feel so fundamentally stupid. I made the biggest mistake in my life when we moved here. I've made us so vulnerable. Just look at us now. *He* found us anyway, so what was the point?

We have to go. We have to get to the hospital in Sprague.

As the pale green self-illuminated digits on the clock on my bedside table flip from 4:59 to 5:00 a.m., I realize it's impossible to stay here not knowing how ill she's going to get, and so far away from all help. I don't care what it looks like out there after the storm, we'll manage, we have to take 'our asses back to civilization' as he so eloquently put it. I hate to admit he might be right about something.

I glance at him, the man who almost killed me once, who stalked me across the country, even past its borders. He is silent and pale, his hair hangs in his face but he doesn't seem to notice. His eyelids are heavy, almost closed, but I know he is no more asleep than I am. I hope I can convince him to take us back to town. Where we'll go from there

I don't know. Right now it all seems so petty. Petty problems. Cecilia is sick.

"Christian," I whisper.

He stirs and turns toward me.

I look into his deep brown eyes, the light from the kitchen illuminates them from the side and makes them glow golden. He doesn't scare me anymore. My heart makes a sudden leap at the unexpected recognition.

"Yeah?" he answers hoarsely.

"How did you get here?"

He frowns. "Why?"

"You must have a car? Where is it now?"

"Yeah, I had my car."

"And where is it?"

"Some ways down the road. Why?"

"We need to get out of here. As soon as it gets bright enough outside, we need to get her to a doctor."

He sits up straighter. "You figure? You think she's that bad off?"

I suddenly feel so infinitely small. "I don't know. How can I tell? Her temperature hasn't lowered despite the Advil and... I don't know. But I don't want to wait and see and then find out it was the wrong decision."

He regards me for a long time. "All right. I agree. I left my car, maybe half an hour's walk, or a little more, down the road, not far off from the box."

"Okay. That's good. It'll probably take us longer, carrying Cece, but that's good. It's not too far."

He nods.

"Will you help us?" I ask, suddenly shy, blushing slightly. It's dark. I doubt he sees it. I hope he doesn't.

"Help? Hell! Of course, Ker. I don't want anything bad to happen to her any more than you do. We'll leave as soon as we can see where we're going."

I sag with relief. "Thank you," I whisper.

When it's been decided, all my nervous, worried energy leaves me in an instant and I can finally rest. Pulling my legs up under the blanket, I occupy one end of the couch and drift to sleep while Christian sits next to me and guards our baby. It should be so ironic, laughable even, that I can come to a rest in his presence, but there's nothing to laugh at. He has really turned into her father tonight. I don't know what to make of that, but my brain is too fried from all the concern and these last few days lack of sleep, so I don't even try to think harder about it.

It is what it is.

Christian

I was so tired I thought I'd fall asleep at any moment, and now I can't stop thinking about what she said. My brain finally works again after these oddly slow, and yet turbulent days, and all the little synapses sparkle to life in every nerve ending. As I watch her sag more and more until she lies like a little curled up cat at the far end of the couch and her slow, even breaths tell me sleep has finally claimed her, I start making plans.

We'll have to wait until it gets bright. Then we'll find some clothes, and eat. Hopefully we'll get the little one to eat as well, but she should be the safest one on this journey, nonetheless.

The car isn't too far away. I'll go get it, drive up here and then we'll be on our way. Sprague. I'm not sure how far that is. Kerry *should* know. How the fuck could she choose to settle in this Godforsaken place.

I know I can't stay with them. Kerry has made it clear, time and time again, she won't ever be with me. I'll always make sure she and Cecilia are protected, and that they'll never lack anything, whether she likes that or not, but I'll drop them off outside a hospital and then I'll leave. Before anyone sees me, before anyone starts asking questions.

It tears my heart to pieces, but at the same time the decision gives me some small amount of peace. It's a relief to have made up my mind. I stand up and stretch my limbs, touching my tender shoulder. It feels less strained but I'm gonna have someone look at it.

And the knee. Fuck. The knee will be hell to walk on tomorrow.

Listening to Cecilia's breathing, I finally pull the blanket tighter and curl up at the other end of the couch, opposite Kerry. I can't remember when I was this tired. Ever.

I wake with a jerk. It's still dark outside. There it is, the sound that woke me. More coughing, and a small pathetic whining, coming from the little body in the bed. I sway when I stand, then I carefully lift her frail feverish form and try to soothe her, rocking her slowly in my arms like I've seen Kerry do. Against my chest she feels no larger than a small bird in a hand.

How can such a little life, having lived little more than a year, without anything significant to say, with no skills, and with the table manners of a dog, still mean so much?

I glance at Kerry. She looks completely out of it and I decide to leave her alone. If she doesn't even wake up when her daughter cries three feet away, then she definitely needs her sleep. I feel such regret it almost chokes me. Tomorrow at this time I won't be with this little kid anymore and I probably won't be able to be this close to her ever again. Right now she trusts me, and I relish the moment.

I know all too well it won't last.

Cecilia's eyelids become heavier and heavier until she's asleep again, her head leaning against my chest. I give her an extra little squeeze before I put her down, awed by her trust.

She doesn't even stir.

Kerry lies with an arm slung over the side of the couch, her hand awkwardly bent as it rests against the chilly floorboards. There's some space between her and the backrest, and I can't resist the pull, my last chance at being near her. I'm a selfish bastard. I know.

Carefully nestling in behind her, I cover us with the duvet and tuck her arm in beneath it. Her skin is cold. I maneuver until her head rests on my shoulder, like she lay once, that one night when we slept together. Kerry stirs a little but doesn't wake. My heart twinges. I'm stealing a little closeness she won't give me. Like she said: I take, take, take. But what else is there for me to do?

SEVEN

Kerry

In the first confused moments, I don't know where I am. I don't recognize the fabric I rest my cheek on, and my legs are tangled with someone else's legs.

I shoot up off the couch when everything washes over me. Christian! I'm sleeping on his shoulder. How the hell did I end up here?

Then I twitch to action. Cecilia! I dart to her side and put a hand on her forehead. She's hot. Her gaze is drowsy and her eyes glazed. "Wate," she rasps and then the coughing starts again. She is ill for real. My throat clenches and a flutter of worry occupies my chest. We need to go.

Now.

When I turn, Christian is sitting up. His gaze is dulled, and he looks exhausted.

"How is she?" He stands and walks over to the crib.

I lift a limp Cecilia and shake my head at Christian as I carry her to the kitchen to get her some lemonade. She needs water and sugar.

"Are you hungry, honey?"

Cecilia shakes her head. I throw Christian a pleading glance and he nods. He understands. We have a new wordless communication we've never had before. In the midst of the numbing worry, it warms my chest.

I busy myself with Cece while Christian packs everything we think is necessary. The most well-dressed will be our daughter. I don't have any decent boots, neither does Christian, and his elegant, expensive-looking coat isn't exactly made for outdoor activities. We grunt orders to each other throughout the morning: remember to take this, don't forget that, open that cabinet, pull that out... short, efficient words, working together like a team.

She's awake but limp, doesn't say much, refuses to eat but drinks a little. She scares me to death.

Christian sees my concern and our preparations speed up.

He rummages around in every little corner of my house, finding everything that could be useful, while I make some breakfast for us. I pack a few sandwiches for the trip too. We eat standing, wolfing down as much as we can manage, the heavy lump in my stomach doesn't allow me more than one sandwich.

"How far is it to Sprague, Kerry?"

"It's about an hour from Middlebro. If the roads have been cleared."

"I hope to fuckin' God they have," he mutters. "All right, it took what, thirty-forty minutes to drive here, so we'll be in Sprague in less than two hours. I parked half an hour's walk down the road. I should be back in forty. We'll be at the hospital in two and a half, three hours." He takes in my agonized expression. "Breathe. We've got this. It'll be all right."

"Okay. Thanks." I try to find comfort in his assurances as I bandage my left ankle with strips torn from my last clean sheet while he does the same with his left knee. The sight would have been laughable if it hadn't been so serious. I'm nervous about how the roads look. I'm afraid for Cece, and I'm worried about what will happen between Christian and me once we get back to town.

I'll cross that bridge when we get there.

I glance out the window. A thin layer of snow has covered everything during the night. With the sun up, it glitters beautifully. It's calm. Some trees have fallen during the storm, but it doesn't look too bad.

Christian lingers in the doorway. His eyes dart between me and Cecilia. "I'll be back as soon as I can, Kerry." Concern is etched on his face.

"Be careful," I say as the door slams shut.

Christian

The outside world is quiet, so different from a couple of nights ago when I chased through the woods in the roaring storm to catch up with a fleeing Kerry. I slip on icy patches as I veer across the snow-covered front yard and then hit the road. I'm haunted by Cecilia's dulled gaze. My knee soon begins to pound. At first, it's just a distant discomfort, but it gets worse.

I count the minutes until I should be at my car and can sit down and just drive back up and get my ladies.

I stop flat at the sight of a large tree that has fallen across the road, and in front of it a rusty, blue pick-up truck, it's engine compartment and front window smashed in. The same one I followed from the hotel, through the woods in the storm some nights ago. Ray. What the fuck?

I walk up to the truck, clear a little hole in the frost and look into it, seeing no one. Where the fuck is he? I try the door, but it's locked. I use my sleeve to wipe off the window better. Maybe there's something in there I can use? I see part of a shotgun, a pair of gloves, and a lot of used paper tissues. On the flatbed lies a shovel and some neatly folded ropes. I can't think of anything I can do with either of them, so I move on, still puzzled over the disappearance of the man.

I freeze, a horrible thought striking me. I recognize this part of the road all too well. It's fucking right where I parked my car. This isn't happening! Fighting the twigs, rocks and roots, I plough through the terrain around the tree, I make my way to the other side, praying to a deity that has never listened to me that the road will be clear.

It isn't. My heart drops to my feet. The huge crown of the tree has fallen onto the side road, blocking it off. There's not a chance in hell I can get past it.

I unlock the car and almost fall into the driver's seat, sweaty and spent, at a loss as to what to do now. My bag lies next to me, filled with useless items meant for another kind of life. A gun. Shirts and pants, a couple of suit jackets, a second pair of black, neatly polished shoes. My phone.

After several attempts, I manage to start a very reluctant engine to get some warmth back. Shaking everything out of the bag, I take the gun and put it in the side pocket of my pants after making sure it's secured, pull off my ruined shoes and put on the undamaged ones. I dismiss the rest of the stuff. I have better clothes on, and I can't bother with the weight, walking all the way back.

The phone is dead. I put it in the charger, but I'll have to recharge it fully at Kerry's and we can call for help. Well, *she* can call for help. I'll have to think of something else, because I don't want to be seen again. I've never left this amount of traces behind me. People who have seen me several times, a whole house full of my fingerprints and DNA. I'm used to being a shadow, of staying under the radar and my spine crawls with the knowledge that I've made myself vulnerable.

I look around me, at the blocked road. If I'd had a chainsaw... But I've never dismembered anyone I've killed, I've never even dreamt of it, and I haven't had any reason to pack one when I go on a mission.

Twitching back to the present, I realize I can't sit here. I turn off the engine, grab the phone and charger and heave my aching body out of the car as my heart sinks. Staring at the key, I wonder if there's even a point to bringing it, but then I shrug and pocket it.

It takes more than thirty minutes to get back, and I'm sweating profusely as I enter Kerry's front yard. I stop flat at the sight. To my right lies an oblong pile of snow. A thick, human-sized, snow-covered pile. All my senses sharpen as I walk up to it.

It's our missing pick-up owner. Guess the filthy little grocery store is closing. I grab his shoulder and turn him. He's frozen stiff, like a massive lollipop. Well, that's that. It's not hard to guess what happened. He left us, nearly got crushed under the tree, turned back... Then I don't know. A thirty-minute walk killed him? Heart attack? I have no fucking idea.

Bad luck. But he wouldn't have had better luck if he'd have made it back to us. I'm really fucking happy he didn't.

I sigh and turn toward the house. The phone has come to life, low on battery, but at least it works. It hasn't found a network, though, and it fills me with dread that slowly turns to anger. I don't do dread; I don't like the feeling.

Kerry

It's the longest wait of my life. I rock back and forth as I cradle Cece in my arms, staring at the clock every second minute. When forty minutes have passed, closing in on fifty, I am nauseous with worry. Finally there are steps outside, almost an hour and a half after he left. I carefully put Cecilia down on the couch and dart up to open the door, but Christian rips it open and then slams it closed, his eyes dark and his face a mask of fury.

"What happened?" Anxiety creeps through my body like a

tingling spreading from my chest, radiating through my limbs. "What happened?" I repeat, breathless with worry when he doesn't answer.

"No car," he grits out.

I shake my head, I don't understand. I don't want to understand. "Why?"

"Because there's no way in hell to get it past the fucking fallen tree!" he roars, making me jolt.

I look at him in despair, my mind a jumbled mess.

"It gets even better."

"What?"

"I found Ray's pick-up."

I don't answer, dread rising in me with the ominous feeling that I won't like what's coming next.

"Whe—"

"It's *under* the fucking tree! Well, part of it. And your friend is lying dead outside."

He shoves his hands through his hair, his ski cap falling to the floor.

"What?" I have to sit down as nausea rises in me. My head spins and I close my eyes. "What happened? What do we do?"

"Where does the side road lead to?"

"Just to an abandoned house. It's a dead end."

"Fuck!" His voice has a dark edge to it that sends flutters through my stomach. "Is there no fucking signal out here?" He holds up a phone, pulls a charger out of his pocket and puts it in a socket next to the living room window, then he turns, waiting for my answer.

I chew on my bottom lip. I don't want to answer. I don't want to prove to him what a fuck-up I've been.

"When—" he growls, "did you lose your fucking mind? You have a brain. I know it. How the fuck did you choose this dump?"

Tears flood my eyes as I look at a sleeping Cecilia. "Can we please not fight?" My voice is hoarse, barely carrying the words.

Christian tightens his lips into a thin line, making my heart jolt. He looks like he'll lash out any second, but then he suddenly sounds all business. He snatches up his cap off the floor and puts it on his head. "Well... either we wait—"

"*Wait?* Wait for what?"

"—or we walk."

I stare emptily in front of me. Instead of seeing the living room, I see the forest, the upwards and downwards slopes, the rocks and the trees. "It's... it's probably a four-hour walk," I whisper, "or more. Oh God."

"There's no fucking God," he snarls, his face grim. "All right, so we walk." He picks up his phone. "We gotta wait a little. At some fucking point along the way we gotta be able to call for help."

I sink down next to our daughter, bone tired. Christian disappears to the bathroom for a while, and then comes back to sit on her other side, his eyes softening as he looks at Cecilia. We don't speak for a long while, only her coughs break the silence.

Finally he gets up and grabs the phone. "Seventy-five percent. It'll do. Got everything you need?"

I give the room a once-over. "Yeah, I think so."

"That's not good enough."

"*Yes.* We've got everything. Let's do this."

"After you, then."

I pull on my jacket and my boots, pick up our sleeping daughter and look up at him. He's holding the door for me and the little breathing package in a red checkered blanket in my arms.

"Thanks," I say and take the first step out on the porch. The sky is clear, the light wind nips at my cheeks. I shudder and look up at him. "Let's go."

"Yeah." He lets the door slam shut with a very final sound.

I glance once behind me, wondering if I'll ever return to this place, and then we both turn toward the blinding whiteness.

Christian tilts his head. "Lead the way."

The ground is slippery and in my rubber boots, walking becomes a nightmare after a mere few steps. I gasp as I see a dark form lying a few yards to the side. His fur hat has fallen off, and his thick overcoat warms no one. Tears well up in my eyes.

"What do you think happened?" My throat constricts as I'm overwhelmed by sadness. He was such a kind man.

"I have no idea." Christian stops, and looks between me and Ray, then he walks up to him and pinches the coat. "Fuck."

"What?"

"I just had a thought. But they're just as frozen stiff as he is."

I back up a step. "You wanted to use his clothes? That's disgusting!"

"He's got no use for them." Christian grabs a boot and fights to get it off him without succeeding. "*Fuck!* It's stuck like glue!" he roars and drops the leg.

I want to vomit at the sight, and even more at the dull thud when Ray's leg hits the ground. Christian is a person I'll never understand fully, that I'll never want to understand fully.

"Can we please just move on?" I ask faintly.

I swear I hear a near-feral growl from the huge man by my side, and it sends a wave of shivers down my spine. We take off down the road. After ten minutes, I have to stop and catch my breath. My heart slams in my chest and my ankle pounds.

"Christian. It's far. Four hours is at a normal pace. We're not looking at four hours."

"I know," he says through gritted teeth.

"It's gonna take us all day." I nod toward the woods. "There's a shorter route through there, we'll have to walk across the mountain, but it'll take us half the time. The road goes all the way around."

He squints and studies the tree line. "Are you sure?"

I nod.

"Let's go then." Lifting Cece out of my arms, he nods in the direction I pointed out. "After you, my dear."

It's not easy. The road was easy, this is insane. I have trekked here a lot, during spring, summer and autumn. Autumn is my favorite season. The beauty in the decay, and the slowing down of everything that lives, soothes me somehow. But that's during snow-free seasons. This is different. We stumble and slip over rocks, roots, and branches. The sun and light are our friends, but it doesn't warm the air anymore. It helps me with direction, though.

And it goes up, up, up. It doesn't take long until I'm flustered, and soon there's a thin sheen of sweat on both our faces. Christian carries Cece the most. He's stronger.

"Stop," I pant. "I have to stop. My ankle... and I... have no... breath." I sink down on a flat rock, not giving a fuck if my butt will get cold and wet.

"You can't sit there for long or you'll catch a cold."

"I have to sit, or a cold will be the least of my worries," I pant and slump forward, my arms resting on my knees. My heart pounds hard and everything aches.

"We left the road an hour ago. How much further?" he asks and stomps to keep his warmth.

I shake my head and gesture to my chest. I can't talk. Not yet.

He hands me our little, sick baby and for the hundredth time this morning, I check her pulse, her breathing and her color. Her cheeks are rosy, but it could be the cold. Maybe she's breathing a little calmer. Just as I look at her, her round, brown eyes open and her pained gaze shoots straight into my heart.

"Hey, tiger," I whisper.

Christian comes and sits himself next to me. "How is she?"

"I'm not sure. How are you feeling, honey?"

"Wate," she rasps, and then her gaze searches our surroundings. "Snow?"

I dig in my backpack and pull out the bottle, placing it at her lips. "Yes, sweetie, we're taking you to the doctor."

"Ai—ai," she says and lays a little gloved hand against her chest.

Her pain transfers to me. I hurt when she hurts. Tears well up in my eyes. "I know, honey."

"Kis?" she whispers. I widen my eyes in surprise. My gaze darts to him and I am stunned by the transformation. It's as if he's been lit up from somewhere deep within. And it's just... beautiful.

"He's here, Cecilia." I hold her up so she can see him. And then I say it. "It's not 'Chris', honey. He's your dad. Christian is your dad."

I can't look at him after that, the need to leave him alone with the moment too overwhelming. He reaches for her and she grabs his hand as she coughs. Then she smiles and her eyes flutter half shut.

Christian frees himself from her hold, and as I glance at him, I see his face has once again become an unreadable mask. "It's time to move on."

"Do you want to hold her," I ask shyly.

The corners of his mouth suddenly pull up and his eyes turn warmer. "Absolutely." He hugs her to his chest, and we start moving again. The steep slope gets to both of us and nothing is said for a long time.

"When does it even out? How much is left?" he pants and hands me our daughter who has fallen asleep again, blissfully unaware of her parents' struggle.

"Soon, I think. It should be an hour left at most." I hoist her higher, changing the grip. She's already too heavy for me and I've only walked a few steps with her this time. "On top of the mountain it'll even out for a while before it starts descending."

"When we get up there, we need to make a real stop, Ker. Drink and eat."

I nod, my chest too tight, gasping for air.

And we continue our trek.

EIGHT

Christian

I keep checking my cell compulsively, but so far, no signal. I'm seriously concerned for us all. Kerry is exhausted. My knee hurts so bad I want to puke. Cecilia worries me like fucking hell. The chilly air nips at our skin, and we're moving constantly. Half a day has passed since we woke up this morning, and she sleeps and sleeps. That can't be good.

It feels right that we are doing something, and that we're not only sitting passively, but on the other hand I'm wondering if we aren't committing suicide. We reach the plateau and the walk gets a lot easier once we don't have to walk up, up, up and fucking up.

'*Kis?*' She *asked* for me. Well... she'll forget about me as easily. '*Christian is your dad.*'

I'll never forget her.

Kerry glances at me and inhales. Then she shakes her head and remains silent.

"What?" I say, happy for any distraction.

She inhales again. "Why did you keep looking for—" She snaps her mouth closed and then adds quickly, "Never mind."

I glance at her and then back at the cold, white wetness as I sigh inwardly at the decisions I've made. "You have to admit it, Kerry. We had something; you know we did. It was there." I want to touch her so badly. My hand hovers in the air close to hers, but I can't.

I don't.

She doesn't answer, but her silence is answer enough. "It was there, yes," she finally says. "I admit that. A long time ago. You ruined that pretty good."

"I... yes. I know."

I glance at her as she stumbles and then regains her footing, changing her grip around our sleeping daughter's form. My whole body tenses as I ready myself to catch her if she falls. She looks up at me, waiting for me to continue.

"I made choices I regret," I mumble, my whole being crumbling in shame. Salvatore threatened my sister, but I could have found a fucking way around that if I had only thought a little.

She raises her eyebrows but doesn't answer. I guess there's not much to say.

I deflate. I've lost everything. Everything that ever mattered to me. And I can only blame myself. Maybe I could force her to become mine, somehow work her, manipulate her. But that's not how I wanna play it. I don't want to play at all, actually. I know I'm going to have to let them go. Shut down. Shut them out.

I'll have to live with it, with what I've done, and what I've lost.

I realize this is my gift to them, my sacrifice. I'll take them to safety and then give them their lives back. This walk through these abandoned forests will redeem me, help me forgive myself if no one else does.

"Is this the top of the mountain?" I need to focus on something solid, something I can still work with, something still in my grasp. "We need a break."

She nods and carefully lowers Cecilia to the ground, snugly wrapped in her blanket.

I drop the backpack to the ground. "I hate trees, and rocks, and roots, and twigs. I'm never setting foot in a forest again. Ever!"

"I'm prone to agree," she pants and plops down next to our daughter.

"You'll get cold."

"I don't fucking care," she grits. "Still no signal?"

I shake my head as I start unpacking. Coffee, two mugs, two sandwiches, a bottle of water, and a second blanket. At the bottom of the backpack there are two sandwiches left. For Cecilia. And that's all there is. I glance up at the wilderness and pray silently we won't get lost. And that Kerry knows where we're going. I eye her suspiciously. I *really* hope she knows the way.

Now that we've stopped and seated ourselves at the edge of Cecilia's blanket, mugs with steaming contents in our hands, and a few chews in on our first sandwich, I realize how sweaty, cold, and deadly tired I am already. And I started this with a not only good physique, but great. Kerry must be so much worse off, but she isn't complaining in the least.

Her hour of a thousand questions doesn't seem to be over yet, though, and with some newly found energy, she starts again.

"Why did you come for me that second time?"

I clench my jaws and pray for strength. Can she just not fucking let this go? I inhale to speak, but she interrupts me.

"Walk me through it, please. I've existed in a void of pain and fear, only surviving. I haven't lived since. Please let me know there was a reason. Help me understand."

I relive the pain in the harbor, the blinding fury after she seduced me with a mere few words and her big, green eyes, and then completely wiped the floor with me, as if I hadn't been the professional and she hadn't been the victim.

"I didn't come to kill you that second time."

She frowns, her hand with the cup stopping mid-air. "No?"

"I wanted to save you."

She scoffs.

"Fuck, Kerry. I didn't want you dead. Ever. Salvatore held an axe over my head. I tried to get you out of it, but he demanded I take you out."

"But... he seemed so reasonable when I talked to him."

I bark out a short laugh. "Don't ever let that man fool you. He's lethal. He never does anything without reason. If he was nice with you it's because he figured it would benefit him."

"I don't understand."

"Cecilia saved your ass."

Kerry glances at our daughter and then back at me. "So... then you saved my life after all."

I frown.

"That night. When you fucked the woman you knew you were going to kill." Her lips twist into a sneer and then she stands abruptly.

"Ker!"

"Let's go." She shakes the last few drops out of the cup and puts it in the backpack. "If I ever see you again, after today... do I have to be afraid?" Her voice is hesitant, careful. "If—if you'll let us go, I mean," she breathes, the last words barely audible.

I frown as I look at her. Her dark eyes are wide and full of questions. "Yes, of course I'll let you go. *Fuck!* I don't know how I can ever convince you!"

She looks away. "Me neither, to be honest. I'm too scarred."

"I know," I mumble. "I don't know what to do about it."

"Maybe we are?" she says softly and glances at me again.

"Huh?"

"Maybe we *are* doing something about it?"

I regard her. Then I nod. *Yeah, maybe we are.*

In minutes we have everything packed and are on the move again. It's my turn to carry our child. I cradle the little life to my chest and take a deep breath. Then we start walking again.

Kerry

Everything aches.

Everything.

My feet, my ankle, my legs, my back—definitely my back, my shoulders, my head, my heart... I glance at Christian. He looks as terrible as I feel.

And I'm wet. My legs and my back are soaked. Wet. But I'm warm-wet, because of the effort. Only my feet are cold-wet. Ice-cold wet. And I keep slipping in my rubber boots. What the hell made me throw away my good winter jacket and my boots when I entered my kitchen window that first night? When I tried to kill him. But he just kept on living, and now I thank whatever God there might be up there. Maybe all things happen for a reason? I could never have made this journey on my own. But hadn't it been for him, I'd have had a working car, but then again... it wouldn't have made it past that tree that lies over the road.

I can't think! I don't know anymore. Everything has gotten so complicated.

Funny how long ago that seems, when I climbed in through my kitchen window. The days and nights have melted into each other and I'm not even sure how long he's been with us anymore. Forever it seems. Maybe he has really been with me forever? Maybe it was always us? Ever since I first met him I've never been fully free of him, not since the moment I looked into his eyes, turning toward him in the bar, losing track of time and place.

Almost two years ago.

Since his arrival here I haven't had the time, or the energy, to dwell much on those old things. Or on anything beyond him, me, and Cecilia. Things have just... happened, and I've had to live them.

I shake my head. I'm exhausted and can't think anymore.

It's straight ahead on the plateau for a while now, and then it's downhill. We should have an hour left. I have no energy left whatsoever, but Christian's relentless marching and Cece's flushed face gives me that extra boost I need every time I feel like just giving up.

"I think we're through the worst," I pant.

He gives me a pale grin. "That's good, Ker. I'm beginning to completely lose feeling in my feet."

"What?"

"My shoes aren't exactly cut out for this."

"Oh my God! We have to take a look!"

"No."

"Bu—"

"*No.* We move on. That's the only thing we're gonna do. No rest. No looking."

I narrow my eyes as I regard him. My chest tightens from the tone of his voice. He's worried. If *he's* worried...

"Okay. Down through there now. Here, let me take her."

He hands me Cece. She squirms and moans. I lay my cheek against her forehead and the lump of fear grows in my chest. She's hot. The adrenaline gives me new energy and we keep walking.

"*Whoa!* Hold it!"

"What?" I glance up from under my ski cap that has slid too low without me even noticing it.

"Are you sure this is the straightest way?"

He's pointing at a sudden slope where the ground seems to disappear into nowhere, a ravine, maybe fifteen feet deep and thirty feet wide. I take a step closer to get a better view, but he stops me as I stagger and slide.

"Careful! Want me to take her?"

I shake my head. "No, I'm fine."

I'm confused. I didn't know this was here, but then again, maybe I've never been all the way up here before.

"Are we on the right path at least?" he asks with a new edge in his voice.

His eyes are dull and tired, his cheeks flushed, and the stubble has begun to grow into a short scruffy beard. He looks like a very tired caveman. I raise my gaze to the pale sun and think of the directions. I'm good with directions, always have been, it's like I have an inner map I follow, a compass guiding me through the terrain. God, I wish I had a similar built-in device for everything else in my life.

"Yes. It's that way." I point right across the ravine.

His eyes narrow. "Are you sure?"

I nod.

He takes a couple of steps closer to the edge and glances over it and then across to the other side. "There's a river down there. And it's too deep, this whole fuckery. We can't get across it here. Do you know where it leads to?"

I shake my head, my mind rapidly filling with dread and despair. This is it. I can't take this. We can't pass and I just don't know what to do. We're not going to make it. I'm so tired. I just want to sit down and—

"Ker!"

I look up at him, unable to hold back the tears. "It's no use," I whisper. "I can't... go on."

He turns fully toward me and takes one long stride. "Get your act *together*, woman," he growls between clenched teeth. "We're in this together. We started this. We endure, and we *finish!*"

His hands squeeze my shoulders so hard it hurts and a jolt of fear surges through me at his hard gaze, but it gives me a very much needed rush of adrenaline. I nod at north-east. Up along the ravine.

"If we go that way, we'll either find a place to cross, or we'll come across the main road sooner or later."

He regards me. "Upstream it is then."

As we continue in the new direction, along the steep edge, I glance at him. I have hated this man with every fiber in my body and now... I don't anymore. I couldn't have done this alone. Even with the car, the worry for Cece... I can't imagine having no one to share it with.

"Christian, I want to— thanks fo—"

I scream as I lose my footing and begin to slide down the steep slope. I keep screaming as I stop with a violent jerk when something hooks onto my clothing, but I lose my grip on Cecilia and she is jerked out of my arms and continues down the slope.

A little mewling packet in a checkered red blanket.

"*Ceeee!*"

Christian is a blur as he flies past me and disappears over the edge at the same moment as Cece.

For a second everything is absolutely still and quiet. Then I tear my jacket to shreds when I free it from the root it has stuck on and slide down to the edge. I'm absolutely numb. Not a thought, not one emotion comes through in my dazed mind.

Then I hear a cry and a roar and Cecilia is suddenly pushed up right next to me. I grab her little body, holding her tight. She's crying, terrified, cold and wet. I can't separate her shrieks from my own wailing as I clutch her to my chest, waiting for Christian to climb back up.

I lose track of time as my mind replays over and over how she slid and disappeared. The pain is indescribable, and my brain doesn't stop the screams of terror until long after my mouth has gone silent.

NINE

Kerry

Finally, I lift my head and look around me. Where did Christian go?

Everything is still and the forest gets increasingly dusky and silent.

"Christian," I say, hesitantly. Everything is quiet. I clutch Cecilia hard to my chest and stand carefully for the first time since I fell. "Christian!" A little louder. No answer. Did he leave us? A claw of a new kind of fear nips at my already battered heart. *"Christian!"* I cry and Cecilia stirs in my arms.

A ghostly echo rolls over the mountain. That's the only answer I'm getting.

I stand absolutely still, at a loss as to what to do. I don't understand. Slipping and sliding, I fight my way up the slope. Then I wedge Cecilia behind a rock, making sure she lies safely before I, with violently trembling legs, walk all the way down to the edge. The ravine is cold, beautiful, and quiet. On the bottom I see the river hurling cold black water over pointy rocks. The sight makes me physically ill. Where is Christian? I lie down prone and slide further to look over the edge, terrified I'll fall if I go too far. I follow the trail of rushing water and then something disrupts the vision, a speck on the cliffs. Frowning, I stare at the object. Realization comes slowly, it's as if my mind is as unmoving as the world around me.

It's a ski cap.

It's a red ski cap. Christian wears a red ski cap.

Wore.

A wave of dizziness rolls over me and I hold on hard not to topple over. I stare at the piece of fabric and it blurs as tears fill my eyes.

He fell.

He's gone.

I'm alone.

In this desolate, darkening forest, I'm suddenly left alone. My heart pounds so hard it feels as if my chest is going to explode and I struggle to inhale. I panic when I can't feel my hands and stare at them, clenching and unclenching them to try to find them again, to see if they're still attached to my body. And then I realize he's *gone!* I don't know what to do. Still on my knees, the cold and wet has started to leak through to my skin and a shudder ripples across my back. A whimper from behind the rock higher up on the slope startles me.

Get up, Kerry. Get up! You continue. And you finish!

His words ring in my ears as I struggle back up to Cecilia, lift her from her cold cradle and start walking, turning my back to him, wherever he is. *Dead.* I shake my head and keep walking. *He's dead, Ker.* My legs march to the rhythm of my heart, faster, faster, downward, faster. *He's gone.* Heavy weight in my arms. Walk. Walk. Walk. Focus. I try to grab onto some of his strength, repeating his words, his last testament to us.

Continue. Finish.

I lose track of time. I don't feel anything but the little body I'm carrying, the burning exhaustion in my legs, back, arms, and the numbing cold. I know we're going to die out here too. And it's all my fault. I made the decision to move here. I made all the wrong decisions.

Darkness falls and the air is getting increasingly chilly. What should have taken a few hours has taken the whole day. I stagger and stumble. I can't continue. I'm lost. It's no use. We'll die. I can't even muster enough energy to care.

"Kerry?"

I'm dreaming someone's calling my name. I don't recognize the voice. A man's voice. Funny. I would have thought it'd be my father, or one of my grandparents. Not some stranger. I fall on my knees, I think I'm still holding on to Cecilia, but I can't feel my arms anymore. I can't feel my body.

"He's dead," I croak.

"Ray's dead?" Another voice.

Ray? Who's Ray?

"Let me take her." Someone takes the weight out of my arms and I clutch the air, knowing I've lost something important.

"Get her in the car."

"Careful."

"Kerry! Kerry! We need to know! Where's Ray?"

I think I know that voice. Anderson. Mr. Anderson. Ste— Stephan? Yes. Stephan. I see the partly snow-covered shape before my eyes. "Cabin," I whisper.

"Steve! Take'em to the hospital. Fast as fuck. They're frozen blue. We'll go find Ray."

I'm moving, rocking, a humming sound, soothing. A car? *Cece!*

"She's right next to ya, Kerry. We're takin' you to the hospital. Ya're lucky to be alive."

I didn't even know I'd said something.

Cold. I'm so cold.

LIGHT.

I close my eyes again. I squint hard and open one eye just a tiny crack. *Light!* I close it again.

Someone's sitting on my chest. I inhale, try to inhale, try to expand my chest, but it's impossible. Then I fight to breathe through the eruption of coughs that follow. I need to open my eyes. Who's sitting on my chest?

Light. Hard, white light. Snow? No. Not snow. White ceiling.

I'm alone. If no one's sitting on my chest, then why does it feel so heavy? A soft, steady beeping penetrates my chilled mind and a stream of cool air fills my nostrils. Panicking, I tear at my face and end up with a thin plastic cord between my fingers.

"Kerry." The voice is soft, female, caring. "Kerry."

I open my eyes to stare at a woman I've never seen before, and a white ceiling I *have* seen before. I recognize her voice. I've heard it in my dreams. *Cecilia!* I gasp and try to sit up but her hand is stronger. "Ce—" I rasp. I cough myself sweaty and not until my chest calms down can I hear her again.

"She's doing fine, Kerry. She's in the pediatric ICU but she's a strong girl, she's doing fine." She reattaches the cord to my face and adjusts it. "Don't take this off, honey. You need the oxygen."

"I need to see her!"

"You need to get well, but we'll arrange for her to be brought here. You're far worse off than her. You're lucky to be here."

I stare at her. I'm not the one who's ill.

"What?"

"When they brought you in you were critically hypothermic and you have bilateral pneumonia. We had to support your breathing the first night."

The first...?

I try to sit up again but she holds me down. "You need to take it easy, love. You need your rest." She adjusts something where bags of fluids are connected to lines that disappear into bandages on my arms. "We'll bring her to you a little later today, okay?"

"How long have I been here?"

"You've been comatose for two days. Today is your third day here."

Christian!

"Have..." I lick my lips and fight the intense urge to cough, I need to ask this. "Have they found him?" My voice wavers pathetically.

A fleeting look of pity passes over her features. "Your friend was found right next to your house. I'm sorry." She lays a hand on my arm and holds it there, for comfort, to keep me still. "You've been through a lot."

Next to my house? How did he get there? Then I realize she isn't talking about Christian.

She clears her throat. "Actually, there's someone who will be very happy to hear you're awake. Officer Tremblay has requested to see you on several occasions."

The door falls closed with a whisper.

THE CURTAINS ARE HALF CLOSED. IT'S DARK OUTSIDE. Officer Frederic Tremblay takes up the whole room.

I lay my hand protectively over Cece's sleeping form in the bed next to me as the hulking giant of a man invades the room. Taking off his cap, he pulls a chair closer, scraping it across the floor, the sound cutting painfully into my over-sensitized mind. He is surprisingly graceful as he folds his body into a sitting position, on a chair that looks like it'll collapse beneath him, before extending a hand to me.

"Kerry Jackson. I'm terribly happy to see you awake." His voice is deep and husky. He sounds like a friend, like a father would. I suddenly miss mine so much my chest tightens, and I grimace from the pain. I wet my dry lips and give him my hand. It disappears completely in his large paw.

"Do you need anything? Water?" He looks around him and then back at me.

I shake my head. "No. I don't need anything."

"Are you sure?"

I have to bite my lips to not start crying as his kindness overwhelms me. "Yes, I'm sure. Thanks."

"Miss Jackson, as you can imagine we have questions about what happened to you and your daughter. There are some inconsistencies in your story. For instance we've found you are divorced. There are no restraining orders or police reports. Yet you have told everybody your husband was after you. Why is that? I don't understand."

"I..." How can I tell? I can't tell. I see Salvatore before me, the man who once ordered my death. I'll be dead if I ever tell the truth. "I was stalked. I thought there'd be less questions if it seemed domestic."

"Who stalked you?"

"A... man I met." I ponder for a moment if I should lie, but no, better to stick close to the truth without ever telling the whole truth. "His name was Christian. Just a flirt on a stupid night out with friends. He got obsessed with me."

"Do you have a full name for this Christian?"

I shake my head. "No, Officer, I have no idea what his last name was."

"He stalked you?"

I nod. "Yes."

"So you fled?"

I nod again.

"Has this been through a court? Restraining order? Anything?"

"No," I mouth.

"Why is that?"

"Because I knew it wouldn't help."

Tremblay is quiet, narrowing his eyes slightly as he holds my gaze.

"What happened in the woods? Ray McGonaghan has been found dead outside your house. We're investigating his death and can't rule out homicide yet. Miss Jackson... we need to know what happened."

"Homicide? But... What?"

"He had head trauma and a brain hemorrhage due to blunt force. There is no blood in his truck, and he walked quite far only to be found dead outside your house. It might be a coincidence. Or it might not."

"Blunt?"

"Something, or someone, whacked him over the head."

I see his body before me, see Christian, compassionless trying to rid Ray of his boots. Did he kill him? But even I could see that Ray had been dead for a while, and Christian was with me the whole time. Right?

For a moment I'm back there, tied up, crying. I fight against the memories. They hurt. "My... stalker. He found us." My voice breaks, the pain too great. "But he didn't kill Ray," I add quickly.

He nods. "Go on."

"I knew he would come after me sooner or later. I kept seeing him. Wherever I went, he showed up. That's why I finally left the US. I thought I'd be safe."

"And this was," he looks at a notepad, "a little more than a year ago? Somewhere in all of this you had a child."

"Yes," I say, defensively.

"Where's the father?"

I don't miss a beat. "I don't know."

He doesn't miss a beat either. "You don't know?"

I shake my head. "I was with someone... Just a night out. I was a bit reckless back then." I grimace and try to mix my real pain into the lie. The pain I felt then, the pain I feel now.

"That's a lot of nights out."

I raise my chin. "So? Is that a crime?"

He frowns, then he shakes his head and scribbles. I'm not sure how to interpret his expression. Drunken one-night stands are as far from me as it gets, and I itch to rectify the lie, to restore my reputation, even if it's only between him and me, and doesn't mean a thing.

"What happened after your daughter was born? Did you come here before or after?"

"I moved here after. I thought we'd be okay..." My voice trails off. My chest feels so heavy, so tight. I try to inhale but end up fighting for air through endless sets of coughs. Finally, I fall back onto my pillow, sweaty. Tired. So, so tired.

Officer Tremblay clears his throat and hands me a glass of water. "I'm sorry I have to put you through all this."

I nod and drink a small sip. "I want to help. Did you find him yet?"

"What happened these last few days, Kerry, may I call you Kerry?"

I nod.

"Did he try to kill you? Force himself on you?"

I shake my head.

"Why is that? I'm sorry—" He waves his large hands in the air. "This is all a little confusing to me. Are you saying he *didn't* try to harm you? What was he after all this time then? Did he assault you in any way?"

I clear my voice. How am I going to put this? Lies *are* best when close to the truth. "I think he wanted to be with me... Like romantically." My voice trails off. "And I think Cecilia's presence made him restrain himself."

He frowns. "An obsessed stalker who develops a conscience... Huh. How long was he with you?"

I bite my lip and try to think. "I'm not sure... the days melted into one another... maybe three days. Or four."

He studies me and his intelligent eyes seem to look right into me.

Tremblay looks like a teddy bear, friendly, harmless, but I suddenly know his looks are deceiving, that he is very good at what he does—a frightening opponent for those who oppose him.

"What happened between the two of you during all this time?"

"The first day... or two maybe, I tried to," my cheeks heat up, "kill him... a few times." I look defensively at him, challenging him to say something. "I had to try to get away."

He nods and doesn't say anything. It encourages me that he isn't judging me. "The last day, Cece got sick and I begged him to help us get back here. At that point I didn't care about what he did to me, what his plans were or anything... I just needed to take her to safety. And he did. He helped us."

"What did he plan to do once you got back into town?"

I shake my head slowly. "I have no idea, Officer. I never asked. I was afraid to ask, actually."

"Tell me about when he left you."

I shudder, reliving the horrifying moment, fingering the soft skin on the back of the chubby little hand I'm holding. "Cece fell—I fell and dropped her—and she slid over the edge of the ravine... and he... and he... threw himself after her, caught her somehow and pushed her back up." I swallow back the tears. "That was the last I saw of him. I think he must've fallen into the river."

"That... or he found a convenient escape."

I grimace. My head spins.

Maybe.

Maybe not.

Christian Russo is the most capable man I've ever met. If there's even the slightest chance he could have lived, he lives. My heart tells me he's alive. My brain says he's dead, that it's just not possible he'd survive that fall and the cold water.

The door slides open behind him and my nurse for the day enters. "Officer! Is this really necessary? You have by far exceeded your stay for today, she's exhausted! You'll have to come back another time." She rushes to my side and pulls a little at the sheet, adjusts some fluid bags and fiddles with something I can't see, showing clearly she wants him to leave.

He takes the hint and stands, cap in hand. "I'll need to come back, though."

I hold his gaze. "Did you find him?"

He shakes his head. "Only the ski cap at the bottom of the ravine, and some smeared blood right next to it. We're looking further downstream. We will find him. If he's there, we'll find him. Don't you worry."

"That's not what I'm worried about," I say slowly.

"If he fell into the water, he's dead, Miss Jackson. He wouldn't last more than a few minutes in that river. We'll keep looking. For closure. But I doubt he's coming back."

"Okay," I whisper and smile meekly.

That's not what I'm worried about. I'm worried they will find him. And that he'll still be alive. And I don't know who I worry about more.

Him.

Or them.

TEN

Kerry

When I wake, he's sitting patiently by my side, his hands folded in his lap. A day passed already? I attempt a smile. "I must be such a good witness," I croak. "You always know where to find me."

He fires off one of his friendly smiles back but doesn't answer.

I fight my way up to a half-sitting position, regarding him curiously. There's something he wants to get off his chest. I feel it. I fear it.

"This man..."

"Yes?"

"He doesn't seem to exist."

I look up at his scraggy features, his stubble is longer, and somehow grayer, than yesterday. "What do you mean?"

"The fingerprints we found on the knife in your kitchen, and around your house, don't match any registered felon, or anyone else for that matter who has ever passed through customs, been in a car accident, been arrested for pickpocketing... anything."

"You were in my house?"

"We're investigating a homicide, Miss, and you housed a man we suspect for the murder."

"I didn't 'house' him. He broke in."

Tremblay bows his head in acknowledgement. "Very well."

I frown. "So then... that just means he hasn't been arrested, right?"

"We're still waiting for the Americans to get back to us, but so far... it's like he doesn't exist."

"But he does!" Suddenly I'm worried he won't believe me. Will he think *I* killed Ray?

"We have fingerprints unaccounted for, a car with the same prints inside, a dead body, your statement. We'll keep looking further downstream when it gets bright again. If he's out there, we'll find the man who did this to you, and to Ray."

"He couldn't have killed Ray, Officer. Christian was with me the whole time. It was a storm. Couldn't Ray have gotten hit by something? I don't understand."

"It's not unlikely his head wound is from the car crash. We'll get the coroner's report later today."

Tremblay stands, fiddles with his cap, taking me in. "Have you heard of Stockholm syndrome, Miss Jackson?"

My heart drops. No. I know what that is, but no. That can't be it. Can it?

He lays a hand on my forearm. "Do you have someone to talk to?"

I look away. I don't want him to see the tears that well up in my eyes.

It's not Stockholm syndrome. Christian was a complex, real person, who just happened to make bad choices. When I think of him, I don't see the furious murderer anymore. I see a father. A man. A man I could have known, and maybe more... had things been different.

I lower my gaze to Cece, sleeping in her little bed with steel bars on the sides. When she's older I'll try to explain to her who he was—to the best of my knowledge. Christian won't come after us again. We're free. But it's not how it feels.

When I look back toward Tremblay, he has left the room.

"WE'VE STOPPED THE SEARCH, KERRY."

One or two more days have passed. I'm not sure. It's hard to keep track of time here.

"You don't think you'll find him?"

"The river is empty all the way down to the lake which has frozen over. There's no use in keep on looking. We'll see what washes up in April."

"You do believe me, don't you?"

"With the statements from people in town who met him, all the blood in the house that matches neither you nor Mr. McGonaghan, the car next to Ray's down the road, yes, everything indicates things happened more or less the way you described them."

I fall back against the pillow. "Good."

"And I read your journals."

I stiffen and stare at him in horror. "You did *what*?"

"We had to exclude you as a suspect. We don't leave stones unturned."

I'm too shocked to respond. Everything is in there. All the things I've never told anyone but Chloe.

Tremblay's eyes bore into mine. "Who is Christian Russo?"

I swallow hard as sweat breaks out on my forehead. This is it. I'm fucked. I wrote his name. Why the hell did I write his name? His full fucking name!

"Kerry?"

My heart turns into a hard lump of pure fear. Tell on the mob and die. I know how this will go. I won't be safe anywhere. I know it won't be Christian. There's not a chance in hell it will be Christian, even if he lives. But someone will find me and end me. A hole opens up beneath me and it feels as if I'm falling into a black, cold void.

Me. And maybe Cecilia too.

That can't happen.

"We do have a few Christian Russos on the north American continent. The car didn't lead us anywhere. We've found no DNA match. Who is this man? Why did you withhold his full name?"

I hear Tremblay as if from a distance. I'm frozen in terror. I can't tell the truth. It's out of the question.

"What I went through, Officer, has nothing to do with what happened to Ray. The man who was with me didn't murder Ray. Whatever happened, it was an accident."

"Kerry. I need your complete cooperation in this matter. Was it this Russo who was with you?"

I wince. "Am I under arrest?"

Tremblay looks a bit taken aback, and then he shakes his head.

"So I'm free to leave?"

"You're an illegal immigrant. You've stayed in our country without a visa for either work, or vacation. Canada isn't the US. You can't just cross the border and make a life for yourself here without a permit."

"I've neither worked nor relaxed," I sneer. "We fled for our *lives!* Is this going somewhere?"

"Are you afraid to talk? Is someone threatening you? Talk to me. The police can protect you."

I scoff. No, they can't.

He nods at Cecilia who is sleeping peacefully next to me, her fever gone, her chest rising and falling evenly. "She's *his* child, isn't she? That's no 'night on the town'."

I look away, my eyes brimming with tears.

"Why didn't you tell us? Did you have a relationship with this man? Explain it to me. I'm a simple man. Sometimes I just don't understand. Are you protecting him right now? What aren't you telling us?"

"Nothing," I cry. "I didn't have a relationship with him. It was a stupid mistake. He stalked me. I fled here. He followed. Saved Cecilia. Disappeared. That's all there is to it. I held back, yes. I was ashamed. But that's the whole truth!" My heart pounds. I don't want to tell him about how bad I hurt. How much I ache for him. It's nobody's business.

He is quiet for a while and all that is heard is Cecilia's light snoring. "You kept the baby," he says quietly.

I sigh deeply. "Are you gonna question that too? Does that make me more or less suspicious?"

He waves his large hands in the air. "You are not suspected of anything. Not anymore. Ray's death has been ruled an accident, so the investigation is closed. I just don't understand all the lies. You said you were married, you said you didn't know who the father was."

I chew on my lower lip and think on the answer for a while. "Life has taught me to be careful, Officer Tremblay. I have a hard time letting people in."

"There's a difference between people and people, Miss Jackson. And lying to the police is never wise." I flinch when I feel his hand on mine, calloused, gigantic on my tiny, claw-like hand. "You have something beautiful there," he nods at Cece, "and whoever *he* is, he's gone. You are finally free."

I look at Cecilia, then out the window. Am I? Then why doesn't it feel that way? I know what he says is true. I just don't know why it doesn't feel like a relief, but... empty.

OUR THINGS ARE PACKED, SOME TOILETRIES, AND A FEW clothes Mrs. Anderson kindly brought for us. The sheets have already been removed from our beds. Cece is playing on the floor with some borrowed toys and we are waiting for the doctor to release us.

There's a knock on the door but it isn't the doctor. It's Officer Tremblay. He holds a bag in his hand and drops it on the bed as he remains standing. Cecilia looks up and regards him curiously, then she seems to decide he isn't what she was looking for and continues with the doll and the plastic yellow truck. Tremblay pats her head and shuffles his feet, looking awkward, uncertain.

"I heard they're letting you go," he finally states.

I smile briefly and nod.

"I brought your journals. I thought you might want them. They're all there." He gestures to the bag.

I clear my throat. "Thank you." I don't know if I even care about them. They're just words on paper. Sad words on crumpled paper. I know what they say. I was there.

"You... You *should* find someone to talk to. You've been through a lot."

I scoff bitterly. Maybe Chloe, maybe not. There's nothing I can tell anyone.

"So... where are you going to go, Miss Jackson?"

I look out the window, at the falling snow; the dusky day is grey, sad and suddenly I long intensely for warm yellow sand and bright days by the sea. "I hate the cold," I whisper.

"I'm sorry?"

Startled to find I still have a visitor, I realize he asked me a question. I look back out again. "Home," I croak.

Then I clear my throat.

"Home. We're going home."

ELEVEN

Middlebro

Christian

My lungs fill with ice cold water as I hit my head on a sharp rock. I twirl and tumble, not even knowing what's up and down. Sky flickers by, then dark water, sky again, but through a mass of water.

Cold. It's so cold. Numbing, shattering cold penetrates my every cell and I'm losing control of my limbs.

I got her. I know I got her, just as she stuck on a ledge. I managed to hold on for one tiny moment and threw her back up. That move is what will kill me, because that was when I lost the grip myself.

Did Kerry get her? Did they fall? Are they alive? Please live. Please don't let my life and my inevitable death have been for nothing.

I have no air left.

Who the fuck said drowning is peaceful? I'll find the fucker and pull him under water. He'll die slowly and painfully. It's a panic-inducing-aching-I'm losing contact with my body and mind-nightmare.

Suddenly I'm tossed against an unyielding object and throw my arms around it, clinging to something. The whirling force around me tears at my clothes, but my head is above the surface and the riverbank is an arm's length away. I cough up water, inhale and literally feel how I pull water deeper into my lungs to get some fucking leverage to draw the next breath. My head spins as I fight my cramped arms, forcing them to let go of the rock and push my body toward the side, where the water is calmer, and I can get hold of solid ground.

I don't feel my fingers. I have no idea if they grip for something to hold on to, or if they're just lying on the ground like dead matter protruding out of my hands. I'm too weak, too numb, and I slip and slide. Something pulls me back and panic surges through my body, but then it's as if I'm lifted, thrown halfway up on the river-bank. Not even the fucking water wants me, but I'll take it.

Coughing weakly, my legs still move back and forth in the stream, I'm too tired to move any further. I fight to stay awake. If I let darkness claim me, I'm dead. I won't wake again.

Cecilia. I want to live for Cecilia. And for Kerry. I never knew love, but I know this is it, that the swell in my heart, knowing these two exist in the world, is love. Will I ever get the chance to prove to them that I'm worthy?

Christian Russo, you fucker, get *up!*

I pull for all I'm worth, my fingers getting bloody, my hands covered in lacerations and bone deep wounds. When I feel solid ground under my thighs, I begin to crawl, inch by painful inch, forcing my knees up, right, left, right again. I cough up water, empty my stomach of foul-tasting liquids, inhaling it when I can't spit it out fast enough. Panic seizes me over and over as air just won't seem to fill my lungs. Finally, no water swirls around my feet, and I'm up. I'm out of the river, alive, which is unbelievable. I have no energy to even lift my head. With my cheek resting on the cold mud, I look around me. I don't recognize the terrain at all, and the pale sun comes from another direction. It took me far, the lethal water. A little further downstream the river flattens into a lake that I only see the beginning of, most of the view covered by a thick nest of trees and bushes, looking wild and untouched.

Deep tremors run through me. I'm definitely hypothermic. My teeth chatter uncontrollably and I barely feel my body.

I have to get up, I have to do everything in my power to find a warm, dry place, or I'll die out here.

Mobilizing my experiences from a life of pain, of surviving street fights, being shot- once in my early twenties, once by Kerry, stabbed, fighting darkness, and blood loss, I scream at my legs to obey me. My roar echoes through the silent forest, bouncing off the distant mountains, or so it seems in my over sensitized mind.

I force one single image into my mind, Kerry sitting cross legged on the floor, next to Cecilia trying to assemble big Lego blocks, a ray of light playing across our daughter's hair, showing a little red in her dark brown locks.

One step. My legs tremble. One more step. I look around me. I have no idea where to go. Wrapping my arms around me, I stop, indecisive. If I walk in the wrong direction, I'm fucked. If there even *is* a right direction.

Where is Middlebro? Which direction were we heading? Where was the sun? It was a little to our right. How much time has passed? I haven't been unconscious. I don't think it's been more than thirty or forty minutes since I slammed against the rock and started fighting my way out of the water. That puts the sun just slightly more to the right, probably at my two. I have washed up on the right side of the river. At least that's some kind of luck.

I take the first step, then I fall on hands and knees and cough up more water. I wipe my ice-cold face with a hand I barely feel, get up again and take the next step. To where, I don't know. Maybe I'll just die out here anyway, but I'm no man if I don't try.

I don't know how long I've walked. I've never felt so ill in my life. I tremble from bone-deep exhaustion, shivering uncontrollably. I can't stop my teeth from chattering. It's as if someone has ripped the skin off my body. I'm raw, as if my flesh is falling off my bones.

Through a haze in the increasing dusk, my vision blurry, I see a squared shape that doesn't look like everything else. It's not a tree, or a rock, or a hill. My heart speeds up as my brain tries to connect the dots.

Is it a house? Is it a fucking house?

I stagger closer, every breath burning and wheezing. Finally I fall to my knees on the ungiving cold stone steps before an ill-maintained door, the dark blue paint flaking, leaving the wood unprotected.

"Hello," I rasp and slam my fist on the door. I slam against it again and try to speak, but no more sounds escape me.

It's as if I'm shutting down. Right here and now. I curl up into a little ball and gasp for air, then I reach out once more and grasp for the handle, getting a temporary burst of hope when it obediently swings open.

I roar in agony as I force my body to move, getting up on my knees, crawling the last few feet into a dark hallway. Pushing the door shut with my foot, I gasp and curl up again, hugging my chest, trying to find an ounce of body warmth.

It takes me a long while, getting a feel for my surroundings. It's inhabited. There's no movement, no sounds, but there's a faint smell of greasy food coming from somewhere, and it's not cold. I'm unable to tell if it's warm, but I know it's not cold.

"Hello?" I rasp. I try to find my core, some part of my body that isn't shutting down, and that can help me live.

There's no answer.

I force myself up on my knees, numb fingers clutch for the buttons in the icy overcoat. I know I have to get this shit off me. When the buttons finally come undone, I shed the coat, dropping it where I stand. I try to toe off my shoes, but I can't feel my feet and can't coordinate my limbs, so instead I pull off the sweater and the shirt, the checkered shirt that used to be Kerry's dad's. I've never seen my skin so pale. Next to me hangs outdoor clothes and thick sweaters. There are gloves and knitted ski caps.

I reach for one of the sweaters and pull it on with jerky moves, almost weeping from the effort, then I stagger deeper into the house.

Someone lives here, and I should worry about who. I can't go to a local hospital. I can't be caught by the cops. We have no leverage in Canada, no contacts. I could go away for real if they find out who I am and what I've done. I feel for the gun in my pocket, it's still there and I fumble forever to pull it up. It's useless in its soaked state, but whoever I meet won't know that.

The sound of a TV blaring some commercial gets louder as I investigate the deeper recesses of the ill-maintained house, the rooms small and dusky, every curtain pulled closed over the windows.

My heart pounds as I enter the little living room. A chair stands with its back to me. A tuft of gray hair and a foot is all I see of the person sitting there. From the TV comes fake laughter from some breakfast cereal commercial.

"Hello?"

The person moves, and an old woman peeks around the side of the backrest. Her face is void of all emotions and she has almost no wrinkles despite her apparent old age. It's obvious the horses aren't in the stable anymore. She's probably far gone in Alzheimer's or some other dementia. Her empty eyes have an eerie light blue color.

"Ray?" says a thin voice.

My frozen mind kicks into action, a series of images flipping through my mind. Ray. Ray in the grocery store. Ray in the hotel. Ray at Kerry's house.

Ray is dead.

"Mom?" I say tentatively, and put the gun back in the pocket. "I'm a bit cold."

Kerry

My fingers tremble when I dial the well-known number.
Mom.
I haven't talked to her in probably six months, and before that... that was before I left Chicago. I haven't told her anything. I haven't dared, afraid she'd get pulled into my nightmare, that they'd come after *her* too. She knows nothing of my life. I never let her come visit me in Chicago. She has never met Cecilia. She doesn't know I'm in Canada. She doesn't know of Christian.

"Yes?" Hearing the warm, slightly husky voice nearly brings me to my knees in relief, and in profound pain knowing how much I've hurt her.

"Mom?" My voice quakes pathetically.

"Kerry? Oh my God! Where are you? Are you in trouble?"

"I'm coming home, Mom. I'm so sorry. I'm so, so sorry." I swallow hard, terrified she'll reject me, lash out. "I've missed you," I whisper.

"I'm— You are? When?"

The hope in her voice makes my chest tighten. "Soon. Really soon. A few days."

"Are you okay? Is Cecilia okay?"

I look over at my daughter. We're being released from care. Finally. She's fine. Maybe a little pale, but it's also winter. Neither of us have seen the sun. She's playing on the floor by my feet with toys we've borrowed from the children's ward. Outside snowflakes whirl past the window. I shudder. I'm not fine. I still have a horrible cough, and I tire easily, even from walking a mere few steps, but they say I'm recovering.

"We're good. How... are you?" My heart feels as if it shatters from having left her right when Dad had just died. I had good reasons, but still. I should have talked to her. Regret has consumed me these last few days when the thought of home has set root.

"It's... Sometimes up, sometimes down. It's getting better. I miss him..."

"I know. I do too."

"Do you want me to do something? Do you need to be picked up somewhere? Do you need money?"

"Mom... I can't get hold of Chloe. My house..."

"I think your friend left town. She left it to me, saying she was leaving for a while. Or well, she sent me a letter in a box with the key."

"Oh..." A stab of disappointment hits me, a feeling of betrayal, which is ridiculous. I haven't kept in touch. She isn't obliged to put her life on hold for an old friend who completely disappeared on her. "My hous—"

"It's still there, hon. I haven't had the heart to sell it. I kept seeing you in it, and Cecilia... her little legs running on the lawn, chasing butterflies —" Her voice chokes up and tears well up in my eyes at the imagery.

"Mom... I've been the worst daughter."

"Well, I'm sure there are worse, but... I have missed you. When are you coming home? Please let me know if I can do something. Can I reach you on this number?"

Mrs. Anderson gave me an old phone. Her husband and a couple of men from town cleared the road and packed up my house. I don't need much. I only asked for my wallet, laptop and our clothes, and Dad's clothes. They're giving away the rest.

"Yeah. I don't even know the number myself yet, but this is my new phone. I'll be home in a few days." An urge to cough rises in my chest, and I fight it down. "I'll call you," I choke out, "gotta go."

I disconnect before she can object, then I can't hold it back anymore and an exhausting series of coughs erupt, feeling as if they'll tear my chest apart.

"Mommy?"

Cece looks at me with dark, worried eyes.

"Mommy's okay," I grit out between the violent fits. "I'm okay."

When I'm done, sweaty and spent, I stare emptily in front of me. I wonder how he died. Was he in pain? I just can't see this magnificent, larger-than-life, human being dead. I press my fists to my chest to quell the ache, the never-ending pain. I wish I could have thanked him for our lives.

I wish I had let him in that last night, when he touched me, showed his passion for me, made me feel again.

I wish he was here.

ELISABETH ANDERSON PICKS US UP. TOGETHER WITH HER husband Stephan she's the owner of Pond's motel. A kind-hearted born and bred Middlebro resident who has done everything for me since I arrived. Now she's also the new owner of the little grocery store.

Mrs. Anderson rolls us out of the hospital in a wheelchair, Cecilia sitting in my lap, gawking at everything we pass. I can definitely walk and it's beyond embarrassing to be wheeled out.

She has found an old, stained child car seat and I buckle up my tired little daughter, panting from the exertion.

"Do you want me to do it, hon?"

I shake my head. "No. I'm okay," I rasp.

"Just let me know what you need."

I smile weakly. I just want out of here. I want to go home. I want my mom, my friends. "Let's just go, please."

She gives me a half smile as she puts the key in ignition. "Tired of hospitals?"

I glance at the large, modern building to my left, glass and concrete, connected to an older red brick building that lies partly hidden behind a large park, everything covered in a growing layer of snow.

"I just wanna go home."

"I hear you."

We make it in time to our appointment at the police station to get temporary passports sorted, then Mrs. Anderson maneuvers us through the dense traffic, leaving the city behind us onto smaller roads until we reach Pond's motel in Middlebro. We'll stay here two nights and catch our breaths. Recuperate a little. The day after tomorrow we're taking a flight to San Francisco. Mom will pick us up and take us home.

That night, with Cece sleeping on a couch next to me in the otherwise empty bar at Pond's, I nurture a whisky, grimacing as it burns hot in my chest. I sit with my laptop, looking over my finances, and weep. It's not that I don't have money. I have embarrassingly too much money. Evan has kept paying, and I have barely used anything for the last year. I cry for the loss of my life. I cry when I look at Cecilia, because she will never know her father. I cry because we will go home, build a life again, and a part will always be missing. Always. She looks so much like him, like Christian Russo, and I will be reminded of that for as long as I live.

"WILL YOU BE AW'RITE, LOVE?"

Stephan Anderson has driven us all the way back to Winnipeg, even though I tried to insist that we could take a taxi. None of the Andersons were having it. Elisabeth has packed us sandwiches and little cartons of juice, trying to wipe the tears out of the corners of her eyes without me noticing.

I want to say that I'll miss them, because they have been nothing but amazing, the townspeople, all of them, but Middlebro will forever be too connected with pain.

I have two suitcases containing everything I own. Watching as they roll out of my sight at check-in, I hold Cece in one hand and give Mr. Anderson a one-armed hug with the other. We're standing in the middle of the bright departures' hall, people rushing by.

"I'm so sorry I couldn't be there for Ray's funeral."

Stephan's face falls a little. "I knew 'im since he was a kid. He'll be missed."

Making a non-committal noise, I shift and take a step back. Suddenly my skin crawls and I can't wait to get on that plane. All I see before me is my house, the steep slopes of San Francisco, hear the squeaking noises from the cable cars, smell exhaust and the salty sea air, the bridge. I fiddle with the passports and glance around me, looking for the security checkpoint.

"We should be on our way."

"Of course. It's been an honor knowing you," he crouches before Cecilia who slides halfway behind my leg, clutching her arms around my knee, "and you, little one."

"Thank you for everything, Mr. Anderson. You've been very kind and I can never hope to repay—"

"Don't you worry about that too, now. Go on home. You're finally free of that bastard. Go start the life you were meant to live. You and the little doll."

AS THE PLANE STARTS MOVING ACROSS THE TARMAC, I throw a quick text to Mom as Stephan's words burn in me. Free? I'll never be free of Christian Russo.

PART TWO
BEGINNING

Twelve

Middlebro

Christian

The memories of the last few days are blurry at best. Or is it weeks? I wake sweaty, haunted by the usual nightmares where I keep losing something important. The scenarios change, but the lingering feeling is always the same.

Fighting to draw my next breath, I clutch for whatever is wrapped around my chest until I remember there never is anything. The tightness is inside my chest, not around it. I can never get enough air.

The sheets I lie on are dirty and smell of unwashed bodies. I'm not sure how long I've been here, coughing myself sweaty, burning up with a fever I try to quell with Advil, crawling between the bathroom and the bed. Ray's demented mother thinks I'm her son. She's getting food delivered that she barely touches. I have no appetite either, but I try to chew and swallow a little every day. I have to get my strength back. I have to get help.

She's thin as a stick, Mrs. McGonaghan, and can't have much time left in this life, but even so far gone in her dementia, her worry about her son, or who she thinks is her son, is palpable.

I feel genuinely sorry for her. When I leave, if I leave, she'll lose everything.

For the first time there's a tiny bit more vigor in me, and I flex my thigh muscles experimentally, wondering if I dare to sit up. I drink a sip of water, fighting the urge to vomit, then roll over on my side and push myself up, swaying, pain searing my chest. I cough. Cough up unmentionable things. Cough until I taste iron, until I spit blood. My attempt at standing fails miserably and I fall on all fours, panting.

She has to have a phone. As I begin to crawl, I pray to a deity I've never trusted, all the mandatory church visits in my life a joke, a charade, the confessions to the priest laughable, the tattooed cross on my arm an attempt in my mid-twenties to find *him*. I never did. But *now* I pray.

Forgive me father for I have sinned.

I have sinned so fucking much, and maybe this is my penance. If he exists, if there is forgiveness, now would be a good time. I don't know if I'll survive this, but fucking hell, I'm not leaving without a fight. Gasping for air, I make my way from room to room. She's in the same chair as she was sitting in when I literally fell into this house the first time. Next to her on the table is a phone that must have been new in the seventies. It must have been white once. Now it's grimy from decades of dirty hands gripping the handset.

At first, I think she's died, but then she slowly turns her head and looks at me, her face as empty as ever. I reach for the phone, clutching it to my chest as I finally allow myself to lie down again, sweating floods, coughing my lungs up.

Thank you, Lord!

With trembling fingers I call the number to my most trusted, most capable brother. He'll know how to sort this.

"Yeah?" comes Nathan's voice through the receiver. I might not have heard anything as beautiful in my life.

"Nate," I croak.

"Who's this?"

"Chris. I... need help."

"Damn man, I didn't recognize your voice. What's up? What've you gotten yourself into now? Don't tell me you're about to throw in the towel again?"

"I'm... really ill. I need—" A set of violent coughs renders me unable to speak. Finally I manage to gasp the next word, "help." I curl up in a fetal position. I don't know if I can get up from here again today. I've used up the little energy I had.

"Where are you?"

Where am I? For a moment my mind is blank. Then I see images, rather than thinking coherent words. Kerry. Her hideaway.

"Middlebro."

"What? Where the fuck is that?"

"Canada. South... of Winni... peg." I'm salivating, fighting the urge to throw up again."

Nathan is quiet, I hear him breathe.

"What's up with you?"

"Fell in... water. Almost drowned. Think I got pneumonia," I whisper.

"Can you give me a little more detail? I'll come pick you up asap, but I can't look through every—"

"McGonaghan. A house in the woods. McGonaghan, Nate. Please come."

"Where can I reach you?"

I look at the phone. No number. I look at the woman, and give up the thought.

"I don't know," I say faintly, a feeling of helplessness creeping into my chest.

"Middlebro, McGonaghan. I'll find you. Gimme a day."

"I don't know if I have a day."

"Sure you do. Nothing fucking kills you. Keep breathing, bro. Keep yourself motivated. Gotta go. Got some phone calls to make."

"Thank you," I gasp, then I let the phone slide out of my grip. I feel for it on the floor next to me, trying to put the handset back in its place, but I'm too uncoordinated.

My head is heavy and deep shudders run through me. I just need to sleep.

VOICES PENETRATE THE FOG. MEN'S VOICES. MY HEART jumps to my throat. They've come for me. The cops. Nathan can't have gotten here yet.

"Chris?"

I'm still on the floor, curled up, my mouth dry as sandpaper, my lips cracked.

"Nate," I croak.

The sound from the TV is too loud. Mrs. McGonaghan is nowhere to be seen. It's dark outside. How long have I been here?

"Chris! What the fuck?" My brother darts to my side and crouches next to me. I've never seen anything so pretty. And he's got a pretty fucking face as it is.

"Hi," I whisper, "took you long enough."

"In here," he shouts.

Steps, a rustle, voices, more people.

"Can you stand?"

I shake my head.

Nate frowns, then looks up, over my shoulder. "We gotta carry him. You got any belongings here?"

"No."

"You owe me a story, dude."

I nod.

Strong arms grip under my arms and legs, steadying me in a tight grip between three men I've never seen before, big, burly. The ceiling comes rushing toward me and I close my eyes as a violent vertigo tilts my world.

Cold. Winter. Snow.

I tense up, the nightmare overwhelming me. My hands and feet hurt at the mere memory.

A car ride. I slip in and out of consciousness.

A whirring sound that increases until it's unbearably loud. The sucking feeling in my stomach tells me we're lifting.

"A helicopter? You clever bastard." I gasp.

"There you are. You had me worried for a while. You went totally offline the whole car ride."

I try to smile, then darkness swallows me.

The whirring decreases. Stops. A door slams, more cold. Wind whips in my face. Tiny flakes of snow, sharp as nails. Lifted. They put me on a gurney and roll me across a roof, through a door, corridors. Nate is by my side the whole time.

"Where are we?" I croak.

"Mount Sinai."

"Huh?"

"Hospital, you imbecile."

For the first time in a long while, I allow myself to relax. My body is heavy on the thin, hard mattress as a sense of calm washes over me.

"Thank you."

Then everything fades.

San Francisco

Kerry

IT'S A LONG, LONG FLIGHT. WE'VE BEEN IN THE AIR FOR eight hours, and I've been on my feet since five this morning. Cecilia is fine. She has slept a lot, oblivious to the changes that are about to take place. Myself, I'm a tight knot of anxiety and pain. Pain for the one I've lost, that I never really gave the chance, and anxiety over meeting everyone again, especially Mom.

I'm exhausted when I pass through customs with my bags on a trolley and Cecilia perched on top of them. She's delighted to be doing something else than sitting on that boring plane, points at everything and chatters endlessly. I've slept, but nothing seems to help against the bone-deep tiredness.

Walking slowly, I scan the crowd for my mom, my stomach clenched in worry that she won't be here, that it won't be all right between us. When I spot her well-known features, I hold my breath until she sees us, her eyes darting between me and Cece. I don't breathe until a big smile spreads on her face and she begins to wave for us to come to her.

I fall into her arms, almost choking from the bear hug.

"Mom."

"Kerry!"

I hold her back at an arm's length. "Mom, this is Cecilia."

My little daughter looks up when she hears her name.

"Ce, this is your grandma."

Grandma doesn't even hold a meaning for her, but as my mom crouches before Cecilia and starts cooing and making funny faces, I have a strong feeling we will rectify that sooner rather than later.

Mom stands again, and takes my hand. "How are you? I've been so worried. You left that letter for me, so at least I had something to hold on to, but in my darkest moments—"

"Mom. Please take us home."

She nods resolutely and grabs the trolley. "Do you wanna see a new city, Cecilia?"

Cece looks up at me, her face full of questions.

"I don't think she has any concept of 'city'."

Mom gives me a strange look. "Oh. Okay. We'll have to do something about that." She turns the trolley and begins to push it through the crowd as determined as when Moses split the Red Sea. "Cecilia, do you like the ocean, then?"

I clear my throat. "I... don't think she knows that either."

"Oh my God. Where have you been living? In a hole?"

Right outside the entrance stands a large burgundy SUV I recognize. "Mom, did you park here?"

She shrugs. "I found it convenient. The parking garage is so far away."

I look at the large concrete building situated right across the street. A walk that would have taken her two minutes. "Aren't you afraid to get fined? Or towed? Jeez."

The doors click open. "Isn't this comfortable, though?" She grins mischievously. "I bought a seat for Cecilia. I hope it's the right size."

I buckle up my daughter in a perfectly sized seat, and help Mom with the second bag, sending me into a coughing fit that feels like it lasts for days.

Mom lays her hands on my shoulders, her face laced with concern. "You need to have someone look at that. I'll call my doctor asap."

"It has been looked at," I gasp. "It's okay."

She frowns and shakes her head. "That is not good enough."

I climb into the backseat next to Cece. "Let's just go, please. I wanna go home."

Mom jumps in. Her vigor amazing for being close to sixty. "My place or yours?"

"Do I have anything at my place?"

"Of course, hon. I stocked your fridge. There are diapers and soap, shampoo, everything. Your bed is made." She glances at Cecilia who is staring at all the people who rush by. "I think we need to buy a bed for her as well."

"You don't have to do everything. And thank you!"

"I've... I've missed you so much. Please allow me. I want you to feel at home. And to never leave again."

Tears well up in my eyes as my chest tightens. I don't ever want to leave again, and I might not have a reason. Salvatore said he won't come after me, and Christian... Christian is dead. A pang of pain hits my chest. I wipe my eyes and nod.

"My place," I croak.

. . .

WE'RE HOME.

My steps echo in the well-known rooms as I close the book and walk up to the giant window. It's night and I can't sleep. Too much has happened. I'm standing at almost the same spot as when I camped here those first days after Christian's attack. The same ache as always clutches my chest and makes me press the heel of my palm to cover my heart. Why does it hurt so much? We barely knew each other, and what I know about him is absolutely horrifying. A life of violence. A killer. How did I ever see something else in him?

Outside it's quiet and still. The bridge glitters faithfully, its lights dimmed in the slight fog over the bay, hovering eerily. The moon is full and blood red, huge, hanging right at the horizon, reflecting in the peaceful ocean. The tranquility of the scenery in a way the same I experienced in the cabin, and still so very different.

I grip my side and fight the urge to cough. If I start it never stops and I know by now that if I subdue the reflex it passes after a while. I know I'm not supposed to, they told me the cough is meant to clear the airways, but I cough until I taste blood, and that just can't be right.

Mom ran errands the whole first day, mobilizing every old lady she knows, finding a crib for Cece, cooking for us, staying way too late.

Christmas has come and gone almost unnoticed. Mom was here for a few hours and doused us with gifts. I should be the one sucking up to her, but she is so happy that we're back that I just let whatever happens between us run its course. It's a strange and a bit strained dynamic, but how can it be natural after everything we've been through?

On New Year's Eve I watched the fireworks light up the sky, standing on my patio with a blanket tightly wrapped around my body. I felt no joy over a new year. I can't see the future. It's a black hole, as black as the void in my heart.

Cecilia is sleeping soundly upstairs, snoring, still having a bit of a cold, but she's healing quickly. Quicker than me. Sometimes my little girl seems to be made out of steel and reminds me whose daughter she is—too. Myself, I haven't lain down yet. I drink tea, think, write a little, and just exist.

Dawn is only an hour away. Yet another sleepless night lies behind me. Yet another warped day awaits, where I'm barely awake, barely believing I'm back here, and at the same time hyper sensitized, experiencing everything so clearly as if through a magnifying glass. Every scent, every breeze, the faint sun on my skin, walking the streets of my hometown, my daughter's breathing, every heartbeat.

Every memory.

> *Cecilia has accepted her new surroundings with a child's amazing capability to adjust. She keeps talking about 'Daddy.' I simply tell her he's gone.*
> *I'm done with lying.*
> *At least to her.*

Tossing the journal on the kitchen counter, I take a sip of coffee and then I smile wickedly at my daughter. "I'm coming to get you! Tickle tickle tickle." She squeals and runs across the room, climbing up on the couch, me chasing after her. I have a coughing fit and fall into a sweaty, coughing, laughing heap, pulling her to me. When she grows tired of hugging, she slithers out of my grip and picks up paper and crayons and starts drawing circles, squares and dots—whatever it is she's drawing.

The dots remind me of whirling leaves in a late autumn storm, and I shudder from the memory. I wonder how much she remembers—how much she will remember. She hasn't asked where he went, why he's gone. Maybe she's too small to follow up on the 'Daddy's gone' statement. And when she's older she won't recall any of this.

Unless I help her.

I don't know how to keep his memory alive. The easiest would be to just not talk about him, but that wouldn't be fair to either of them. How will his heritage affect her? She was conceived in deceit, and her father was a murderer, and not just any murderer. He was a professional assassin.

It's a pedagogical nightmare.

Cecilia comes running and pushes a drawing into my hands, then she runs off to her writing corner again. As I try to think of Christian's good traits, at least one, I study the multicolored circles on the paper. *She* trusted him from the first moment. She saw something in him I couldn't. I'll tell her about that. About how they found each other despite everything. He did save her life. I cling to the memory. That is something to hold on to and to let her know about.

. . .

NIGHT COMES. AS ALWAYS HORRIFYING IMAGES HAUNT ME. Fear. Darkness. Violence. Death. My daughter sleeps without a care in the world, my worry grows. I'm postponing something. I owe Christian the truth. I need to tell his family that he's dead.

I have to go to Salvatore.

THIRTEEN

Luciano Salvatore

Not a lot of things surprise me, but when Ivan knocks on my door and announces that Kerry Jackson is standing outside my gates, requesting to see me, my jaw drops. Miss Kerry fucking Jackson who went completely off grid with her baby, our newest Russo addition, in tow. Christian has looked for her ever since, for more than a year, and come up with nothing.

"Let's see what she wants, then." I nod for him to go get her. "Bring in the young lady."

Ivan doesn't let one single emotion cross his face as he backs out, talking in his radio.

I stand and walk over to the window. Staring at the robot lawn mower as it zig-zags across the well-trimmed green surface, my thoughts sprawl in all different directions. How long has she been in town? Did Christian know this? Did something happen to the kid? If she's endangered the child, she'll be really sorry she came back.

Christian lies in a bed attached to a ventilator, in a medically induced coma in a hospital in New York. He'll pull through, but the fucking doctors won't give us any useful information about his future. We still don't know what happened to him and how the fuck he ended up in the near-wilderness in rural Canada, but I have lost one of my best men, that much is clear. If I can find out the hows and whys of that, if there's someone I can make pay for the damages to the closest thing I have to a brother, then I'll destroy that person with my own bare hands.

A knock brings me out of my reverie, and I spin around in time to see the little redhead entering my office. Her hair isn't red anymore, though, it's black with red roots, short and choppy. It looks terrible. She's thinner than before, with dark circles under her eyes and hollow cheeks. Her beauty lingers under the surface, more fragile than ever, again awakening the predator in me. Weakness is to be exploited and my mind immediately begins to process how I can use that. I'm not a good man. I don't protect the weak, I crush them.

"Miss Jackson. To say that this is a surprise doesn't quite cover it."

Her eyes widen and it's obvious she's terrified. She jumps when the door whisks shut behind her. I move up to her, past her, and discreetly lock it, pocketing the key.

"What are you—" she gasps, staring up at me as I tower over her.

"You and I need to have a word. And I don't want to be disturbed."

Her eyes dart around the office, no doubt taking in the other two doors, one leading deeper into my mansion, the other to a bathroom.

"I came here of my own free will. You said you weren't gonna hurt me!"

"That was over two fucking years ago, Miss Jackson. Things change. People change."

She pales and takes a step back. I don't follow.

"I have a child. Please!"

"State your business. Why are you here?"

Her mouth opens and closes a couple of times. "Please unlock the door."

"No."

"Are you—"

"Focus," I snap.

Her cheeks turn red in an instant. "I can't focus on anything except you locking me in!"

I purse my lips as I regard this little hellion, then I grab her arm and pull her with me toward my desk.

"Hey!"

"Sit!" I push her down on a chair. "Explain yourself. Simple words will do. I'm not a morning person and I've only had one fucking cup of coffee, so get to it."

She presses her lips into a thin line, staring back at me in defiance. Something dark wells up in my chest. Her baby might be family, but

Kerry isn't as safe as she thinks she is. I lean in close, nose to nose, making her recoil.

"Look, young lady, I'm no stranger to hurting a woman. I'm no gentleman, that's not how I've built my business. Where *the fuck* did you go? Why did you disappear? Why have you come back?"

Her eyes dart between mine and the door. I grab the back of her neck and force her to meet my gaze. "Forget about the fucking *door*," I growl.

"I ran," she whimpers. "I ran for my life. I thought Christian was going to kill us!"

I let her go and straighten as I look down on her. "I told him to stay away. I told you you were safe."

"Well, he didn't stay away!" she cries. "And you didn't tell me I was safe. *You* told me he was out to get me and that you couldn't control him!"

I narrow my eyes. Did I? Maybe I did. "You could have come to me."

Kerry scoffs. "Sure. Right back into the claws of the man who wanted me dead."

"And yet here you are. Again."

"Because I'm stupid," she says, more to herself than to me.

I have to agree.

"Where did you go, Kerry? We looked for you."

"I moved to Chicago."

"I *know* that." My impatience grows, crawling in me like slithering snakes. "Go on."

"Canada."

I twitch and stare at her. I don't believe in coincidence. "Where. In. Canada," I say slowly through clenched teeth, heat rising in me, a cloud of rage. If she has something to do with Christian's situation, I swear to all that's holy—

She stutters, no doubt sensing that I'm ready to pounce. "A—a little town called Middlebro."

"You fucking bitch!" I snarl and grab her by the throat, pushing her back against the backrest.

Kerry cries out and clutches at my hand, but she's like a mouse in the hands of a lion and has no leverage. Her face turns beet red. "Please," she mouths. "It's Christian, he's—" She swallows, wincing with pain.

I snatch back my hand and she darts up, taking several steps back, toppling the chair. "You're all the same!" she cries, tears streaming down her cheeks, her hand flying to cover the reddened skin on her throat. "You're all assholes."

"I have never claimed to be anything else, Miss Jackson. And neither has my nephew, or anyone else in my family. We haven't gotten to where we are by being cuddly. Now what about Christian."

"*He's dead!*" she screams. "He died!"

I go still, processing what she's saying. What makes her think that? She is very close to having been right, but how is she involved? How did Christian end up with double-sided pneumonia, a temperature through the roof, his body filled with fluids and his organs close to shutting down?

"Go on."

"He found us," she whispers as new tears drip down her cheeks.

"And?"

Kerry chews on her plump bottom lip. Her nostrils flare as she stares at me. "He... Cecilia got ill, and we had to walk to get her to the hospital. He fell into a ravine, a river, and disappeared."

"Why did you walk?"

"Everything went wrong! There was a storm. The road was blocked." Her eyes turn distant, as if she's not in the room anymore. "We had to." Her last words are nothing but a hoarse whisper, filled with pain.

"So let me get this straight. You fled from nothing, settled in fucking nowhere, my nephew found you, and because of *you*, he's now dead? Did you kill him? Push him? Did you find a convenient opportunity to get rid of your stalker?"

Her green eyes widen. "N—*no!* It wasn't like that!"

"Then what was it like?"

"That's none of your business!"

I close the distance between us in a fraction of a second and push her until I slam her into the bookshelf, a little bronze statue of Athena falling to the floor with a loud bang, my hand around her throat again. Her pulse thuds like mad under my palm, and fear oozes off her making my cock twitch, waking the monster in me that always lurks under the surface.

"Sweetheart! You have *made* it my business."

"Can't— breathe," she gasps.

I ease a little on the pressure, but she's going nowhere until she explains. "Well?"

She swallows, and her soulful eyes nearly do me in. A part of me just wants to caress the tears off her cheeks and let her get on with her life. I do see the appeal. I have no problems understanding why Christian got so obsessed with her. She's strong, intelligent, brave, and so fucking beautiful she almost burns my retinae, and she doesn't even know it.

"I don't know how to explain it." Her lower lip trembles.

"Keep it simple."

"He found me. We fought. Then we didn't, and..."

"And?"

"We almost found... something... again. Between us. Then Cecilia got ill, we had no way of getting out of there unless on foot. He fell. I didn't hurt him, but I feel like I'm to blame anyway."

"Funny, that's how I feel too. If you hadn't run, none of this would have happened."

Her expression turns fearful. "I didn't know."

I remove my hand, take a step back and regard her.

Her hand flies up to her throat. "Please don't hurt me."

"Where's Cecilia."

"With my mom."

"And where is Mom?" I ask silkily.

She stares at me and snaps her mouth shut.

"Never mind. We'll find her."

Kerry darts forward and grips my shirt. "No, please! Don't hurt her!"

I take her little hands and bend her clutching fingers until she is forced to let go. I keep her hands in mine, holding tight, a little too tight from the wince on her face.

"Miss Jackson. From now on you stay in town. If I come knocking, you open, if I tell you to come here, you'll get your fucking ass here, if I tell you to jump, you jump. Are we clear? And no hiding the child. She's a Russo. You're nobody, but young Cecilia is family, and the child of my nephew. That means a lot to me."

She's not nobody. A kid needs their mother. I was forced to learn that a long time ago, first when I lost my own, and then again when a surprise pregnancy gave me David. Kerry doesn't need to know that, though. I prefer a healthy dose of fear.

"You're a monster," she whispers.

I laugh. "You've learned."

She bows her head, her shoulders slumping in defeat. It's an unexpectedly saddening sight, watching the fight drain out of this strong woman.

"Can I go?" she asks weakly.

I throw out my hand toward the door, following her as she takes a few quick strides toward it, so eager to flee.

"I'll be in touch," I say as I pull out the key and unlock it.

"I bet," she mutters.

There it is again, her defiance. Temporarily down, but not defeated. I like it.

When she's left, I realize I forgot to tell her Christian is still breathing. Well, she's probably relieved he's gone anyway, so I'll leave it the way it is.

Kerry

My back crawls as I leave the mansion. The guards follow me with their eyes as I kick my scooter alive and take off down the street. Right around the corner, out of sight, I stop, tear off my helmet and throw up in the bushes by the side of the road, chills running down my spine, sweat breaking out on my forehead. I feel like I've escaped death by a hair's breadth.

If I felt like a prisoner before, hiding from Christian, fleeing, having no life, it's nothing to what I feel now. I'm just a puppet in Salvatore's game, disposable. He said it. I have no choice but to do what he says, or I'll be looking over my shoulder for the rest of my life. My stomach clenches and a bitter taste of bile lingers in my mouth. Shuddering, I push the helmet back on, hop on my Vespa and fly down the long, winding road as if I have the devil on my back, tears streaming down my cheeks.

I miss Christian so much. I think I could have talked to him. I think he would have listened, stayed on my side.

Or am I wrong? Am I brainwashed? A victim of Stockholm Syndrome?

When I have locked my door behind me, I run up the stairs and curl up on my bed, images rushing through my head. Christian when we first met, his black eyes glittering, his touch hot. Christian with death in his eyes. Christian becoming a father, transforming into the true meaning of the word. Christian being a mobster, a murderer, a close relative to the monster I just escaped.

I should be glad he's dead, but it's not what my heart screams during sleepless nights.

My heart weeps in sorrow.

FOURTEEN

Christian

I t's all too familiar. The sharp smell of antiseptics, the low beeping from monitors, oxygen tickling my nose. I have no idea where I am, except that it's obviously a hospital. I fucking hate hospitals! Every breath feels as if something squeezes my chest, as if something pushes back every time I inhale. An attempt at a deeper inhale makes me cough until I almost throw up.

"Mr. Russo. You're finally awake."

The voice is female with a slightly husky quality to it I recognize. It's not *her*, but close. Too close.

"Kerry?"

"I'm Rhonda, I'm a nurse here at Mount Sinai."

"How..." I open my eyes and take in the dark-skinned woman in her pink scrubs as I fight for a breath. "How long?"

"You've been here a little over three weeks."

"What? That's not..." I gasp, "possible."

"I'll go get the doctor. They'll be happy to know you're with us again."

I grip her arm, shocked at how weak I am, much much weaker than I was after being shot a couple of years back. "Nathan. Get me Nathan."

"Your brother?"

I nod.

"Will do, Mr. Russo."

The door whispers shut behind her and I'm left alone. I try to feel my body, feel what's left of me. I wiggle my toes and then lift a leg experimentally. It falls back, heavy as lead.

Kerry. Cecilia.

With the images of them everything else comes rushing back, the water, the numbing cold. Panic claws at my chest as my heart speeds up, tightening it impossibly, choking me.

THE DOCTOR IS TALL, HIS THICK SALT AND PEPPER HAIR neatly combed back. He's got an impressive tan in the middle of winter and something about him screams avid golfer. He looks slick, superior. I dislike him immediately.

He drones on and on about the state I'm in, the state I've been in, what they've done, but I zone out.

"Did you get hold of my brother?"

The doc snaps his mouth shut and throws an annoyed glance at Rhonda as she darts to my side. "He's on his way here, Mr. Russo."

I close my eyes. "Good. Leave me alone, please."

"BRO."

"Where the fuck were you?" I grit out.

"Aww. Got lonely? Me and Ang have taken turns sitting here, watching you sleep. It's boring as fuck."

"Angela's been here?"

"Of course, she's been glued to your side, dude, but she's got classes and shit she's gotta attend, or she'll lose her position."

"Kerry? Cecilia?"

Nathan goes serious and my heart plummets. "It's like the two of you are connected. Kerry and your kid resurfaced in San Francisco yesterday. She just popped up at Salvatore's. He almost freaked. And there's not much that rattles that bastard."

Everything stops. Inside me. In the room. There's a low hum from the air conditioning, and that's all I hear.

"Chris?" Nathan's voice penetrates from afar.

"She's alive? The baby?"

"Seems that way," he says.

"And back home?"

"Seems that way."

"Did she mention me?"

"Luci didn't say shit, just that she was back."

I'm so fucking stupid. Why would she wanna see me? Why would she ask for me? She must think I'm dead, and maybe she's better off that way? Maybe, this time, I really should stay away? I've paid my dues, redeemed myself, I know that. If I seek her out, I'll just fuck everything up again, because that's me, that's what I do.

"Nate."

"Yeah?"

"Get me out of here. Now. I can't stay a minute longer; I can't breathe in here."

Nathan regards me a long while, then he nods. "I'll take you home."

I grab his arm. "Your home. I can't... I can't go back *home* like this."

My brother, one of two, maybe three people in the world that I trust, grabs my hand. "No worries, dude. I got you."

"Don't tell Luci I'm awake."

Nathan frowns. "He probably knows already, Chris. He's footing the bill. They're all his staff. Look, I don't know what you think will happen, but he's been worried sick."

"*Him?* Worry?" I manage to grit out a laugh, which I regret when it sends me into a coughing fit that never seems to end.

"You're fucking lucky to be alive." Nathan tsks and shakes his head.

"Lucky," I say bitterly. "It'd have been better for everyone if I'd died."

"Dude! Don't go fucking depressed on me, or I'll leave you here to rot. Get yourself together and get up on your legs. You'll be fine.

I scoff, but snap my mouth closed. He's right. I'm wallowing. I don't wallow, I don't feel, I act.

I'll bounce back. I'll be fine.

San Francisco

Kerry

I visited the center today.

There was only one person I recognized, an elderly lady I haven't talked a lot to. Chloe hasn't been seen or heard from in a long time. It hurts. She was, along with Mom, the one I really longed for. They think she moved, but no one knows a forwarding address.

I called Gayle. She screamed. I'm gonna have to tell them something and I'm petrified. I've been away from people for so long that I don't know how to get back into socializing. But somewhere deep inside it feels amazing that they'll take me back even though I pushed them away.

I feel blessed

THE DOORBELL CHIMES SOFTLY. I THROW THE JOURNAL IN A drawer and rush to the door, then I hesitate, terrified. But these are my friends. I've known Gayle since I was a teen for God's sake. I unlock and open and two beautiful women trickle into my hallway, wine bottles in hand, large pots with flowers and plants, bags with cute children's clothes from expensive stores, chitter-chattering.

Gayle has changed so much I can't believe it. Gone is the mousy, shy girl. Her hair is jet black, short and spiky, her eyes are sooted, there's a piercing in her eyebrow and another in a nostril. She's got a half punk-vibe going on.

Rebecca is as vibrant as ever, and she looks happy, she's always a ray of sunshine, but there's something about her, about them both really, that makes me itch to ask what the hell happened because these last two years have transformed them. Maybe it has changed us all?

I didn't know how much I had missed people. Friends. It just hurts that Chloe has left and I wonder if that's got anything to do with me. My insides freeze when I realize that she knows secrets she shouldn't have ever heard about. What if she's in danger? Or worse?

"We need wine! Lots of wine. You still drink, right? Red or white?" Rebecca holds up two bottles.

"Red," say Gayle and I with one mouth.

Rebecca laughs, a light, tinkling sound, as she disappears into the kitchen. "I knew I could count on you guys," she half-shouts over her shoulder.

"So, you've got some 'splainin' to do, girl." Gayle turns to me. "And where is this little miracle we've heard of?"

"Oh..." I didn't consider they'd want to meet Cecilia. "She's with Mom for the night."

"Kerry! You're the first of us to have a kid, a very secret kid, and you hide her away?"

My mouth goes dry. In a way she doesn't know how right she is. Except I can't hide anymore.

Rebecca comes back and puts a glass of wine in each of our hands and we salute each other. I down more than half the glass in three quick swallows, then I nod toward the dining table, a big heavy oak piece in a rustic style.

"I'm... not hiding her, I just— just wanted it to be us, uninterrupted," I stutter.

Rebecca aims her glass toward me. "Next time, girl."

I nod. "I promise." My heart swells at her words. Next time. There's gonna be a next time? They want to see me again? I haven't taken anything for granted. I've been the worst friend imaginable. And daughter. And mom.

"Evan's been asking about you," says Gayle as we sit.

"Evan?" asks Rebecca. "The slime ball?"

Evan. My ex-husband. The first man who played with my emotions and spat me out a wreck, but that was only for a short while, until I realized what a snake he really is and how lucky I am to have dodged that bullet.

"What did *he* want?"

"He said he missed you, can you believe it?"

I groan. "I *so* don't want to see him. Is he still with that blonde? His secretary?"

"I have no idea," says Gayle. "My interest in his life and whereabouts is zero."

"Kerry, girl. Talk to us," says Rebecca. "You went missing without a word. Chloe said you had to move and that she couldn't say more. It was kinda hurtful, especially to Gayle. She's been a mess. Then *Chloe* went and disappeared too."

"Yeah, Mom told me. When was that?"

"About a year ago," says Gayle. "Everything seemed normal, and then she was just gone. She left a note in her apartment, but it just said she was fine, and it was too weird. Something just didn't add up. Her folks were desperate. It's been a mess."

"A... a year?" After I disappeared to Canada. Ice trickles through my veins. No, it has to be a coincidence, why would she—

Christian.

Christian would be looking for me. Christian knew she and I were close.

Nausea rises in me and my head spins. *No no no!*

"Gotta— bathroom," I squeak, jump to my feet and rush up the stairs. Throwing open the toilet lid, I empty my stomach of the wine, and the sandwich I had earlier. Sweaty and spent, I fall back, leaning against the bathtub. I wipe my mouth with the back of my hand, then I smear out my makeup as I try to dry the tears off my cheeks.

It's him. Of course it's him.

A knock on the door makes me flinch and my heart jumps to my throat. "One moment," I shout. I get to my feet and look at the flushed mess that is my face. Oh fuck.

"Ker?"

"Coming! I just got something in my eye." I wash my face in ice cold water and then rub it dry as I unlock the door.

Gayle's wise, light-gray eyes regard me. "Talk to me. What happened to you?"

I study her new face, the unfamiliar jewelry, the dyed hair, before I sink back to the floor and pull up my legs, hugging my knees. "I'm dangerous, Gayle."

She crouches before me. "What do you mean?"

"There are people in my life who would hurt me if I talk."

Gayle's face turns serious. "What? Why? What did you get yourself into?"

"There's a world out there we aren't supposed to know about. Ruthless monsters. I met a man, and I thought we had something. He turned out to be someone else. Dangerous. He stalked me. I had to run."

My friend shakes her head so the black, spiky tresses bounce. "You're not making sense. Are these not people? Monsters?"

I grip her arm, tight. "They're mafia," I whisper, "I tried to, but I can never get out."

Gayle pales. "Kerry... you're scaring me."

"I'm scared too. Day and night."

"Cecilia," she says, "is she... his? This man's?"

I cringe and look at my feet, then I nod, whispering, "Yes."

Gayle puts her hand over her mouth, widening her eyes. "Oh my God. But you're back? Are you safe now?"

A half-hysterical laugh escapes me. I hug my knees tighter and rock back and forth, trying to calm my racing heart. "Please, don't ask more," I manage to grit out, fighting new tears that threaten to soak my cheeks.

"Can I do something? Anything?"

I look up at my friend, my old friend, and new friend by the looks of it. "Just be my girl again? I thought I'd lost you all, for sure. I've been so lonely. I can't pull you into my shit, but I need you so bad."

"Of course," she says and throws her arms around me. "Always." Then she pulls back, and grabs my shoulder, holding me at arm's length. "What do we tell Rebecca?"

"Not everything! Not that word I mentioned. She's a little..."

"Gossip-y?" suggests Gayle.

"Yes!" I laugh. "I was gonna say chatty, but yeah, that."

"We'll trim it down to a Rebecca-sized truth. Don't worry. You wanna come down? Or are you done for the night?"

I get to my feet. "No! Give me wine. I think I got some tequila somewhere. Probably some years old, but—"

"*There's* my Kerry!"

The rest of the night is drama free. Between the two of us, we serve Rebecca as much of the truth we think she can handle. We eat and they update me on everything that's happened in their lives since we last saw each other. I sit opposite Gayle and struggle with the twinges of guilt.

After the main course, and a couple glasses of wine, I'm beginning to relax. Rebecca has found a steady acting gig in a TV-show and has a new boyfriend who snores like a troll and she is seriously considering getting rid of him for that reason only. Gayle offers repeatedly to let 'the poor man' sleep in her bed, because apparently he's an Adonis, and they engage in a lively discussion about what's hot and what's not in a man.

Gayle plays bass in a band, and makes us listen to their mix of grunge, punk, and rock on Spotify. It's not bad, and I promise myself that I'll listen with a little more focus some other day, because tonight I'm not quite here.

I sit with my mouth open and listen to their chatter. They seem so young. Was I like that once? Before I met a tall, dark man who turned my life upside down.

I feel so old.

When they leave, I'm exhausted, drunk off my ass, and my chest filled with joy.

Until I close the door and tonight's realization comes rushing back. Christian is somehow behind Chloe's disappearance.

His black eyes burn in me that night, through sleepless hours, and deep into my dreams. They filled with rage and regret, hope and fear.

I wish I could have asked him.

FIFTEEN

New York

Angela Russo

"You're thin as a stick, brother."

His eyelids flutter, but he doesn't wake. He sleeps a lot, my big brother. Or, he used to be big. Now he's nothing but a shadow. My chest clenches with worry at what will become of him. Will he ever be himself again? My strong hero and protector. Chris has been both my mother and my father through my whole life.

I poke him. "Hey, dude. You gotta eat some. I made you a smoothie. It's got kale, and carrots, soya milk, three raw eggs, and a ton of fresh strawberries."

"I'm not a fucking rabbit," he mutters, and I exhale with relief. As long as there is snark in Christian Russo, there's hope.

"Well, from where I'm sitting, you're helpless as a baby, and you do what I tell you."

He opens one intense, deep brown eye and regards me. "Or what, sis?"

"Or you'll starve to death. You'll get bed sores and die in your own shit while flies feast on your rotten flesh."

"You're as charming as ever."

I laugh. "Always."

"I've missed your laugh, Ang. Everything is always so fucking serious."

"It's always life and death with us, isn't it?"

"It's the way of the Russos."

"The Russo way sucks. I don't ever wanna see you in a hospital bed again. You scared us. You scared *me!*"

He pushes himself up until he half-sits against the big fluffy pillows behind his back. We're at Nathan's. The room is big and bright, the ceiling high, the floorboards a beautiful light wood, a whole wall of windows with a sliver of a view of the Hudson river, right now covered in long white curtains. The bedside table is filled with half-full glasses of water and crumpled tissue.

"I scared myself good too."

"What happened? Who's Kerry? You keep talking about Kerry in your sleep."

He flinches as he reaches for a glass of water. "I don't fucking talk in my sleep!"

I hold out the smoothie for him.

"Keep your kale to yourself, you hippie. A real man needs steak."

I shrug and take a long sip of it myself, shuddering. Not my best work. "You talk all the time. Kerry, Cecilia. Storm. Water. Middlebro. When you sleep you're a babbling mess."

Christian groans and closes his eyes, falling back against the pillows. "You might as well forget you heard that. It's not gonna go anywhere anyway."

"Who are they?"

He opens his eyes, and the depth of the despair in them makes a shiver run across my back. "What am I, Angela?"

"My... brother?"

"What am I?"

I swallow. "I— I don't understand."

"What do I do?" he growls, so loud that I twitch.

"You're a hitman for Uncle. Is that what you want me to say?" I spit.

"And as such, what do I do?"

A chill settles in the pit of my belly. These are the things I never want to touch, never want to acknowledge. "Kill people," I whisper. "You kill people."

He's silent.

"This Kerry... is this someone you killed?" My voice barely carries. This feels important. Whatever it is, this has had a profound impact on my God-like brother. It's as if a piece of his soul is missing, as if his aura is flickering, being consumed.

"No. She's alive, but I might as well have killed her."

"What did you do?"

He grabs my hands, clutches them in his large paws. "I hurt her bad, Ang. Really bad. I don't know if she'll ever forgive me."

"What did you do. Tell me everything."

"It's... it's too dirty."

I scoff. "If you lived it, if *she* lived it, I can fucking hear it. Tell me, or I'll force feed you kale. I have the fridge stocked."

"You're an evil bitch."

"I've learned from the best, bro."

Seeing my brother clenched up, his gaze empty, tears me to pieces. I caress his thick hair, longer than I've ever seen it before, as I stare emptily at the tattooed cross on his forearm. Religion. God. These Italian macho men all go to church and pray and make their confessions, then they go out and keep hurting people. It's all such a farce.

"She was a hit. Luci ordered me to kill her because she knew something she shouldn't. But she was beautiful, Ang, inside and out, just amazing. I couldn't. I should have stayed away, but I couldn't. She... I seduced her. I don't think I gave her an option to be honest."

My heart speeds up, the faint memories of the rape threatening to resurface from deep into that dark void where I've pushed them.

"Tell me you didn't force yourself on her," I exclaim.

He twitches and looks up at me. "No. Fuck no. It wasn't like that." He looks over my shoulder, at the windows, and his gaze turns distant.

I wait for him to continue, pushing and pushing to put the lid back in place. I can be okay for months at a time, and then something triggers me, and it rips me right back to when I was a proper little sixteen-year-old, very naive, very Catholic, very, very stupid and trusting of an old neighbor.

"What was it like, then?"

"After... I had to kill her anyway. Luci, he—" Christian gives me a look that makes yet another shudder run through me. "He didn't give me a choice."

"That's sick. You slept with her and then you were gonna kill her? Like what? Right there, in bed?"

I'm nauseous. How can I love Christian, and Nathan, and my other two brothers, Matteo and Luca, knowing what they are? Am I just as sick as them?

He groans. "*No.* Anyway, I failed. She beat the crap out of me. Shot me, nearly killed me."

"Oh! Was *that* when you were in the hospital last time?"

"Oh yes," he sighs.

"One day your luck will run out, Chris."

"It already has," he says darkly. "Turns out we made a baby that night, a little girl who's my spitting image. Long story short, she ran from me, I followed. I found her, in Canada, shit happened, and some good stuff too. And here I am."

"You have a daughter? Is it Cecilia? Oh my God. Where are they now?"

"Apparently she's back home."

"San Francisco?"

He nods.

"You gotta go see her. Them."

"No. You don't understand. She thinks I'm dead. For two fucking years my existence made her life hell. You didn't see her, she was a shadow of her former self."

"So are you."

He shrugs. "She's finally free. She's better off."

"But you don't wanna hurt her again? Right?"

"Fuck no!"

"Then explain to her—"

"No!"

"What the fuck? You're so stubborn. All of you. You're hopeless."

"Unlike you, sis?"

I stick out my tongue at him.

"Angela, I'll just hurt her more. It's all I do. I can't be the man she needs."

"There's good in you, Christian! You have to believe that."

"I don't *do* your New Age stuff. I don't believe in shit like that. You are what you are. I'm a monster."

"New Age," I scoff, "that's *so* the eighties."

"Vegan shit, then? Buddhism. Whatever. A man is defined by his actions. My actions speak loud and clear. I can't ever go near them again or I'll destroy them."

"I think she's already there."

"What do you mean?"

"Nate said she went to see Salvatore."

Christian's eyes darken, but he doesn't answer.

"And you two have a child together, a *Russo*. I think she's already there, in the dark. She's in the worst shit imaginable if Salvatore's got his eye on her. And he has, you know it."

Christian suddenly sits up, sweat beading on his forehead. "Give me that smoothie, but you gotta get me some real proteins too, red meat. I need to get back on my fucking feet."

I stand. "Now we're talking. *There's* my brother. I wondered who that whining puddle in bed was."

A wicked grin spreads on his face and I see a little bit of myself in there, in the dark determination to get what I want. Whatever it is he needs to do, he'll do it. There are no other options.

"Ang," he says, "you're fucking brilliant."

"I know. You owe me one."

"No. I owe you a million. Now go get me some real food, woman!"

San Francisco

Kerry

I used to think of him a lot because I felt like I had to in order to survive. I needed to keep my focus and never forget. Now I have moved back home, where the open ocean soothes my need for air and the bright sky lifts me up. It helps a little. No. It helps a lot. But he still lingers.

He's dead. So why do I keep feeling this pain? Why doesn't it go away?

It hurts just as much every time as I see him throw himself after her before disappearing into the ravine. He gave his LIFE for her...

And how did I treat him? What did I make of his last days? Cecilia's father.

God. I'll never be free, will I?

"KERRY!"

I spin around when I hear the all too well-known voice, light and slightly raspy. A ghost from the past. Cecilia is asleep in the stroller, I'm walking along the docks, enjoying the sun, warm on my face, and the scent of salt in the air.

"Evan," I say, trying to come up with some measure of polite enthusiasm.

He throws his arms around me and scoops me into a tight hug, way too tight, sending me into a coughing fit. Evan takes a step back, but a hand remains on my shoulder, making my skin crawl, his eyes darting between me and Cecilia.

I shrug off his hand and look him over. He's got a receding hairline and has shaved his head to a short blond stubble to maybe hide the fact. He was always vain. A thick blond beard covers the lower half of his face. His blue eyes glitter. Evan is thinner than I remember him, and a few wrinkles have appeared on his forehead. He's still handsome, but I can't for the life of me remember why I ever saw anything in him. I married him out of convenience that I mistook for love in my young naivety.

I'm still not sure I know what 'love' is, except for the love for a child, but I sure as hell know passion, and that's something he and I never had between us.

"Fancy meeting you here!" he exclaims, still cheerily. "I haven't seen you in ages! Doing well, I see. Who's the lucky father?"

I freeze. "What's up, Evan? What are you doing down here in the middle of a work day? I thought you catered to the high and mighty over in the fancier districts, selling them ridiculously expensive apartments."

"Yeah, I... That didn't— Hey, let's go grab a coffee! Come on."

I really don't want to, but I can't see a way out of it. What harm is a coffee anyway? We spent eight years together, five as married, and he still pays me enough every month to keep me afloat, almost to the point where I've begun to feel guilty about it. One more year, then I'm gonna have to start fending for myself in earnest.

"Sure." I nod and force a smile.

"Fantastic!"

We turn our backs to the docks and begin walking side by side. "A kid, Kerry! My God. I didn't know you'd married! Honestly... I think our agreement on the money—"

"I'm not married," I say quickly. "There's no father."

Evan side-eyes me and frowns. "Really. That's not like you."

"You don't know what's like me anymore, Evan. Things happen, sometimes they don't go as planned."

His gaze darkens. "Tell me about it."

An unease creeps into my stomach. There's a tension in him, something different, an underlying sense of desperation.

"So, does the father pay up at least?"

"He's dead," I snap.

Evan's mouth forms into an O, and for a moment he looks like a fish out of water. "I'm sorry," he says, and he does sound like he means it, making me soften a little. This is just Evan, after all. He's not inherently bad, just really stupid. He cheated on me, sure, but I'm lucky our marriage ended, I'd have been miserable in the long run.

"Thanks. It's fine."

It's not, but isn't that what you say between strangers? Everything is fine, no need to lay your burdens on someone else.

Evan comes to a halt and pushes open a door to a little coffee shop, old-fashioned, dark wood, cramped with tiny tables and only two other customers, huddled over a laptop each at the far end of the little room.

We have to lift the stroller down two stone steps and Evan keeps the door open with a foot while we maneuver past the obstacles.

"Couldn't you have found a smaller place?"

He laughs. "I like it here. They have a mean espresso. What can I get you?"

"Chocolate muffin, and a latte."

"Coming right up." He turns toward the counter as Cecilia throws up her deep brown eyes and peers curiously around her.

"And a carton of apple juice, if they have any," I half-shout.

He waves in acknowledgement.

"Hey, sweetheart. Wanna sit on my lap?"

"Sit. Come," she exclaims and raises her chubby little arms toward me. I unbutton her yellow spring jacket and pull it off her before I hoist her up.

"Mommy, nam-nam?"

I laugh. The little sweet-tooth. "Mommy's only having coffee." I wince when I realize I'm lying. "And we'll share yum," I add.

Cecilia beams up at me and then takes stock of our surroundings as Evan comes back with two cups, one small and one large, placing them on the table. On instinct I immediately push mine out of Cecilia's too-long reach.

"Hey, little one," he says and bends over to catch her attention. Her eyes fixate on his beard and her mouth falls open as she reaches for him. "Look what Uncle Evan's got!" He holds up the apple juice and a big grin spreads on my daughter's face as she glances between me and the packet. Cecilia looks more and more like Christian every day, and when she smiles, it's almost as if his soul makes a brief visit. It still hurts. It's been almost six months, and I wonder when I'll ever be free of him.

I pull myself back to the present and nod. "Go ahead. It's for you, sweetie." She reaches for it, and I mouth a thank you to my ex-husband.

"So, Kerry, what've you been up to? And a baby? Oh my God!"

"Are you still with that blonde?" I counter. I don't care, he can have a harem of blondes, or any color of women, but I want to deflect that question.

He has the decency to blush. He always did blush easy. "No," he mumbles. It only lasted a few months."

"Way to go to end a marriage over."

"Ker, I never told you how sorry I am."

"Yeah, you did. I think that was all I heard for about seven months while our lawyers settled the deal."

Evan looks at his espresso. "I fucked up," he mumbles.

"Yeah, you really did."

Cecilia reaches for the muffin, and I break a little piece for her.

"I'm not doing well, Kerry."

Something in his voice makes me look up and study him closer. "What happened?"

"I really screwed things up at work. I... borrowed some money..."

"Borrowed?"

Evan squirms. "I was stupid."

I tense. My alarm bells go off. Something is off. Way off. "Exactly how stupid?"

It's obvious that he itches to speak, that he carries a burden he can't manage on his own. I'm not the one he should talk to, though. We haven't spoken in years. There's gotta be someone else.

"I re-married."

My eyebrows shoot up. That was unexpected.

"She was really into my lifestyle, high maintenance... My credit cards literally burned."

I doubt they *literally* burned, but whatever.

"So...?"

"I crashed. It all crashed. I took bank loans. My apartment was worth millions and it was my security."

Oh, yes. I lived it. He made a ton of money on real estate. I gave him my everything so that he could focus on his career.

"Then the banks wouldn't lend me more so I... I took some money from the firm."

"You did *what*? You stole money, Evan?"

I can't believe what I'm hearing. He was always a little bit naive, but that's *so* not like him. He always knew right from wrong. *Did he?* says a little voice at the back of my head. *He cheated on you. For six months he went and fucked another woman.*

"I was terrified of losing everything."

"You could've come clean with her."

Evan licks his lips and looks out the window. Cecilia pulls out the straw from the juice packet, spraying us with little drips. I put it back down.

"Let it stay there, honey." I give her another piece of the muffin that I have yet to try myself, but I have no appetite.

"She's so cute," says Evan as he grabs a napkin and wipes his face. "Her eyes, hair, she's really dark, nothing like you. Is— Was the dad dark?"

I inhale raggedly, the reminder of Christian aches. "Yes. Why didn't you just talk to her?"

"I... When the company found out I stole from them, they threatened me with prosecution."

"Naturally," I say.

Evan presses his lips together. "I guess," he mutters. "Anyway, I got them back the money and they settled on kicking me out and never pressed charges."

"Where did you get that money?" A crawling, nasty foreboding is settling in my stomach. He did something bad, something really bad.

"I borrowed from Suzanne's dad."

"Okay. And?"

"He really wants his money back."

"I can imagine he would. What does your wife say about this, then? Does she know?"

"She left me."

"Oh."

"I gave her everything, and she fucking went and annulled the marriage, as if what we had was worth nothing."

Pushing down the rage that threatens to flare up, I laugh inwardly at the irony. He gave her everything? Much like I did in our marriage.

"Her dad's not a good man, Kerry. He's threatening to break every bone in my body if I don't pay him back, and I don't have the money, I can't."

"What the fuck, Evan? How can you be so stupid?"

He hangs his head. "I don't want to die," he whispers. "They'll kill me."

"Who is he?"

"He's not a good guy. Better if you don't know his name."

An awful suspicion makes my heart suddenly slam in my chest, making the room tilt.

"Evan! Tell me his name! You have to tell me his name!"

"Charlie. It's Charlie Richter, Ker. He owns casinos in Vegas, a bunch of them. He's loaded. And dangerous."

I don't know any Richter, and it seems I should be happy for it.

Leaning back in my chair, I exhale with relief. For a moment, I was so sure it was Salvatore. Not that I know if he has a daughter eligible for marriage, but I was just so damn sure.

"Mommy! More!" Cecilia pulls at my sleeve, pointing at the crumbled remains of the muffin.

"Sure," I say absentmindedly.

"Evan... the alimony."

"I'll pay it," he says quickly. "You were the only good thing that ever happened in my life. I will honor our agreement."

"Where does the money come from?"

"It's... from the loan." He winces and looks down at his hands. They're clutched into tight fists, his knuckles white.

Suddenly I feel genuinely sorry for him. We did have good times. We were friends once, laughed, shared our lives.

"Evan. I don't want the rest. Please stop paying. I'll talk to my lawyer and put it on paper."

A slight relief lightens his features. "No, I insist. It's not your fault."

"*Evan!* Don't you see? I don't want dirty money! I won't take it." My life is so full of dirt anyway. I wade in it. I don't want to be involved in even more. "Since how long?"

"How long what?"

"When did you steal from the firm?"

"Kerry—"

"*When?*"

"It's... about three years ago."

I shake my head. Poor, stupid Evan. "I'll pay you back every dime since that moment. Maybe that will help some? With this Richter?"

Evan winces.

"You borrowed much more?"

He scoffs. "Yeah," he says on an exhale. "A lot more."

Clenching my jaw, I fight down the anger that wells up in me. "No matter if it helps or not, I don't want that money. If you won't take it, I'll give it away to charity."

Evan suddenly leans forward, grabs one of my hands and kisses it. "You're amazing. You always were amazing. You're so wise, and good, and kind, and—"

I scoff inwardly, bitterly. I am *so* not wise. I'm so incredibly stupid. But that's nothing I'll share with Evan.

"I need to go." I stand and grab a napkin, wiping off the crumbs from around Cecilia's mouth. Her hands are sticky and she puts her fingers in her mouth, sucking them.

"Muffn," she says and looks questioningly at me.

"Muffin," I correct her.

Evan shoots to his feet. "I'll help you."

We make our way up the stairs. My stomach churns as I look at him. I don't like that he's in trouble. He's made some really, really bad choices, but he doesn't deserve to get hurt over them.

"I'll be in touch," I say.

Evan attacks me with a firm hug. I pat him awkwardly.

"Thank you, Kerry! For everything. I'm so happy I met you today!"

I'm not, but I give him a skewed smile and turn the stroller back toward the docks. I feel as if my life just took a turn for the worse. How will this affect me? Why did he have to show up and unload his shit on me? I have enough trouble as it is. Salvatore hasn't been in touch. Yet. Every day I live in terror, fearing the call, fearing men suddenly appearing in front of me, demanding I come with them. It's a nightmare I can't wake from. I really didn't need more of the same.

Sixteen

Kerry

I stand outside the university. It's been settled with the dean and I can pick up where I left off. I have a lot of catching up to do, and I decide to wait with any other commitments. I paid back everything to Evan, everything from when he stole from his company. I know I could keep it, but it makes me sick. I don't want to see him get hurt, I don't want to know what he does with the money. I still have savings, but I'm gonna have to look for a paid job soon. Mom has a contact, some old friend of Dad's. I really do want to work with kids and his wife runs a daycare for children with special needs. It would be perfect. I hope that it will work out. I don't want to be dependent.

I've found a daycare for Cecilia. She'll be two years old soon and she is very social, very easy to get along with, and very curious about other people. It's not fair to keep her hidden. I clench up at the thought of not keeping her in my sight at all times. What if Salvatore just takes her? What if she's gone one day when I come to pick her up? But seven months have passed, and there's been nothing but silence. I've slowly begun to relax, to allow the fear to subside. The only thing that remains as strong as ever is the aching hole her father left in me.

The sky is cloudy, orange-tinged, and the air is humid. There's talk of a storm rolling in tonight. They come early this year, it's still spring. I can't help but smile, thinking about how I'll sit with a glass of white wine and rest my eyes on the fury of the ocean as the waves pummel the beach.

Twisting the tendrils of hair at my neck, flipping them between my index and middle fingers, I turn the stroller north and start walking along the narrow sidewalk, avoiding the largest cracks in the concrete. My hair is still short, but it has a ragged style to it I like very much, a styled style. I had the hairdresser get rid of the black. They had to dye it red, but it's close enough to my natural color. I wonder what *he* would have thought of it.

And I really don't know why I just wondered that. I have to stop thinking about him. He's a monster. He helped us, sure, but at his core, he's like Salvatore, a stone-cold murderer.

I'm so happy I can start studying again. I need it for my sanity, for my mind. I need to feel like I'm doing something. I can't just drift.

Cece sleeps like a log, her dark hair curled against her forehead in the moist heat. I walk on light feet until I reach the shore where I struggle against the wind for a while before I hail a taxi that takes us home.

San Francisco

Christian

SHE DOESN'T KNOW I'M WATCHING HER.

She doesn't flinch when strangers pass too close, and she doesn't glance over her shoulder time and time again. If she did know I was here, though, she'd know she has nothing to be afraid of.

I really do hope she'd know that.

They are beautiful together. Cecilia has grown since I last saw her. She's a self-conscious little lady, trotting next to her mother, cute, her dark hair tied into ponytails, bouncing as she runs in circles, jumps, runs back and forth. Just as active as ever. I smile when I see her. I can still recall the feeling of the little body in my arms, fever-hot, still, a heart thumping rapidly. An involuntary shudder passes through me, as always, when I remember how she slid and disappeared over that edge.

I want to touch them.

Them.

Cecilia.

Kerry.

Her hair has grown, it's back to its beautiful red, and I do believe she's actually paid for a haircut because she doesn't look like she ran over herself with the lawnmower anymore. They look happy, relaxed, but I detect a briefly passing haunted look on Kerry's features from time to time, like an underlying sadness. I can't imagine why. Everything has turned out for the best for her. As far as she knows I'm dead, she has no need to look over her shoulder anymore. And still... she kind of does.

I should keep away. But I already know I won't.

I can't.

SEVENTEEN

Christian

S
he's on her way to the university again. It's the third time since I started watching them. This time is different, though. She has left Cecilia at a small daycare. Seven kids. Different ages. I checked the staff. Just a couple of speeding tickets. No pedophiles. Had there been one, I'd have killed him. Or her.

I'm conflicted.

I want her to be with our daughter and not leave her in the hands of strangers.

Her eyes were sad when she jumped in her car after leaving Cecilia, but when she went home that afternoon she had a new posture.

Proud. Alive.

Something I remember from a very long time ago.

"HOW'S EVERYTHING WITH MY FAVORITE NEPHEW?" Salvatore sits with his feet propped up on the table, a newspaper and a cup of espresso next to him.

I stick a new toothpick between my teeth, dropping the one I just broke on the table. Salvatore looks disapprovingly between the little piece of wood and me, but doesn't comment on it.

"I need something to do."

"I don't know what to use you for."

Pain laces my chest. I'm worthless to him. I know nothing of any other life. I don't know what to do with myself.

"There's gotta be something."

"I have people managing my paperwork, and you're not trained for that. You're muscle, Christian, not brain. No matter how much it pains me to say it, in your current condition, there's nothing for you."

"I know security systems like my own back pocket. I can do tech."

"Yeah, got no use for that. I want my men capable in a fight, no matter what else they do."

I'm quiet, my mind spinning. I'm weak, useless, damaged.

"You were my best man, Christiano. You're still the closest thing I have to a brother, and that will never change. You'll never lack anything, I'll provide for you, but right now... I can't put you to work for me. If shit went down, you couldn't defend yourself and you'd put every-fucking-one at risk, and you know it."

I lean my elbows on the table and rub my hands over my face. "Fuck, Luci. I'm going insane."

"You have something beautiful out there, that you refuse to acknowledge. Why don't you go pursue her? Them? You asked me to stay away. I'm staying away. But if you don't get your shit together and go get your woman, I'll fucking bring her here, her and the child, because my patience is running out."

"She's happy, you fuck! She's making a life for herself, finally, the life I took from her. I can't fucking barge in and destroy it all over again."

"Mind your fucking language when you're addressing me! I don't know who you are anymore, Chris! You've gone soft. You're a fucking wuss. Go claim your woman, or I'll do it for you. I'll get her here and make her and the little one live under my roof. Don't think for a moment I'd hesitate. You've got one week to pull yourself together. You hear me? I'm fed up with your wallowing. Maybe, if you start acting like a man, I could have use for you, but as it is now... it makes me sick just looking at you. One week. Now get out of my sight for fuck's sake."

I jump up, nauseous. One week. It rings all too familiar. He's always making demands. Last time it was for me to get between her legs before he would have someone kill her, and I fucking went for it.

I leave my uncle without another word. I went for it, fucked her, destroyed her. All because I did what he told me. Am I just gonna do what he tells me again?

Yes. Fuck me, but yes, I am. That's why I'm here, back in San Francisco. She has a pull on me that I can't deny, and I need to be in her life. If not as a lover, then at least as their protector, because God knows she needs protecting.

I rev my engine and speed off down the steep road, my heart lighter than it's been for years.

I know what I must do.

WEAK AS A NEWBORN BABY, OR AS I FIGURE THEM TO BE, I'VE had to start from the beginning. I spent months in physiotherapy in the Big Apple, and I keep at it. Military exercises. Simple. Legs. Back. Chest. Arms. Repeat. Repeat. Repeat. And when I take breaks, I take rides. The university. The daycare. Her place.

I can't seem to get enough air, enough strength. I don't recognize my own body and it scares me. I go see a doctor. He hums and listens, and huffs and creases his forehead. After an X-ray, I find myself in his office later the same day and he looks even more concerned and asks me what I've been through. I tell him to fucking spit it out.

The earth is trembling underneath me as I'm back out on the street. My lungs apparently look like shit, scarred and stiff, and I'll never regain my old physique. I sway. I don't know what to do with the rest of my life. I only know one thing—how to fight, how to hurt people.

I refuse to budge and go back to my regime. Legs. Back. Chest. Arms. Repeat.

On the sixth day after my last, tumultuous visit to Salvatore, I realize I'm stalling. I'm stalking again. Stalking and stalling. Pathetically. Who the hell called me pathetic once? I am strong enough now. And if the fucking doc's right, it won't get much better than this. I hope she won't try to kill me when she sees me because she might very well succeed. I hesitate for a moment. Would she?

It's Friday evening and by now they will have eaten and are watching cartoons on TV.

It's time.

I listen for a moment. There's music coming from inside the door. I recognize the song immediately. I always did like Creedence.

They sing of trouble that's on its way.

I can't help but grin at the accidental meeting between my knuckles on her door and John Fogerty's foreboding words.

I hope I'm not trouble. I don't think I am. I hope she'll welcome me. In fact, I'm terrified she might not. I hesitate a moment longer. This could change my life forever. It can go either way. She can throw me out, and then there'll be only darkness. Or she can welcome me into her light, into her bright house, where all the life, and everything I've ever cared about exists.

I almost touch the door, and then I pull back.

I could destroy her life all over again, rip away the safety she has felt since she returned. I think of leaving her alone and immediately reject it. I need to know she has forgiven me. I need to know what I once did has been undone.

Then I knock.

Kerry

Cece is watching the Disney Channel, some cartoon I think is just a little too violent for her age. The hollow sounds of fake laughs and characters beating each other to a pulp are increasing and I realize she must have found the volume control again. The noise from the TV mixes painfully with the music I have on in the living room. I am just about to enter her room to switch to another channel when I hear the knocking on the door. Not the doorbell, nothing that should be even remotely startling, but just a couple of soft knocks.

I...

I stand indecisively in the upper hallway, staring at the stairs, then at Cece's open door. I take a few quick steps inside her room and lower the volume.

"Mom!"

"Too loud, hon. Bedtime soon. Hop in your PJs."

My mind is already completely preoccupied with the stranger outside the door, Cece's choice of children's show and my concerns about it already forgotten.

It's just...

I don't know who it can be. A twinge of fear makes my heart tremble for a moment. Salvatore? Then I get angry with myself. It's a neighbor, maybe the new one who moved in after Mr. Edwards apparently was moved to a care facility. Or Gayle. It's a considerate person who knows it should be about bedtime for Cece. I drop the remote on Cecilia's bed, run down the stairs and walk with determined steps through the hallway, unlock and open the door. At the same time the CD has come to its end and the music stops.

I know the moment I see even a part of the dark suit. My knees nearly fold and on instinct I scream and try to slam the door shut.

His foot sneaks into the gap and stops the motion. "Kerry," he rasps, "don't shut me out."

I only hear his voice. *His* voice. And see the tip of an impeccably polished shoe. He pushes the door open enough that we can see each other. I have tunnel vision and all I see is his eyes while I hear the still too loud, clanking sounds from the silly children's show from upstairs. His voice is desolate and his eyes are so dark. I see him throwing himself, without concern for his own safety, to save Cecilia.

You died!

You're alive!

"Please," he says, holding a hand on his side of the handle, his foot still preventing me from shutting the door.

I let go and stagger back. The hallway is dark and the only light enters from the narrow ray from a streetlamp that shines between the frame and the door. Then the ray gets wider as he slowly opens the door and enters. He's my whole world in that moment. I don't hear anything else, see anything else. Him and me, that's all there is.

I think I'm going to faint. Or throw up. But I do nothing.

When he shuts the door behind him, we're thrown into near darkness, only the light shining from the kitchen allows us to see anything at all. And the sounds from Cecilia's room return.

"I thought you died," I finally whisper.

He is quiet for a moment. "Did you really think that?" he whispers back.

Did I?

No. Not really, really. He's like a force of nature. Like energy. He can't ever truly cease to exist.

I shake my head and he nods in acknowledgement. We're like accomplices, partners in the sham. I could have told the policeman from Winnipeg, Officer Tremblay, it was very likely that Christian would turn up again. That he always does. But I didn't. The moment he saved my child—our child—was the moment he also earned my protection, what little I can give. I want to lay my arms around him. I want to lean my head against his chest and hear if there's really a beating heart in there. I am so incredibly relieved he is alive; I want to touch him to feel if he's real. The urge surprises me and I clench my hands, my arms glued to the sides of my body. *No.* Instead I get angry. Angry at myself for even thinking of wanting to touch this monster, this *murderer*. Angry for all the agony he's put me through these last months when I thought he was dead.

I open my mouth to speak, to reject him again and to let that anger well up, when his gaze shifts and he's looking behind me. I spin on my heels and see that Cecilia, true to her nature, has dropped the less exciting thing for the more exciting. She's standing on the last step of the stairs, peeking around the corner. I glance back at Christian, finding him crouching, transfixed by my—no, our—daughter.

"Hey," he whispers.

Cecilia gazes at me for a moment, then she hops down the last stair and walks straight up to Christian and takes his hand. "I am Cecilia," she says, loud and clear, exaggerating every syllable, pronouncing them perfectly.

I stay out of their way for the next hour, letting Cece show the interesting stranger her room, her drawings, the contents of her wardrobe and every little bit and piece of her world. She chatters vividly, as cheerful as always, and I hear Christian's soft murmuring answers.

Walking back and forth in front of the panoramic window, I'm beginning to wonder how long it will take before I've made a groove in the wooden floor. I'm clutching a cold cup of tea, and I haven't taken a sip in probably the last half hour. Every nerve ending I've got is directed toward his presence. I feel him more than I hear him. I'm exhausted from the constant fear that I'll suddenly hear the front door slam shut and find them gone. When he comes up to me from behind, I turn deliberately slowly. I don't want him to know how on my toes I really am.

"She's yawning."

I stare at him. He's thinner than I remember him, his hair has lost some of its luster, and he seems older, even though only a few months have passed. I still can't believe what I'm seeing.

He clears his throat. "I think she's tired, I figured you'd want to do the bedtime thing."

I force myself to snap out of my self-induced trance. "Why didn't you let me know?"

His eyes dart between mine, a pained expression on his face. "Can we talk later?"

I nod numbly. "Okay."

His gaze makes my back tingle and burn all the way until I've turned the corner where I fumblingly support myself on the wall as I make my way upstairs to my daughter's room. I have to stop and lean my forehead against the cool wall. *Oh. My. God.* My life is once again turned on its head, I'm losing my footing and I don't know how much more I can take.

When I read to her, I have flashbacks from when I put her to bed that first night, with him in the cabin, and I can barely breathe. It hits me hard. How afraid I was. How angry, disgusted, and filled with hate. I try to feel her soft, warm skin against mine as I help her into her pajamas. I try to be here and only here, to cherish the moment, because God only knows what awaits us in this next round in our lives. But I fail. I'm not here. I'm far away as I put her to bed. I'm back in the cabin. I'm listening for any sounds from outside her room, trying to keep track of his movements in my house. I'm anywhere but with my daughter.

Our daughter.

I taste the words and realize I can't hide from them. He has earned the right to be with her, to get to know her. If that's what he wants. *What if he wants more?* The voice in the back of my mind is small, but persistent. I shut it out. Am I afraid? *Yes. Of course.* Will he hurt us? No. At least not intentionally.

She's been asleep for awhile and I've been hugging her little body for comfort for much longer than she needed, but not for as long as I need. My brain feels like it's melting from all the swirling thoughts and images and I'm exhausted before we've even talked.

EIGHTEEN

Kerry

He has pushed the large sliding door to the side and stands there, tall, magnificent, his broad back to me, staring out into the dark. In the far distance the lights from the bridge break the monotony of the darkness. The breeze ruffles his black tresses. My heart jolts when he turns to me. I can't believe I still find him so beautiful despite everything he's done to me.

"Hi," he says in a hushed voice. "Thank you."

I stare at him a moment longer, still unable to process what I'm seeing, then I force myself out of my reverie. "For what?" I busy myself with some plates, gathering them, piling them along with the knives and forks, every part of me hyper aware of his presence.

He shifts and pushes his fingers through his hair. It's shorter than when I last saw him. "For allowing me to spend time with her."

I drop the plates with a slam, that makes us both jump. "I thought you were dead! All this time—" My eyes fill with tears and I have to look away, unable to meet his piercing gaze.

"I thought that was what you wanted."

"I—" I swallow and try to pick up the plates again, but my hands shake too much. "You could have just fucking let me know. How long have you been back?"

He hesitates, takes a step toward me, stops. "A while."

"What's a while?" Anger rises in me. I should be happy. He's alive. Or should I? Does it start again? "Did you follow me?"

"Ker, honestly—"

"What do you want from me? Honesty? What a joke. You've done nothing but fool me since the first moment we met! How the fuck could you not let me know you were alive, you piece of shit?"

"It hasn't all been a lie—"

"Bullshit!"

"No." He shakes his head. "Fuckin' hell no. Not everything was a lie, Ker."

I grimace and sit. He sets himself opposite me at the table. I can't even believe there's anything to discuss. "You played pretend right from the start, Christian."

"You already know this part, Kerry. Are we really gonna go through this shit again?"

I jerk as his hand shoots out and grips around my forearm. His touch is electric. I can't believe how he can touch me like that. I wrench out of his hold and massage my skin where his fingers made contact.

"Shut up," I snarl.

"No," he says. "I won't shut up. No matter how fucking wrong it was, it was still real between us, and you know it."

I'm so cold. I shiver despite the warm night and I stand abruptly to close the sliding door, feeling his eyes on me as I move. I sit back down on the chair again and pull up my knees, hugging them, my jaw so clenched it hurts.

"Y... ou h... urt me," I manage to croak.

A look of concern crosses his face. "Are you okay?"

"I'm so c—cold." I hug my legs even tighter and rock back and forth. And I really am. I'm frozen deep into my marrow. I can't control my shuddering. The shock from seeing him before me again suddenly rolling over me with its full force.

"I'll get you a blanket, hang on." He stands and disappears before I can even say something. I still can't move an inch as he comes back with my blanket, draping it around my shoulders, making sure it stays on before he goes back to his spot. "Better?"

I stare at a piece of macaroni, lying alone on Cece's side of the table. *You hurt me. Nothing can make that better.*

"Do you want to talk about it?"

My eyes look up to meet his. He's looking straight back at me, and at the same time I get the feeling he's having a hard time holding my gaze, that it's his sheer willpower that makes him meet my pain.

"About what?" I ask, my voice hoarse. Even though I know.

"About... what I did to you." He licks his lips, and his gaze flickers.

I scoff. "What good would that do?"

He shakes some stray strands of hair out of his eyes and leans back, his gaze hardening, becoming more distant. "Why the fuck are we at this again? *How* can you not see that all I do is try to redeem myself, for fuck's sake?"

"Shut up!" My heart slams against my ribcage as I jump up. The blanket falls to the floor. "Get the fuck out of here!"

He shoots to his feet and storms toward the door.

"How *could* you?" I ask to his squared shoulders.

He stops and turns. "It was my fucking *job!*"

"*You hurt me!*" I scream.

"I hurt you because we had connected. Right, Ker? It wasn't my gun to your head that hurt the most, was it? It was because we were something more than just killer and victim. Weren't we?"

"No," I mumble unhappily.

"And you couldn't believe that *I*, of all people, could do that to *you*, of all people."

"*No!*"

"And you thought more of me, didn't you? That I was a better person. That because you felt something for me it meant I had to be a *good* person deep down and not who I really am."

"*No!*"

"Yes. And it has hurt ever since. That *you* fell for *me*. That your judgment was so flawed."

"Shut *up!* Get out!" I'm shaking. I need to throw up, but I won't do it when he's anywhere near. "Get out of my *house!*"

"Kerry." His voice is suddenly calmer, subdued. "I didn't mean... We need to get this shit out of the way."

"You're *defending* what you did!" Nausea washes over me like waves of muddy water.

"That's not what I'm doing."

"That's what I hear."

"Then you're hearing it wrong."

"*Really?* Then *tell* me how I should hear it." I pick up my blanket again, wrapping it tight around myself, making it my protective shell.

"I can't undo it—"

"That's true at least," I snarl.

"When we met... I didn't intend to put you through that."

"You came to fuck me and then kill me! You *knew* you were going to kill me. You tied me up, scared me, beat me."

He regards me, something dark flashes through his eyes for a brief moment, making my gut churn. "I should leave. And you *need* a fucking spanking for being so *fucking* mouthy!"

"You're an asshole," I spit. "You're just like your boss, like that *shit* Salvatore! I hate you all!"

He blinks and throws out his hands. "What do you want from me?"

"I thought you wanted to talk."

"You're so hostile. This isn't easy for me either."

"Do you think I care what's easy for *you*?"

He bites his lower lip and his eyes narrow. Then he turns. "Bye."

"Don't!" I blurt out, suddenly afraid he'll disappear again. I look at his back as it slumps. He puts his hands on either side of the door-frame. His shoulders rise and fall rapidly. He doesn't turn, but he doesn't leave either. I swallow hard before I say it. "Please, don't leave." I close my eyes to shut out the moment. Why didn't I just let him go?

He still doesn't move.

"Are you?" I ask and open my eyes.

He turns slowly and leans against the doorframe, his arms crossed defensively over his chest. "Am I *what*?" he spits.

"Are you a better person?" It feels as if my whole life hangs on the answer.

He closes his eyes and presses his lips together into a thin line, looks at his feet and then up at me. "What do *you* think?"

That's not the answer I wanted. Not the answer I crave. Like always. I look away from him, out into the blackness. What do *I* think? My image of him is so blurred, so complex. I've seen so many sides of him that shouldn't even exist within one person. I close my eyes and swallow hard.

"Are you killing people?"

He looks at me. As the moment stretches, my stomach clenches more and more. "I'm not."

"Will you?"

He waits a long time before he answers and his voice is suddenly slow, measured. "That would depend on the situation."

I raise my eyebrows. I can't imagine even one situation where I'd ever consider murder.

"How?" I croak.

"If someone, or something, threatened Cecilia, or you, or me."

"And if *I* threatened you?"

He grimaces. "You're not making this easy."

I shrug. "I just wanna know how deep this do-good urge, and the miraculous change for the better goes. And what would turn everything around again, back to the Christian I know and distrust."

"I have *no* fucking intention of hurting you, Kerry."

"Now?"

"Ever."

"But you did—" I look away, "have that intention."

He hesitates. "Maybe. I don't know anymore."

I groan. "You and your half-answers, the way you twist everything around... It's driving me insane."

"Welcome to the club," he says with a grimace.

I scoff. We're not getting anywhere. Maybe we won't ever? But if this is it, then we've still come a long way.

"Do you want me to make us some tea, Ker?"

I gape from the sudden friendly offer, as if this is just a normal night in a normal life. "Yes, please. Blackberry." As he turns his back to me, I suddenly bombard him with the questions I've held inside me since he arrived, some of them since when he disappeared. "How did you survive, Christian? Did you fall into the river? Where did you *go*? They were looking like mad for you, you know."

"That's a long story," he says, his back still to me as he pours water into the kettle.

"The night is long."

"I found a house. I almost died. It's been a long road to recovery."

"Who... who was in that house? Did he survive?"

Christian stops for a moment, becomes absolutely still, and something goes cold inside me.

"She did."

I exhale a breath I didn't know I was holding. "Why didn't you get in touch earlier?" I ache to tell him about my pain, about how out of my mind I've been, but I swallow the words. I fear making myself vulnerable to him again.

He finds two bright yellow mugs in my cupboard and then tea bags to put in them. The sound from the water boiling increases and then, with a sharp snap, it abruptly dies out.

"I thought you'd be happier without me."

I snap my mouth shut. "But you came anyway?"

"I wasn't left with a choice," he grits out.

My stomach plummets. "Your uncle."

Christian spins around. "My uncle is a selfish piece of shit. He also considers Cecilia close family, and he will never let you go, Kerry. Never. He wanted to rein you in. I had to step in."

Fear crawls along my spine and it feels as if my skin shrinks. "He'd do that?" I croak.

He raises his eyebrows as he places the steaming cups in front of us on the table. "Salvatore does what Salvatore wants. He's really not pleased with you."

My whole face feels numb. "Why? But he's stayed away?"

"Because I told him to." Christian sets himself in front of me, the cup untouched before him. He licks his lips and looks away for a moment. Then he looks back at me, his face serious.

"Why?"

"Because you deserve to be happy, and being in the clutches of Luci does not make a person happy."

Warmth spreads in my chest as I take him in. I can't believe he's here, that I'm looking at him again, that he's alive. What does this mean to me? To us? Then realization hits me.

"Am... Am I in the clutches of you now?"

Christian looks at me for a long while, then he stands and moves toward the door.

"Christian," I half-shout.

He spins around, his face darkening, his eyes suddenly reminding me all too well of the killer.

"You are," he says. Then he pulls the door open and disappears.

I stare at the door as it slams shut, all I hear is my own heartbeat roaring in my ears.

You are.

What am I? A pawn in these people's game? I'm nothing, nobody, Salvatore made that clear. Only my daughter is worth something to them. Is that why Christian came back? To claim what's his?

My head spins and I have to support myself on furniture and walls as I make my way to the door and lock it.

Walking up the stairs on trembling legs, I realize I forgot to ask him about Chloe. I stumble, and fall to my knees, moaning from the pain of the impact. *Chloe.* He hurt Chloe. I know it. Oh my God.

There's no doubt in my mind that Christian will be back, and I'm not gonna let him get away. He *will* confess!

Christian

She let me in.

I sit in my car. The engine is off. My body is on fire.

She let me in. She trusted me. She had missed me. She had fucking missed me! I can't believe she let me in and let me spend time with Cecilia. I can't understand how she can be so generous after all I've done to her.

I told her the whole uncomfortable truth, concentrated into two words only. *You are.* Kerry won't like it one fucking bit, but the moment I laid my eyes on her, she was doomed.

The moment she chose to speak to Salvatore for the first time, she doomed herself to death.

The moment she let me drive her home that first night, she doomed herself to be mine.

The one, single time, we fucked, when we made Cecilia, was the night that changed my whole existence. Women to me had been for one thing only up until then. I've had lovers, short-time girlfriends, and more one-night stands than I can count, but I've never felt such a rush of power over her submission to me. I've never felt such a deep need to be with someone, and to keep her as mine, forever.

Kerry Jackson *will* be mine again, and soon, because I can't stay away. I won't stay away. I need to have her warm little body under me again. Flashes of the reddened, slightly mottled skin on her butt, her fearful eyes as I tied her up, make me rock hard in a second.

Do I woo her, or do I just take her?

I have no fucking idea how to court someone. Fuck that. I know she needs me just as much as I need her, and this time she's not going anywhere. No Chicago. No fucking Canada. She stays.

I have half a mind to storm back inside and push her up against the wall, ripping the clothes off her body. I have waited so long. Too long.

She's mine. Finally.

NINETEEN

Kerry

I'm putting the casserole in the oven when my phone chimes. I let the oven door slam closed and glance at the clock. In thirty minutes Rebecca and Gayle will arrive, and in about an hour Mom will come and pick up Cecilia. They adore Cece and have demanded to always meet her at least a little before we throw ourselves into our girls' nights.

My kitchen counter is a mess, with remains of cut fresh herbs, slices of tomatoes, and the skin of a salmon tossed to the side. My hands stink of fish. I find the phone beneath an oven mitten. It keeps chiming. I don't recognize the number.

"Yes?" I squeeze the phone between my shoulder and my ear as I rinse the spoon and quickly lather and rinse my hands.

"Ker?"

I drop the cell. It slides down my chest. The wooden spoon flies through the air and water splatters everywhere as I manage to catch the phone. The spoon bounces as it clatters to the floor.

"Evan!"

"Oh thank God. I wasn't sure it was the right number."

"How'd you get my number?" I pick up the spoon, turn off the faucet and regard the mess as I drop a towel on the floor to soak up the worst of it. The front of my blouse is wet and... fucking Evan!

"Ehh... at the center for autistic children, they—"

"They aren't allowed to give away my phone number!"

"I... might have introduced myself as your husband."

"What?" I shriek. "Why'd you even do that? And why wouldn't you have my number if you were my husband? Why are you calling, Evan? I can't give you more money, I'm sorry."

"Hey, can't I call as a friend?"

No, I want to scream, but manage to moderate my answer somewhat. "I don't think we can be friends, Evan, I'm sorry, but that ship sailed a very long time ago. Honestly, I hope you'll solve your shit, but don't pull me into it, I've got enough as it is."

"Cecilia—" he says, *"is she a Russo?"*

Everything goes absolutely still. The only noise that is heard is the oven fan that gives off a slight humming sound.

My voice doesn't sound like my own as I answer him. "What makes you say that?"

"So she is. Whose? Did you fuck a Russo, Ker? What the fuck?"

"I don't think that's any of your fucking business," I hiss. I try to disconnect, but I tremble so hard that I keep missing the button. I hear him speak, but I don't hear what he's saying.

Fuck him, fuck him, *fuck him!*

Finally I manage to cut the call and fall to my knees, right into the puddle of water, clutching my constricting throat. How did he know? No one can know! I can barely breathe.

'Did you fuck a Russo, Ker?'

I crawl over to the couch and climb up, hugging my knees. Why does this shit keep happening to me? But I know why. I'm in their claws. I danced with the devil, even if it wasn't by choice, and these are the consequences. This is my life.

Christian's words from two nights ago ring loud and clear in my head. They've been eating away at me since he left, all through classes, conversations with classmates, all through the nights—again with the sleepless nights.

'You are.'

I'm his. His property, the mother of his child, his to do whatever he wants with.

'Did you fuck a Russo, Ker?'

No, I didn't. But a Russo fucked me.

I groan and wipe my cheeks. Cecilia is up in her room, transfixed by cartoons, and hasn't noticed anything, thank God. I have twenty minutes until my friends arrive, I have to pull myself together, wash my face, change clothes. I'm gonna have fun tonight. My life might be shit, but I won't let it destroy the few windows of light-hearted fun I get to have.

I SWAY A LITTLE AS I HUG GAYLE AND REBECCA GOODBYE. I refused to let the call from Evan ruin my evening, even though it has been nagging at the back of my mind, but by God, it did make me drink a couple of glasses of wine I shouldn't have. My mind is pleasantly buzzed, and I feel light, carefree.

On Friday, Gayle is taking me to one of her concerts. She wanted to set me up with a date, but that's not happening. She doesn't know Christian is alive and back in town, and I'll keep her safe from that knowledge for as long as I possibly can, because it's my burden to carry and no one else's. It'll be fun, though. I really look forward to seeing her on stage.

Locking the door behind them, I start up the stairs, stopping when the doorbell rings. Did they forget something? I sail down and quickly twist open the locks, swinging the door open.

It's not Gayle, and it's not Rebecca.

A tall, hulking figure stands in my doorway, his eyes pitch black, his hair hanging in unruly tresses over his forehead.

Christian Russo.

'Did you fuck a Russo, Ker?'

'You are.'

I scream and try to shut the door, but he slams a palm against it and stops the movement. I don't know why. He's been here before. It's only Christian, but something is different tonight. Something about him screams danger.

"I'm going to bed," I gasp. "It's not—"

"Perfect," he says darkly, spits out a toothpick and invades the hallway with his looming presence, pushing the door shut behind him.

I'm unable to move, and he's standing way too close.

"What are you doing?" I whisper.

"Kerry," he says as he raises a hand, letting it follow the contour of my head, my shoulder, my arm, but without touching me, setting the air between us on fire. "I can't stay away anymore. I won't."

"What are you saying?" I manage to croak, while it feels as if my insides liquefy.

Christian leans in, I take a step back, he follows, I hit the wall and jump from the abrupt stop, glancing around me for an escape. He slams his palms to the wall, one on either side of my head. He smells of whisky and sandalwood with a slight hint of citrus to it. His scent does me in. It always does.

"You know fucking well what I'm saying. I'm done playing."

"I didn't know we were playing," I whisper, transfixed by his dark gaze.

"Trust me. I'm not one for games." He leans in, his eyes level with mine, his breath hot on my lips. "Don't move."

His mouth descends on mine and my knees buckle with instant, primal need I had forgotten was ever there. He coaxes my mouth open, pushing his chest against mine, trapping me. I push back, the instinct to keep defending myself against this man so deeply rooted in me after nearly three years of fleeing.

"Christian."

"Shut up."

"No! Chr—"

"Not a word, Kerry."

His hand moves to my throat and I inhale raggedly, tensing up, then it caresses down along my vulnerable neck, taking a moment to trace my collar bone before he cups my breast, roughly, tight, bordering on painful.

I squirm and don't quite know what to do with myself. I know what's happening. There's no doubt in my mind why he's here, and there's no one who can help me, who can interrupt us. It's two a.m. and I'm slightly dizzy from the wine, even though I woke up good when he showed up. My body is responding to his even though my numbed mind screams danger.

His hand descends along my stomach, following the curve of my hip, down along the outside of my thigh where he begins to bunch my dress in his hand, pulling it up.

His mouth is still devouring mine, and the hunger for him grows as the tips of his fingers suddenly meet with the naked skin on my thigh.

My legs barely carry me. "Christian," I mumble. I don't know anymore if I'm trying to object or if I want him to go on.

He pulls up my dress in one rough yank and puts his large, rough hand between my legs, his thumb rubbing against my clit while his fingers push against my opening, only my panties between his feral desire and my aching core.

"You're soaked, Ker," he moans. "You fucking need me as much as I need you." He keeps rubbing, a little too hard, and I don't know if it's good or if it's bad anymore. "Tell me, have you been with someone else?" He pushes the panties to the side and slides along my wet slit, teasing, back and forth. "Have you?"

"No!" I gasp. "There's been no one."

A shudder runs through him as he pushes his rock-hard bulge harder against my belly. He leans back a little and regards me, his eyes darting between my swollen mouth, my eyes, my hair, back to my eyes. "You ruined me for all others, Ker. I need you more than I need air."

He thrusts his fingers inside me, spearing me. I cry out incoherently, unable to support myself on my trembling legs.

"Come here." Without further ado, he lifts me, and I wrap my legs around his waist, letting him carry me up the stairs.

Throwing me on the bed, he pants heavy and beads of sweat pearl on his forehead. "You've been a bad, bad girl, Kerry, and you keep on resisting me, fighting me, when all you had to do was keep your promise.

I scramble back as he moves in on me. "What promise?"

"You told me once you were mine. I'm gonna hold you to that. Get the fuck out of that dress. I want to see you."

His? What's he talking about? Then it dawns on me. "What the *fuck*? That was before you tried to kill me!"

"Get. Out. Of. The. Dress. Or I'll rip it in two."

"You wouldn't!"

I try to move back further, my head connecting with the wall behind me. Christian sets a knee on the mattress and strikes, his hand gripping my ankle, pulling me to him with ease. My dress rides up to my waist and he grabs it.

"No! Wait!"

My hands shake violently as I take his hand, removing it. I force myself up on my knees, my whole being screaming at me that this is not how it's supposed to be, that a lover should be gentle, not threatening, tender, not demanding and rough. Shuffling over until I got my back to him, I show him the zipper.

"I need your help," I whisper.

The groan he emits sends a wave of heat to my pussy. Warm fingers caress along my back, deliberately slow, as he pulls down the zipper and my dress falls to the sides, revealing my whole back down to my butt. With a feather light caress, he pushes it off my shoulders, and I let it fall to the bed, bunching around my knees.

"Beautiful," he moans. "Bend over." He puts a large palm between my shoulder blades and pushes.

As I fall to hands and knees, I know I have to obey.

I remember last time. My strength is nothing to his brutal force.

I remember last time, and my heart rate spikes.

I remember pain, fear, lust and want.

I remember caresses and him spanking me. I know I'll have to submit. He won't take no for an answer.

His palm is hot and calloused, caressing my butt. "You're so soft, Ker. So pale." The smack comes unexpected, shocking me to my core. I dash forward, but he grips my hips and pulls me back. "You tried to run from me." His hand is treacherously tender, then he slaps me again and I scream.

"I want a safeword, Christian!"

"You don't need a fucking safeword," he growls. "You're mine. I won't hurt you. Much." His palm connects with my skin again, and I bury my face in the mattress as I cry out in fright mixed with growing heat.

"I'm yours!" I gasp. "I'm yours. I'll be yours, but you have to give me *something*. You scare me."

He doesn't move. I listen to his ragged breathing.

His lips on my tender ass are soft and soothing as he blows a stream of cool air on raw skin. "Does it turn you on then? Being scared?" I whimper when he nibbles at my soaked panties before he pushes them to the side, and licks a path along my wet slit, all the way down to my clit. "Because you're so fucking wet, babe."

Does it? I know it does. I don't know why, but it's as if Christian's brutal soul was made to match my softness, as if his rough edges find a fit in the crevices of what makes up Kerry. It's as if together we're whole.

"A little," I whisper, too ashamed to say it out loud.

I yelp as he bites down on an ass cheek and then grabs my panties, tearing them, ripping them off me.

"I thought that was just something they do in the movies," I gasp.

Christian scoffs. "I don't like obstacles." He buries his face between my legs again, his tongue circling my clit, hard, flicking it, sucking on it as he pushes his fingers inside me again, thrusting, slow at first, and then harder, faster.

I clutch the sheets and whimper, rocking back, meeting his eager touch that brings me closer and closer to the edge. My head spins as my whole focus turns to one single point. His skin on mine, his tongue and fingers making me moan louder and louder as I begin to shake, teetering on the verge of losing my mind, forgetting who I am and who I am with.

I cry when he stops and pulls back.

"No!"

"Want me now, do you?"

I groan into the mattress.

"Tell me!" He slaps me hard, too hard, and all air rushes out of my lungs. The next slap is even harder, and I scream.

"Christian, no, *please!*"

He leans in, grabbing my chin, his eyes meeting mine, darting to the tears on my cheeks, and then back up to meet my gaze.

"Tell me you're mine."

"Give me a word," I hiss.

"Not until you tell me you'll submit to me and stop fucking fighting me."

I clench my lips together and stare defiantly at him. Fuck him!

"Kerry," he growls.

"You can't just come and take, and take, and take. You fucking ass!"

Christian laughs, and as his features lighten, my heart jumps at how beautiful he is.

"I can. And I will."

He backs up and pushes me down onto the mattress, hard, his palm heavy on my lower back. I kick out, trying to get leverage, trying to get away, but he sits down on my thighs.

"Do you remember that first night?"

I'm still struggling, but go still as he speaks. "What?"

"When I pushed you up against the kitchen counter?"

Do I remember? What a joke. Every second with him is etched into my memory, burnt into my soul.

"Yes."

"I almost took you there and then. With or without your consent. Do you know what made me stop?"

I exhale with a shudder and shake my head.

"Me neither. Do you think anything will make me stop tonight?"

I gasp, fighting to take my next breath as primal need starts a renewed furnace between my legs. Then I shake my head again. No, I don't think anything will make him stop tonight. I can only pray there's some little decency in him. He *has* said he won't hurt me. He's always said he won't hurt me, except that one time when he really was out to hurt me.

"Good girl." His voice is hoarse, aroused, and that alone makes me squirm again. I want him, and I want to run.

"Please."

A hand lands on my butt with a loud smack, and a second time, a third. Again. And again. I lose count. When he stops, I don't know if I've screamed, but my throat is raw. He caresses me, dips in between my legs, finds my desperate flesh.

"Say you're mine." He keeps caressing, building pressure. When I don't speak, he stops. "Tell me." Short, short circles around my clit, a barely there finger in my tight channel, unsatisfying, teasing, a promise of fulfillment.

"You're evil!" I bury my face in the comforter that I've bunched up in my arms, clutching it for dear life.

"Yeah?"

He stops again. I ache. I'm so close. So, so close.

"I'm yours! Fuck you! Fuck me!"

His deep, dark laugh rumbles through his chest as he spears me on his fingers, thrusting, adding his thumb pushing at my tight rear hole, pushing, gaining entrance.

"Oh God," I cry.

"Touch yourself, Kerry. Come for me."

I swallow hard and push my hand between my legs, my pussy is raw, tender, tingling. My swollen clit only needs one last caress before I lose it, coming completely undone in his hands.

Christian

Kerry convulses on my thrusting fingers, her back covered in a thin sheen of sweat, her heart shaped little ass pushing back, inviting, beautifully reddened, her skin mottled from my brutal palm. I haven't even gotten her out of her bra yet. I haven't even gotten my aching cock out of my pants yet, but I enjoyed it too much, seeing her pain, and her pleasure, seeing her so unsure, and still so wild for me.

With a last shudder she goes absolutely still, only her chest heaves. My fingers are still in her warm, tight pussy and my cock screams at me to get the fuck in there, into her tightness, into that wet heat.

"Don't move." I stand and undo my pants, kicking them off me.

"I can't," she moans.

I laugh. Well, good.

"Safeword," she whispers. She looks absolutely beaten, almost on the verge of broken. But I know she isn't. I know she'll fight me if she thinks it's needed. And she might feel that way.

"What do you want, then?"

I may be brutal, like it rough, but I have no intention of assaulting her.

"Canada."

I slap her ass, making her jump. "Fuck no. Something else." I pull off my shirt and my briefs, taking my rock-hard cock in my hand, stroking it, almost trembling. Kneeling on the bed, I nudge her thighs apart. "Come up with something quick, Kerry, or you'll have none."

"Red," she gasps. "Red!"

I put a hand on her butt, and she twitches, making me grin. I don't want Kerry to be afraid of me. Out of bed. In bed, though, I want her hot, weeping, terrified and in rapture. My fingers find her wet, slick core. She squirms as I caress her, fill her, pushing, preparing her.

"Very well." I line up my cock, my head to her entrance, teasing up and down, finding the right spot, making her arch up her butt to meet me. "Don't abuse it." I push inside in one hard thrust. Kerry squeals. Her knuckles whiten as she grips the sheet.

It's pure fucking heaven. Nothing has ever felt this good. She's tight, wrapping my cock in her soft, silky channel.

"Don't resist me," I whisper as I begin moving in her. I lean forward and grab her wrists, pushing them hard to the mattress. "Don't ever resist me again. I want you; I know you want me. No more games."

Thrusting hard, knocking the wind out of her, I flip her over onto her side. I hug her thigh to my chest as I thumb her clit with my other hand. Kerry's wide eyes are dark, a deep hazel-green, framed by natural thick dark eyelashes. She stares at me in wonder, her eyes hooded with lust.

"I," she pants, "haven't, oh God—" The muscles in her neck tense as her whole body arches back. I intensify my thrusts as I keep massaging her clit. An intense flush has crept up on her cheeks. Redheads. They bruise and flush so easily. "—haven't played," she finally grits out. "I'm gonna come again!"

She rocks her hips, meeting my thrusts, screaming as the walls of her pussy convulse, squeezing me hard. I intensify my pounding, absolutely loving the sight of the thrashing woman on the bed before me.

Every nerve in me focuses with a razor blade's sharpness into one single point.

"Fuck, Kerry," I groan. "Are you protected?"

"No!" she cries, and her eyes fly open. "Don't come in me."

For a moment my mind spins. Why not?

I pull out. So fucking close. I may be a monster, but I'm not forcing a child on her.

Again.

Even though it turned out amazing the first time.

I grab her arms and spin her around, leaving her lying on her back with her head resting on the edge of the bed, right in front of my cock.

"Don't move. And don't fucking safeword anything."

"That's not how it works," she gasps.

"Shut up and open your mouth."

A shudder runs through me as I push inside. I let her taste me and my cock twitches in anticipation. Then I push deeper, and deeper, and begin to thrust, and oh my fucking God. It's incredible.

Kerry gags and pushes at my thighs as tears drip along her cheeks. I let her draw a breath, and as I thrust in her throat again, I lean over and put my hand between her legs, sliding along the wet slit, finding her rear entrance, pushing inside both holes, matching my thrusts.

Heat rushes to my cock, immense, scorching heat, and my mind goes blank as I come in her mouth. Hard. Her pussy begins to spasm around my fingers again, as does her ass. I already know I'm going there. I'll tie her up, I'll make her come until she begs me to stop. I'll make her fucking safeword her own pleasure, because she just can't take anymore.

I pull out and fall to my knees, cupping her cheeks in my hands. Kerry lies absolutely still, only her eyes move, darting between mine. I tilt my head, trying to compensate for her upside-down position, then I look her over, wondering where my load went. "Did you swallow?"

Kerry scoffs, turns over on her belly and pulls the comforter to her, trying to drape it over her back. "I had no choice or I'd choke."

I can't help grinning. "I fucking love you."

Sitting up, groaning when her butt touches her heels, and quickly changing position, she gives me a dark gaze. "You're not right in the head."

"Don't go mouthy on me again."

Her eyes soften and a shudder runs through her. "I'm cold," she whispers.

"Come here, babe." I lift her and move her so I can lie down beside her, then I find my way under the comforter too, pulling her into my embrace. For a moment she resists, holds back. There's distrust, and I don't like it, but I don't blame her. I'll never be her knight in shining armor, but I'll protect her, and our baby until the day I die, and she'll learn to trust that.

When Kerry finally relaxes, and snuggles closer, my heart jolts with pure happiness. I caress her hair, her cheek, letting my thumb follow the contour of her lower lip.

"You're so beautiful," I whisper.

She's quiet. I look down, meeting her eyes. A whole slew of emotions pass through them and I can't believe how someone can have so many expressions. She looks me over, hair, eyes, nose, mouth, back to my eyes.

"So are you," she finally says.

I almost crush her to me. She can't possibly know how much she means, how deep she has rooted herself in me. I can only hope she feels at least a fraction of the same for me.

I WAKE FROM THE SOUND OF FLUSHING WATER IN THE adjacent bathroom. Stretching, I feel like a big cat who got his cream. There's a sense of calm in me. We'll figure this out, we'll find our way in the mess that is our lives. We'll sleep some more, but then I'm taking her again. Images of how I tie her up, fuck her, spank her until she matches her word with the color of her butt – *red* – flash before me, and my cock twitches. Or maybe we won't sleep.

When she emerges, she has pulled on sweatpants and a T-shirt. Her eyes are glossy and the tip of her nose is a little red.

"That's not—"

Kerry crosses her arms over her chest, her lips tightening. "What did you do to Chloe?"

For a moment I'm completely blank. Who the fuck is she talking about?

"My *friend*. What did you *do?*"

Chloe. *Fuck.*

The friend.

When I couldn't find Kerry, after she had run from Chicago, I got desperate and sought out the only one I figured she might have confided in. I was in a dark place. I might have been a bit rough.

"Who?"

Kerry takes a step closer. "You know fucking well who I'm talking about. I swear to God, if you won't tell me the truth, I'll never let you in again. I'll never let you see Cecilia!"

I explode out of bed, stark naked, and stride toward her, towering over her as dark rage rises in me. She's in no position to make any fucking demands.

She doesn't move. She has to lean her head back to hold my gaze, and hers is firm, unyielding.

"Did you kill Chloe?"

"What the *fuck?* No!"

She didn't die. She didn't fare particularly well, but she was alive last time I saw her.

"But you did *something*. I know it. Tell me. I know you'll come here. I know you'll demand me to be with you, command me. I know I'm not going anywhere, because you, or your fucking uncle, will make sure of that, but know this Christian: I'll *never* trust you again, for as long as I live."

My stomach churns. I can't tell her the truth. It's too ugly. But I can't lie to her either. I spin around and locate my clothes, putting them back on as I try to come up with what to tell her.

Hell.

When I turn, she still stands in the same position, her features frozen.

"I met your friend once. After you'd disappeared from Chicago."

Kerry doesn't speak.

"I wanted answers. I thought she knew where you were. She kept denying it." I take a deep breath and wait for her to say something. She doesn't. This is the Kerry from the harbor. The Kerry that first day in the cabin. The tigress, the darkness in her that makes us such a good match. "I— I had to convince myself."

"Stop squirming, you fuck," she snarls.

I move forward and push her into the wall, my hand gripping her chin. "You've gotta watch that fucking attitude!"

"I don't *care!*" she screams in my face. "What did you do to Chloe? Where is she?"

I let her go and take a step back. Pushing a hand through my hair, I wince. She's not gonna take this well. "I beat her up."

"What the *fuck?* Get out!" She pushes at my chest, as if she could move me even an inch. My stomach clenches when I see her tears, angry tears, and her resolute face. "Leave, Christian! *Leave!* Get the fuck out of here!"

"You wanted the truth," I snarl. "I beat her up, but I left her alive, some broken bones, nothing she'd die from for fuck's sake! I had no idea she was missing."

Kerry's eyes narrow as she presses her lips into a thin line. "I hate you! I could never love you! Never. I hate everything you are! Get the fuck out of here."

I stumble back, not from her physical little attempts at moving me, but from the force of her words. Pain shoots through my chest. I don't *do* pain, I deal pain. Feelings make you weak, and I'm fucking done.

"This isn't over," I growl and storm down the stairs. Where my heart should be there's nothing but a swirling dark void, the monster in me roaring in fury. I have no idea if I can mend this, but I'm nothing if not persistent. I'll wear her down. She's mine. She's always gonna be mine, no matter what. She and my daughter.

TWENTY

Kerry

I flinch when the door slams closed so hard it seems the whole foundation shakes. I inhale and exhale ragged breaths, my heart slamming in my chest. My rage is mixed with a profound sorrow that I already know is going to eat me until there's nothing left.

Christian can't be anything to me, and yet he is my whole world. He's the only one who makes me soar with a dark passion I never knew existed. He's the father of my child, and despite what he is, there's an obvious deep devotion to Cecilia there.

When the first raw sob tears through my throat, there's nothing stopping the wave of cries that brings me to my knees. I curl up into a little ball on the thick rug and wail until there are no more tears.

The guilt suffocates me. It all my fault. Completely and fully my fault, from start to... end? No. There's no end.

If I hadn't talked to Salvatore that morning? If I hadn't had such a vivid imagination when little David talked about the red he'd seen. If I hadn't involved Chloe. If I hadn't run.

If, if, if.

It's a little past eight in the morning. Mom and Cecilia must be up. I want my mom. I want to be little again. I want all of this to just go away. It hurts too much.

My hands shake when I splash some water on my swollen face, then I grab my keys and phone and flee my empty house, echoing with memories of our night together. I'm not sure if enough hours have passed since I had my last drink, but I can't wait. I have to be with people who are good, with people who love me with simple words and actions.

There's not a lot of traffic early Sunday morning in San Francisco. Cabs. Garbage trucks. People who work odd hours. The occasional early bird tourist with out of state plates, driving too slowly, switching lanes erratically. And me, driving too fast, my vision blurred with tears, fleeing the devil. Stabs shoot through me when I think of my friend. Again and again. I need Cece's warm little arms around me, her devotion and unconditional love. She's my rock and the center of my world.

Gravel crunches under my tires as I park on Mom's driveway. A curious head peeks out from behind the curtain in the kitchen window and I exhale with relief that they are awake. The door swings open and my mom's confused face meets me, confusion turning into a worried frown as she takes in my disheveled appearance.

"Kerry! What happened?"

"I'll explain," I choke out. "Where is Cecilia?" I take a step into the hallway and walk toward the sound of the children's show, coming from a room to the right. Dad's old office, still with his large oak desk by the window, but otherwise turned into a guest room.

Cecilia looks up, a surprised look on her adorable little face, her dark eyes widening. Then she slithers off the bed and rushes toward me, throwing her arms around my legs. "Mommy!"

"Pumpkin!" I fall to my knees and hug her back, holding her tight, reveling in the feeling of her body tight against mine, her chest heaving, her powdery scent.

I'm surprised by the nickname. I've never called her that before. It's almost as if Dad just channeled through me.

"Bears, Mommy!" She points to the TV. "Come!" She grabs my hand and I follow her, cozying up next to her on the sofa bed.

Mom stands with her arms crossed over her chest, leaning against the doorframe. She's already dressed in an impeccable, wrinkle free blue dress, complete with flawless makeup and her hair perfectly in order. Very much my mom. Appearance.

I look a mess, and I know it.

"I'm making coffee," she says and spins around.

"I'll come in a few," I half-shout at her disappearing back, then I hug my daughter tighter and try to let our love, or closeness, seep into my soul and chase away the worst of the thorns.

Finally I carefully free myself from her arms. She barely notices, engulfed in the show. Filled with trepidation, I make my way to Mom, who sits on the couch, two cups in front of her. I sit down next to her and lean my head on her shoulder.

"Mom, I'm not well. It's not good."

"I can tell, hon. What's happened to you? Are you in trouble?"

"Yes," I whisper.

"Do you want to tell me? Can I do something?"

"Yes, and no."

I don't give her names, but I tell her almost everything. I don't mention mafia, I don't mention the existence of Salvatore, only Christian. I don't tell her he almost killed me, only that we met, made Cecilia, that I thought we had something, how he stalked me and finally found me. I tell her about his sacrifice, his devotion, and now his obsession. I tell her how much it hurts.

"You have to go to the police, Kerry!"

"Mom, I can't. Please don't ask me why, but I'll be in danger if I do, if you do, if anyone does. Please trust me."

"Have you been alone in this the whole time?"

"I've talked to Gayle, and Rebecca a little. Mom... Chloe, she's missing, and I think he's got something to do with it." Tears well up in my eyes again. "I can't!" My voice breaks and Mom scoops me into a tight embrace.

"There are things you're not telling me," says my clever mom.

I nod. "But I really can't. I just hurt. It hurts. He's my everything, but I don't want to see him ever again."

"Are you in love with this man? Kerry, he sounds dangerous!"

"He is," I whisper, "but he would never hurt Cecilia and me."

"You can't know—"

"No, I know. It's all those other things... He's not a good man. I need a good, kind man, not... What have I done? Why did it have to be him, Mom?"

My mother doesn't answer. There is no answer to that.

"Someone like Evan?" she finally says.

"Maybe."

"He is a good man."

I think of the cheating, and now the stealing, all his stupidity, that is really just naivety. But all our years of friendship meant something too. It was a calm life.

"Someone like him."

"But not him?"

"No, Mom!"

She has never quite grasped that he cheated on me, that he was fucking a blonde at the office the last six months of our marriage, but I've tried to tell her so many times, and she keeps living in denial. Initially it even felt like she blamed me for not being wife enough, but at least that passed. She really loved Evan.

I stay for hours, until past lunch, when I've finally come back to myself a little. There's no solution to the mess I'm in. I shouted at him to stay away, that I won't let him see Cecilia, but that's a threat that's impossible for me to keep. He'll take what he wants, and do I really not want to see him ever again? The thought makes me hurt. Everything hurts. Will I ever find peace again?

In the car heading home, my phone rings. I vaguely recognize the number but can't place it. Putting the call on loudspeaker, I answer. "Yes?"

"I'm so sorry for calling again."

"Evan?"

Oh my freaking God. *Did you fuck a Russo?* His harsh words from last night ring in my ears, but at the same time: isn't he right? His judgmental tone hurt, but today I feel he's right.

"Ker, I just wanna say I'm sorry for last night. I didn't mean for it to come out that way."

"How did you know?"

"I just happened to talk about you with a friend, about you having a kid. It shook me a little, I'm sorry, I just had to vent, and he knew whose it was."

Apparently not exactly whose, but way too close.

"Ker. Wanna grab a coffee today? I just want to make peace. Bring Cecilia, she's so cute. It makes me wanna have kids myself. I've made so many wrongs, but I know now how I'm gonna make them right, and then I'll get my life in order. Meeting you inspired me."

It's not Evan per se. He's not the one for me. But someone like him, and he catches me at the exact time when I just want to see one normal person. Or, close to normal at least.

"Sure. Same place?"

"Yes! Three o'clock?"

"That'll be perfect." It's one p.m. now, and I'll have some time to shower, put on some makeup and get myself together.

. . .

EVAN IS PACING THE STREET OUTSIDE THE COFFEE SHOP. I honk and wave as I look for a spot to park my car. He spins around and stares, then his face lights up and he waves back, eagerly, almost childishly.

As I park along the street, backing in between two cars, he comes darting, crossing the street without even looking, and pulls open my door right as I kill the engine. Pocketing his phone he lifts his hand in an awkward salute.

"Cecilia with?"

"Yeah."

"Want me to help unbuckle her?"

I laugh. It's liberating after half a day of misery. "Sure."

I leave the stroller in the trunk. The cafe is right across the street. Evan carries Cecilia who sticks her hands in his thick blond beard and pulls at the hair.

The sound of an engine revving and tires coming to a screeching halt on the asphalt right next to us makes my heart jump to my throat. I grab Evan's elbow to pull him out of the way. The back doors of the black van slam open and three black clad men with the lower halves of their faces covered jump out. One grabs hold of me, Evan hands Cecilia to one of the others. I'm thrown to the ground and everyone jumps into the van. Evan gives me one last glance.

"I'm sorry. I had to."

I scream as the doors slam shut and the van shoots up along the street, disappearing around the corner in the next intersection.

"*Cece!*"

My mind is empty, but my heart hollers in agony and I don't know if the sounds in my head also come out of my mouth. I'm on all fours on the asphalt, feeling as if my chest has just been torn open.

"Miss!"

A man comes rushing. Behind him stands a young couple, their faces white, their eyes wide. He reaches for me, trying to pull me to my feet.

"I've called the cops! I tried to look for the plate, but I couldn't see any, it all happened so fast. I think I can describe the man you were with. Come, please."

"My daughter," I gasp as the tears come. "They took my daughter!"

There's a void in me that keeps growing. It's beyond anything I've ever felt before. My soul has been ripped out, a part of me is gone, torn out of my body. Where is she? Who were they? Where are they going? Why? Is she afraid? Evan?

Evan!

I fumble with my phone, still sitting on the street, the man next to me talks, but I have no idea what he's saying. I flip through last calls and hit the number Evan called from.

It's been disconnected.

No!

Cars honk.

"Miss!"

Someone's pulling my arm.

I get to my feet, numb, staring at my phone.

Cecilia!

Then I know.

I don't have Christian's number, but I actually have a number for Salvatore, from way back when I looked up his address, all those years ago. Something has made me keep it. I hope it's still active.

The man pulls my arm, his voice pleading, and I stumble after him to the sidewalk as I thumb through my short contact list. It just says S. I tap the number and pray.

"Yes?"

I don't recognize the voice. My voice shakes as I speak, and I swallow against the panic that threatens to engulf me.

"I need to speak with Salvatore," I gasp breathlessly.

"Mr. Salvatore is in a meeting. Who is this?"

"Kerry. Kerry Jackson. Please! It's about Cecilia! It's urgent! She's in danger. Please get him. Or Christian. *Please!*"

Silence. I'm just about to speak again.

"One moment, Miss."

"Miss, the cops are on their way. Come inside." The man leads me inside the cafe and pushes me down on a chair. I clutch the phone and listen to the silence. The man disappears behind the counter and then comes back with a glass of water.

"Miss Jackson. This is a surprise. Again." Salvatore's smooth voice makes me flinch

"I need you," I whisper, my throat thick.

"What's happened?" He's suddenly not so smooth. His voice changing, getting sharper.

"Cecilia—" My voice breaks. "She's been kidnapped. Please come."

"Where are you?"

"They took her," I whimper.

"Where are you, Kerry?"

I have no idea where I am. I look up at the man who has helped me, who keeps pacing, hovering anxiously as he repeatedly glances out the window.

"What's the address?"

I repeat to Salvatore what he says.

"Someone will be with you shortly. Did you call the cops?"

I'm suddenly afraid that was a wrong move, but there's no way hiding that, and even as I think it, I hear blaring sirens in the distance. "Yes."

"Good. Cooperate with them. Stay where you are."

"Okay," I whisper to no one. The call has already been disconnected.

I clutch my midsection, my mind spinning. The imprint of the man who grabbed me lingers, making my skin shrink in disgust. I feel Cecilia in my arms, warm, trusting, happy. Or rather, I feel the empty space where she should be. It's unbearable. Tears keep streaming down my face. A tissue has been pushed into my hands, but I'm too numb to care. I don't know how to draw the next breath.

I want Christian here. I need him!

I almost jump through the roof when my phone rings. I don't recognize the number and for a confused moment I think it's the kidnappers. It's Christian.

"Kerry. Just stay put. We're on our way. Don't worry about the cops. Tell them everything."

A police cruiser comes to a halt right outside, double parking outside the line of cars along the street, blue and red lights flashing. Two burly cops enter the little space.

"They're here," I whisper.

"Good. See you soon. Hang in there."

I disconnect as the cops approach me. They ask. I answer. Something. I don't know what.

The man from the cafe waves his hands, points and talks. I hear everything as if from a distance.

The door flies open, and three men enter, all dressed in suits and elegant overcoats, dark, imposing. Salvatore's gaze searches the room and lands on me. Behind him is Christian and a man I remember seeing in the mansion.

Salvatore walks up to the cops and shakes their hands. Christian darts to my side.

"Kerry!" He's breathless, his voice thick, almost unrecognizable. "What happened."

I lean toward him, needing the comfort but unable to take the initiative. Christian sinks to his knees and takes me in his arms, hugging me tight. "Tell me everything. Absolutely everything. Don't leave one single detail out."

Melting into his embrace, I tell him about meeting Evan, how it all happened within mere seconds.

"It was planned," I whisper. "Evan planned this. He knew you were the father. Or... that someone in your family was. He had a debt. Richter. Charlie Richter."

I look up at him, searching his face for something, for comfort, for reassurance that he'll make this undone.

His features are frozen, and I realize he's just as afraid as I am.

"Christian, there's been a demand." Salvatore has come up behind Christian who stands and turns. Salvatore holds a phone in a gloved hand. His eyes move to me and in his gaze there's compassion, protectiveness, concern, and murder.

"Ransom?" asks Christian, still holding my hand clutched in his.

"Yes. Nothing we can't handle."

"Do you know a Charlie Richter?" asks Christian.

Salvatore frowns. "I do. Not in person, but I know about him. Owns a bunch of casinos in Vegas."

"Seems he's behind this."

Salvatore doesn't move a muscle, then he tilts his head toward me. "Take Kerry with you to my place, take care of your woman. We'll solve this."

Christian pulls me to my feet as Salvatore walks over to the cops, talks and shakes their hands again.

"Come, Kerry. We'll get Cecilia back."

My mind spins. I'm wobbling next to him, his arm around my waist, tight, my feet moving even though I can't feel them.

"Ransom?" I ask as the word penetrates through my fog.

"We'll fix this, love. I promise you that." He opens the back door to the large black SUV and ushers me inside.

Salvatore and the other man hop into the front seats as Christian settles next to me, buckling me up, holding me to him. As we move way too fast through the streets of San Francisco, leaving the city center behind, moving toward the affluent suburbs on the hills, I lean into Christian, soaking up his warmth, his strength. No matter who he is, I need him so bad right now that I think I'd die without him.

TWENTY-ONE

Christian

Ivan drives fast, but he knows what he's doing. Salvatore is on the phone more than half the drive, then he turns and looks at Kerry and me.

"We'll get her back today. They called my lawyer and made a ransom demand."

"We have to pay them," gasps Kerry.

Both Luci and I look at her with pity. She doesn't know how we solve things in this family. When the sun sets there'll be no one left of Richter's men, and the man himself will be hanging in the meat locker in one of our restaurants, being skinned alive. I'll gladly do it myself.

I hold Kerry tight and, despite her trembling, I feel how she calms a little in my embrace. I know very well the last words that were said between us, I have agonized over them the whole day, clueless as to how to fix this. I can't undo what I've done, the ways I've hurt her, all I can do is keep trying to redeem myself.

"We'll get your daughter back, Kerry," says Salvatore. "Trust me. Trust your man," he nods at me. "Can you do that? You did good, calling me."

She exhales, her dark green eyes darting between me and Luci. "What if they've hurt her?" Her lower lip trembles and her voice is shaky.

"They have no reason to, Ker," I say. "She's too little, they won't have to worry about her being a witness against them, they've made a demand, and that is a good thing. She's alive, she's not hurt, and we'll get her back before you know it."

I don't know for sure that what I'm saying is true, but my insides are nothing but a black void of raw fear and I have to hold on to something or I'll fall into it and be of no use to anyone. My heart pounds so hard that my pulse roars in my ears. Cecilia's little, warm, trusting shape is etched into my arms, and it feels as if the ghost of her sits on my lap. I've never felt such a physical sensation of something that isn't there. I remember how I clutched for her when she was no longer in my arms, as I tumbled into the cold water in that river, but that was different, nothing like how it feels now.

Emptiness can be palpable.

Kerry weeps. I swallow against the lump in my throat.

"The police?" asks Kerry. "Are they looking?"

Salvatore glances over his shoulder. "Of course. They're doing their part. They report directly to me. If they learn something, I'll know it in a minute."

I look down at her, at her confused expression, then at how it dawns on her. Her mouth shapes into an O, and she doesn't answer. Kerry knows better than most that we have contacts in the San Francisco Police Department. Lots of contacts who get paid well to do what we tell them.

WHEN WE MAKE OUR WAY INTO SALVATORE'S MANSION Carmen, the young mother of Salvatore's son David, comes rushing, her face laced with concern. She grabs Kerry's free hand. I'm holding the other one, and Kerry hasn't tried to pull out of my grip, which secretly pleases me in the midst of it all.

"I heard!" Carmen looks up at me, her eyes flashing. The curvy little Colombian rarely comes into Salvatore's house. She lives with her husband Lucas in the house next door, David living mostly with them, so for her to be here, she's really engaged.

"Kerry," she says, catching Kerry's attention who now stares at Carmen, almost as if she's looking but not seeing her, "we don't know each other, but I think we spoke on the phone once, a long time ago. I'm David's mom."

Kerry's eyes dart between me and Carmen, then she nods. "I remember."

"Let me take care of her," Carmen says and turns to me as she narrows her eyes. "You go do what you do best, and..." she chews on her lip before she continues, her deep brown eyes darkening, "do it well. *No one* fucks with this family!"

The vengeful words take me by surprise, Carmen loathes what the rest of us do, I've felt her distaste more than my share, and she stays way out of the business. Her husband once worked for Salvatore, but now he teaches high school, and they're just two, seemingly normal, people who happen to live in somewhat abnormal circumstances. I shouldn't be that surprised, though. Carmen is a lioness when needed. She once beat Salvatore at his own game. There's a fire in her and right now it blazes red hot, scorching anyone who would dare to get in her way.

I give Kerry a squeeze. "Go with her. I have things to do. Don't worry."

Kerry scoffs, her face swollen, her eyes glossed and red-tinged with fresh tears hanging in her eyelashes. "Do what you need to do," she says, her voice broken. "Bring back Cecilia."

I know that she knows what she's asking. She's giving me permission to be the monster she hates, the demon she fears. She's asking me to be everything that I am, to use everything I've learned throughout life, to annihilate the ones who threaten our little dysfunctional family of three.

And I will.

"Go with Carmen, hon." I lean in and give her a quick kiss on the head, inhaling her scent, her vanilla and strawberry scented soap, mixed with the sweet essence that is Kerry herself. Oozing off her is also a dank smell of sweat, of fear, of agony.

Carmen lays her arm around Kerry's shoulders. Kerry holds my eyes one moment longer, then she leans in and listens to whatever it is Carmen says. That gaze stabs right through my chest. I follow them with my eyes until the front door falls closed behind them. Carmen will look after her. She is one of the most capable people I know, and that's really saying something in my family. Carmen is fiercely loyal to the ones she feels need her protection, and it's clear she just included Kerry in that.

It means I can focus.

It means I can push Kerry to the back of my mind, resting in the knowledge that she's as good as she can be in these circumstances.

I walk toward the dining room, where I last saw Salvatore head. He sits with Ivan, Johnny, and a couple of his muscle that I know the faces of, but not the names.

Ivan turns to me. "Cops called. They got a few possible locations."

I sit in front of him, next to one of the men I don't know.

"Adrian, Francesco." Salvatore gestures to the two men.

I shake their hands in turn, but don't introduce myself. Everyone knows who I am.

"How many?"

"Five. They're confident they haven't left town, though."

"Any way we can narrow that down?" asks Salvatore. "Do we know anyone in their organization?"

"Not that I know of," I say, "but they have someone in ours."

Everybody turns to me. I explain what Kerry told me. There's no fucking way her little shit of an ex-husband could have known one in our family fathered Cecilia unless someone from our ranks told him. That's what this is. He's paying off his debts to Richter. He's gonna die in pain. I'll make fucking sure of it. There are ways to make a man suffer for a very long time before he dies, and once Cece is back in her mom's arms, I'll let him pay for the pain he's caused Kerry and Cecilia. And me.

Salvatore's face is a mask of fury, seemingly calm, but with death lurking in his eyes. He glances at the two men next to me: Adrian and Francesco. They both go pale.

"Boss, we swear!" says Adrian, and the other man nods eagerly holding up his hands, as if in defense.

Salvatore whips up his gun, pointing it at them. "I can only trust my closest men. Go with Ivan and Johnny. Don't make a fuss."

"Luci?" Ivan shapes his hand into a gun, hidden from sight from the others. He asks if they're killing them.

Salvatore shakes his head. "Just lock'em up."

The four men leave the room, two of them with dread etched on their faces. I regard Salvatore, waiting for him to speak. He waits until the door closes, then he turns to me.

"Ivan and Johnny?" I ask.

"I trust them as my own family. But it's someone close. I need you to call Matteo. Have him tap into everyone's account and look at every transaction made for as long back as needed, see where my men are getting their money, and if there are purchases that don't match their income. Cars. Gambling. Hookers. Houses."

"Everyone?" I raise my eyebrows. We're talking about hundreds of people.

"No. I'll give you a list of names. Give me a moment, call Matteo and keep him on the line. I'll be right back."

He disappears, his steps echoing in the vast rooms. I haul up my phone and tap the number to my second youngest brother. As I wait for him to pick up, my chest clenches, thinking about trusting little Cecilia in the clutches of men who don't care about her well-being, to whom she's just meat to be used for their own gain.

I'll kill every-fucking-one of them. That's a promise.

Kerry

"Sit, honey, I'll get you something to drink."

Carmen pushes me down on a couch and disappears with rapid steps, her high-heeled shoes clicking on the hardwood floors. A few moments later she's back with a glass with a strong-smelling, clear content, putting it in my hand. I try to give it back to her.

"I can't drink alcohol," I say numbly, clutching my chest. It feels as if I'll crack open from the pain. I want to stay alert; I can't dull my senses.

"It's Tequila," she says, as if that makes any difference. "You need it. Do as I say!" Her voice is firm, as if she's correcting a disobedient child.

I look at the glass, then I drink it in three swallows, coughing as my throat burns and heat rushes to my cheeks. "That was strong," I gasp, for one moment welcoming the feeling of something else than fear.

"Of course." Carmen wraps a throw blanket around me and sits next to me. "Tell me what happened."

"How did you know?" My voice is hoarse, broken. I barely recognize it.

"Luciano called me and told me to take care of you."

I stare at her, stunned. I never thought he'd care about me.

"He needed your man."

Christian? "He's not my man," I say quickly.

She cocks her head and regards me. "It sure looks like that, the way you two look at each other."

"He's Cecilia's dad." I can't control my chin as it begins to tremble again, and new tears fall. "I'm so afraid, Carmen!"

The little woman scoops me into her arms and hugs me tight. "Kerry," she says. "Luciano and Christian, and their men, they'll get your daughter back. They'll stop at nothing. This is the wrong family to ever set your foot in, but right now you couldn't be in better hands."

"None of this would have happened if it hadn't been for them," I say bitterly.

"You wouldn't have had Cecilia either," she says quickly. "Or Christian." Her voice is a little coy and I glance up at her. Carmen reaches out and wipes off my cheeks with her thumbs, then she throws me a quick smile. "You'll have her back."

"You can't *know* this," I cry and hug my chest, rocking back and forth.

Carmen hushes me and then just holds me. For a long time she lets me cry in her arms. There is nothing else to say, nothing for us to do. I want to run out on the streets, look in every house, scream at them to show themselves, but they could be anywhere. It's impossible.

"What can they do?" I whisper.

"Luciano?"

I nod.

Carmen is quiet, emotion flickers through her gaze. "There's nothing he can't do," she finally says. "He knows everyone. If you're on his bad side, you're not safe anywhere."

A shudder runs through me. Old wounds. Oh, I know this.

"Do you know how I met Christian?" I ask.

The beautiful little woman next to me shakes her head. "I stay out of that nest as much as I can."

"That's clever."

"I have my reasons."

"But... you're David's mom... right?"

Carmen nods. "Yes."

"So..." I chew on my lip, "you and Salvatore—"

"It's a story for another time. How did you meet your man?"

"He's not my man!"

Carmen gives a half-shrug, as if I can say anything, she has her mind made up anyway.

"I was his hit."

Tilting her head, Carmen frowns as she studies me, then she shakes her head. "I swear, these men... What happened? If you don't mind?"

For the first time ever I have someone I can talk to absolutely freely about this. I can tell her everything. She knows them. She's also trying to make time pass, to take my mind off the current absolute disaster, and I'm eternally grateful as I start from the beginning. When I stutter and blush as I try to describe Christian's dark passion, how he scared and enticed me, she grabs my forearm.

"Kerry, love. I was a prostitute. I worked on the streets for two years, then for some months in one of Salvatore's brothels. There is nothing I haven't heard, seen, or experienced. There's nothing to be shy about."

I'm stunned. I had no idea.

Carmen smiles. "It's okay. No need to beat around the bush. I have a feeling you and I are going to see a lot more of each other, and we might as well come clean with all the dirty details." She flips a few strands of long, curly black hair over her shoulder. "And these men don't play nice. Not out of bed, and most certainly not in bed. Did Christian hurt you, Kerry? Is that why you have this wall up between you and him?"

I clutch my midsection as renewed pain shoots through it. The memories of our first night together brings me right back to the present, to Cecilia, to the raw, horrifying emptiness inside. "Do you have more of that Tequila?" I whimper.

"Sure." She shoots up and disappears out of the room, returning a moment later with the whole bottle, pouring a little more at the bottom of my glass. "I'm not letting you get drunk. You need your senses. You're grieving, and you need to live through that."

I down the glass in one swallow. "I don't want to," I whimper. "I don't want to feel this pain."

Carmen lays an arm around my shoulders. "I know," she says. "I know. I'll take care of you until you have your beautiful little daughter in your arms again. Now tell me about you and Christian."

So I do. Resting in the arms of Carmen Moreno-Payne, despite the pain wracking my soul, I tell the whole messed up story about Christian Russo and Kerry Jackson.

TWENTY-TWO

Christian

Luci is pacing back and forth before his large floor to ceiling windows in the ballroom next to the dining room where I'm sitting, waiting for a phone call. I follow him with my eyes every time he passes the doorway. His whole body exudes held-back fury. He clutches his phone. So do I. We're both holding our breaths, frustrated in this impotent rage. We can't assemble our men until after Matteo gets back to us, because we need to know who *not* to include. When he does, we have to locate the snake in our ranks and make him talk.

An hour has passed since Kerry called, wailing, her cries loud enough to be heard across the room to where I sat on the couch with a cup of coffee, reading the paper, trying to sort my feelings from the night, and the disaster that was the morning.

Luci nearly jumps when his phone rings and with a curse, he puts it to his ear. My phone rings a moment later and I tap to connect the call as I move into the kitchen to get some privacy.

"Yes?"

"Bro," says Matteo. "I've got three men with enough interesting financial activity on their accounts. One Laurence. Got huge gambling debts. Fred, apparently a love for expensive cars, also bank loans up over his ears, and Rusty, large sums being put on his account, but he doesn't buy shit. I think—"

"Rusty's our man," I say. The other two are just plain stupid, but

Rusty, whoever the fuck that is, is laying low, biding his time, trying to be clever about it.

"I agree," says Matteo.

"Thanks, bro." I disconnect and stride through the rooms, finding Salvatore by the bar, a tumbler with whisky in his hand.

Relaying the info to him, his gaze darkens. "Rusty," he growls. "I fucking raised him." He hauls up his phone. "Ivan, release the guys, and the four of you locate Rusty Alfonsi and bring him to the meat locker at The Milane. We're going to have a word with him. You don't have to be nice about it." He disconnects. "Come," he growls. "It's time. Are you up for it?"

I don't answer, just walk up next to him as we stride through the mansion. I might not be in the best shape, but I know my uncle won't question my participation in this op. It's eerily quiet. This house is always full of people, there's always something going on. Now it's dead. It feels ominous, worrying. Nothing is normal anymore. My soul is split, reaching in two different directions, one toward Kerry, the other toward our daughter.

Luci drives, his jaw clenched. Neither of us says a word. When his phone rings, he puts it on loudspeaker.

"Talk," he growls.

"Got him. What do you want us to do with him?" Ivan sounds determined, dangerous. He's a man of few expressions. Hearing emotion in his voice is almost a shock. This whole household is in uproar.

"Don't do anything, just keep him in place until we get there."

"Yes, Boss."

Ten minutes later we pull up outside the closed restaurant. Francesco stands right inside the heavy glass door and opens it for us. I nod a greeting to him as he closes and locks the door behind us.

In the cold meat locker stand four men. Ivan, Johnny, Adrian, all with semi-automatics pointed at a very pale Rusty Alfonsi, a baby-faced, short guy, who's about to regret the day he crossed Salvatore.

Luci walks with measured steps toward the group, then he veers to the side, picks up a crowbar that leans against the wall, walks calmly up to Rusty and then swings it with full force against his knee. The screams are deafening as the man's leg bends in the wrong direction and he falls to the floor. Luci taps the crowbar against the tiled floor, the clunking sound barely audible over the hollers from Rusty.

"Rusty Alfonsi. What do I do with you?"

"Boss!" screams the man. "Boss, why?"

Luci raises the crowbar as if to beat him again, but then lowers it and nods to Ivan. "Tie him and hang him. I want him upside down."

Johnny takes a step to the writhing man and shoves a rag in his mouth, muffling the whimpers somewhat, as Ivan grabs a pile of ropes off the floor. When they begin to tie them around Rusty's ankles, uncaring that the broken leg twists and bends, the noises intensify.

Luci taps his elbow to mine. "Come."

I glance at the scene one last time, then I trail behind, wondering what he's up to. "How long have you had Rusty?"

Luci walks up to the espresso machine, huge, polished metal, imported from Italy. He starts it up and expertly begins to prepare two cups. "He's been with me five years. He's twenty-two, impressionable, hungry. He's proven himself loyal over and over. Worked with us through the near-war with the Irish the other year."

I nod. I was there too, even though I didn't meet this guy. "Not that loyal."

Salvatore hands me a cup and opens the fridge, picking out a bottle of soda water. "No," he says through clenched teeth and slams down the bottle on the counter. "Not that loyal."

"Boss?" Johnny's voice from behind makes us both turn. "He's ready for you."

As we walk back through the kitchen I don't even bother to ask to get the answers out of this guy. Both Luci and I have good reasons for wanting Rusty to speak, but my uncle is so obviously determined that I'll just let it play out. Watching him in action, doing his business, is almost like enjoying an art form.

Rusty hangs upside down. His arms tied behind his back, the rope around his ankles secured on a meat hook. Salvatore rips the rag out of his mouth and a stream of pleading pours out of the man. Tears and snot have dampened his hair as it streams along his forehead.

"Rusty, my boy." Salvatore sounds unreasonably calm. "My little relative has gone missing, and it has come to my attention that a Charlie Richter is behind this."

Rusty's eyes widen for a second, then he shakes his head. "I don't know— what you're talking about," he grunts out.

Salvatore sighs, unscrews the soda bottle he brought with him, takes a swig, then he grabs the back of Rusty's head, gripping his hair and pours soda in his nose. Rusty gargles and his body contorts as he gulps, coughs, cries.

"I suggest you don't inhale it," says Salvatore, his voice stone cold.

I find a toothpick in a back pocket, stick it between my teeth and lean against the wall, crossing my arms over my chest.

"*Boss!*" screams Rusty between gasps. "*Please!*"

"Where are they keeping my little niece, Rusty?"

"*I don't know anything!*"

Salvatore pours more soda up the young man's nostrils. It may seem like mild torture, but the cold fizzing liquid tickles the surface of the brain through the thinnest layer of bone, and this is incredibly painful and panic-inducing.

Rusty resists a few more minutes then he begins to babble. "I can give you names!" he squeals.

"*Where is my niece!*" roars Salvatore, so viciously even I jump.

"*Address,*" he wails, "I have. Let me down! Please!" His voice breaks on the last word.

"Give. Me. Everything. Rusty, and I'll consider your future while I take care of some things."

"Yes!"

Johnny starts tapping down the info on his phone as Salvatore looks over his shoulder, making sure it matches what Rusty says. The young man talks and talks. I glance at the clock. We've been here thirty minutes. Cecilia has been gone two and a half hours. I'm filled with dread, my heart dark, and I clench my fists. I want to do something, hurt someone. Now!

"All right," says Salvatore. "You, you, and you, with us. Francesco, you stay behind."

"What about this ass?" asks Francesco.

Salvatore looks the man over, not hiding his disgust. "Let him hang. Help yourself to whatever the house offers, espresso, Grappa, there are nice meals in the fridge, leftovers from last night."

As we leave the little room, Rusty starts screaming again, pleading, crying. Francesco picks up the rag and shoves it back into Rusty's mouth before he follows us out into the restaurant, letting the heavy metal door to the cold storage slam closed.

WE MOVE FAST THROUGH THE CITY, SPLIT UP IN TWO LARGE black SUVs.

"Christiano," says Salvatore, making me twitch out of the grueling darkness that threatens to swallow me. "Call in Simon and his guys, we need five of them. Tell them to meet us one block south of this address." He sticks a note in my hand.

"This is where they're keeping her?" I thumb up Simon's number in my contact list and put the phone to my ear.

"Supposedly," says my uncle, his voice grave. "It matches one of the addresses the cops gave us. Rusty's in for a world of pain if he's lied, and he knows it."

Simon answers promptly and I relay the information, telling him to drop everything he's doing. Simon and his men are bouncers at our illegal gambling clubs. Many of them veterans, and former mercenaries. They know exactly what they're doing. With their work hours they sleep during the day and work at night. It's late afternoon and they should be free to mobilize within minutes.

"They'll be there," I tell Salvatore as I disconnect. He doesn't answer, just nods, his expression grim. I know he has two concerns. Cecilia's well-being, and the fact that he was betrayed. The latter led to the first, so I'm fully and completely with him.

We pull up in an alley a block from the office building where Cecilia is being held. The other car comes to a halt behind us a moment later. Ivan jumps out and opens the back door, unzipping two large bags.

"Help yourselves," he says and gestures to the assortment of weapons. We're ready for war. We always are. It's part of our lives, ingrained in our genes.

We gear up. Adrian and Ivan leave to scope out the premises. Thirty agonizing minutes later the two men return at the same time as two more SUVs arrive, approaching fast and coming to an abrupt halt right behind our vehicles. Five black-clad giants pour out, already fully equipped. Simon, whom I've worked with on a number of occasions nods at me as he walks up to Salvatore.

"Three exits, a six-floor building, signs of activity on the first and the fourth floor, a guard visible by one of the side doors." Ivan hands out earbuds and radio equipment as he relays what they've seen.

I assemble my gear as I listen to Salvatore explaining the situation to Simon and his men, emphasizing that there's a child in there who can in no circumstances be harmed. My stomach churns and the feeling of urgency intensifies.

"Boss." Johnny comes around one of the vehicles, a phone in his hand. "You wanna hear this."

Salvatore grabs the phone and puts it to his ear, his features darkening as he listens. He hands the phone back with a slight tremble to his hand. "There's been a second demand. The price has gone up and in an hour a body part will be delivered if we don't pay up according to instructions."

Nausea shoots through me. "Let's move. Save fucking no one," I growl.

We move through the shadows, splitting up in three groups, one for each entrance. Outside ours stands a man. None of us cares who he is, if he's just an innocent bystander, or if he's with Richter. With the silencer there's a dulled popping sound, and with a clean headshot he goes down. One of Simon's men darts forward, crouching below a window and checks his vitals before he nods for us to come. Salvatore gestures for Adrian to stay behind and take out anyone who exits.

My heart rate increases as we move inside, through a semi-dark corridor with a dirty concrete floor. A shadow next to me makes me spin around and bury my knife in the throat of another man. He falls with nothing but a quiet gurgle and a slight rattle of his weapon as it hits the hard surface.

The radio comes to life with a slight crackle. *"Main entrance clear,"* says a low voice in my ear.

"Two down left rear," I whisper back.

"Rusty said he thought seven men," mouths Salvatore. I nod, as does Ivan.

As we move forward, we find no one else on the lower floor. Reuniting with the two other groups we advance up the only stairwell while one man stays behind guarding the elevator in the entrance. We've also put one on the lookout on the rear right exit.

The remaining seven of us sneak through the building, dividing and reuniting, floor by floor, room by room. On the fourth floor there are voices from behind a closed door. Someone sounds agitated, someone else seems to be calming the first one down. I hope to fuck one of these people are Richter, but I know the chances are slim. He's probably not even in town.

"Check the rest of the building," whispers Simon. "The girl might be held somewhere else. If we find her first, it would make things easier." He gestures to three of his guys as well as Johnny and Ivan to move on.

I grab Ivan's arm. "You stay. I go."

Ivan glances at Salvatore who nods and waves for us to keep moving.

My heart slams in my chest as the voices of the kidnappers fade. Cecilia is here somewhere. I feel it with my whole being. It's been four hours since Kerry's frantic call. Four hours since our world was torn apart yet again. It's my choices that got us here. My way of life is what keeps circling us back to pain and devastation.

Fifth floor is empty. Sixth floor is the last one and we split up in two different directions. Around the corner stands a man, the smell of cigarette smoke heavy in the narrow space. I shoot, but so does he as he throws himself to the side, crying out as he's hit in the thigh. I shoot again, and so does Johnny, this time hitting home in the middle of his chest. Our weapons are silenced. His wasn't. Two floors down all hell breaks loose, screams, shots, loud slams, more shots. I quickly feel along my body to check I wasn't hit. I'm so stoked on adrenaline I doubt I'd feel a bullet. I glance at Johnny who does a thumbs up, then I stare at the door that was guarded. I don't do prayers, I don't do religion, but for the second time in my life I turn to the God of my childhood, asking not for me, but for an innocent little girl, soon to be two years old.

Please God, let her be in there, please God, let her be unharmed.

Johnny tries the handle and the door opens with a squeak. We can't know for sure no one else is in there and throw it open as we rush to either side of the door opening, our weapons ready.

Not a sound is heard from within the room and I take the chance, taking a quick peek around the doorframe.

On a naked striped mattress in the far corner, under a dirty window, lies a sleeping little dark-haired girl, clutching a stuffed animal. I rush forward and crouch next to her. Her cheeks are covered in dried tears but she's intact and breathing calmly. I lay a hand on her back, shaking with relief.

"Fucking hell," whispers Johnny, his voice awed.

I glance up at him. "Go make sure it's safe to bring her down."

He nods and disappears.

I inhale. Exhale. Listen to the soft whispers of my little girl breathing. My eyes water as tension slowly leaves me. I hadn't acknowledged how afraid I really was, but now it overwhelms me. I never knew how deep love for another human being can run, but I love this little lady, and I love her mother. I'll do everything in my power to make sure they're happy and safe.

I jerk when the radio cracks to life in my ear.

"It's all right to come down," says Salvatore. *"There's no one left."*

"Okay. Be right with you." I shake Cecilia slightly, trying to wake her, but she keeps sleeping.

"Is the little one all right?" asks Salvatore.

Horror rises in me as I shake her again and then lift her limp little body. Clutching her close, I start down the corridor, down the stairs.

"On my way," I grit out, my throat tightening. *Fuck!* "I think they drugged her, Luci."

Salvatore doesn't have time to respond before I'm by his side. He pushes Cecilia's hair off her face and regards her, then he hauls up his phone. "I'm calling the doc. Let's move."

In the car, as Ivan drives us to the hospital where a crew of medical staff will be meeting us, Simon leans over Cecilia, checking her pulse, lifting her eyelids.

"She'll be fine. They've probably given her a benzo. She's got good vitals."

"How do you know?" I growl, fear having seized all my senses.

"I'm a trained medic, military. It's cool. You should call her mother."

I exhale raggedly and haul up my phone.

"Yes?" Kerry sounds out of breath, her voice barely recognizable.

"Cecilia is fine. I've got her."

The wordless wail on the other hand makes me jerk the phone away from my ear and everyone in the car turns to look at me.

"Ker?"

"Yes," she whimpers, *"is she with you?"*

"She is. She's safe. We're passing the hospital for a check-up, but we'll be home soon."

"Which hospital? I'm coming."

No, she's not. I'm not letting her see Cecilia in this state.

"Stay with Carmen. We'll be home before you know it."

I disconnect.

A moan makes me look down. Cecilia's long dark eyelashes flutter and then she opens her eyes. She's drowsy, but she's awake! I give Simon a grateful look, appreciating his earlier words.

"Kis?" she whispers and frowns.

I hug her, careful not to squeeze the little body too hard. "Daddy's here, honey," I mumble as I bury my face in her dark locks.

Salvatore spins around from his seat in the front. "She's awake?"

I nod and can't help the probably goofy smile that spreads over my face as Cecilia reaches for the scraggy stubble on my chin. My phone keeps buzzing, and the voice messages and texts keep coming in. All from a frantic Kerry. I text her back that she needs to calm down, because it's all good, then I turn off the phone. Maybe a bit harsh, but I've told Kerry what she needs to know and she has Carmen by her side. Right now I want to focus on our daughter.

The visit to the hospital is quick. Cecilia's vitals are good, just as Simon said. I'm gonna talk to Salvatore about getting that man a promotion, because he fucking saved my sanity back there.

As we drive up to Carmen and Lucas' house, I tap Salvatore on the shoulder.

"We're not done."

He turns and nods, a grim expression on his face. "I'm gonna wipe out Richter's whole organization. Down to every last man."

"My guess is Richter isn't in town."

"We'll have to make do with two traitors today. Rusty and that other piece of shit, Evan."

"I'll rip Kerry's ex-husband apart with my own fucking hands," I growl.

"I'll let you have him."

The car comes to a stop. The front door to the house slams open and Kerry comes rushing out, barefoot, her face white. I climb out to meet her, Cecilia safe in my arms. I want to hug her forever and never let go, but we have things to do, and she and her mother need each other.

There's always a war, always a new disaster, blood, damage, pain.

Such is my life.

TWENTY-THREE

Kerry

Christian, tall, dark and with a frightening look of held-back rage and determination on his face, carrying a little girl dressed in a yellow dress, white socks, and a white cardigan. In the early evening, with the sun setting in the background, it's a surreal vision. Cecilia's brown locks bounce as she looks around her and then fixates her eyes on me.

"Mama!" she raises her chubby little arms and in the next moment I clutch her to my chest. It'll take a long time for the wounds from today to mend, the hole it ripped in me too deep, but right now everything is perfect. I pat her down, lift her cardigan, frantic to see that she's okay.

"She's fine, Kerry." Christian's voice is calm, and it makes my racing heart slow a little.

I look up at him. He's standing so close I can smell him, almost feel his body heat. "Thank you," I whisper.

He moves in and lays his strong arms around us, a promise of protection, of never letting go. "Always," he chokes out.

"Christiano." Salvatore's voice makes us both jerk. "We've got work to do."

"Be right with you," says Christian, then he turns back to me, dropping his arms. "Kerry. Evan, is it Evan Jackson?"

My lips are numb as I answer, and it feels as if all blood drains from my face. "Evan Thomas Linden." At the look of surprise on his face, I add, "I changed back to my maiden name."

Christian nods, his face grim.

"Christian!" I gasp, "Don't hurt him!"

"What?"

"Let me take her, Kerry." Carmen's voice to my right makes me spin around. She reaches for Cecilia.

I stare at her, then back at Christian. "No." I don't know who I'm answering.

"Kerry!"

Both speak at the same time, and it's just too much, it feels as if my brain is going to explode. I let Carmen take Cecilia and rush toward Christian, grabbing his shirt.

"Don't kill him!"

"You don't get to make that decision," he growls, his nostrils flaring as he looks down on me, his eyes are hard and cold.

I let him go as if I had burned myself, tightening my hands into fists. "Please! He was..." My voice breaks. "He doesn't deserve—"

"He deserves pain and fucking death! Look at what he did! *He* did that, Kerry! *He* put you through that!"

"You said you'd changed," I whisper, unable to hold back the tears, "but you're just the same. Always."

My legs are heavy as lead as I make my way back to the front porch of Carmen's beautiful house. Behind her stands her husband Lucas with three little kids clutching his legs, staring wide-eyed at the scene on their front yard.

"*Kerry!*" Christian's voice is commanding and pleading at the same time.

I don't turn. Carmen hands me Cecilia again. Lucas and the little ones make way as I walk inside.

"Mama," says Cecilia and I bury my nose in her nape. "Everything's all right now, baby. The bad men are gone."

The door falls closed behind us, and for a moment everything is silent, then one of Carmen and Lucas' kids comes running. "I'm Benjamin," says the little three-year-old.

Cecilia's head snaps around, her mouth falling open as she takes in all the people. She reaches for Benjamin who takes her hand.

"Wanna see my Legos?" he asks.

"Mama," says Cecilia, "I have Lego."

I smile through the tears. "Yes, you do. Do you want to see what the boy has?"

Cecilia nods and squirms to get down. She looks tired, but she trots after Benjamin, and Carmen and I follow. I am not letting her out of my sight again.

"It'll be all right," says Carmen and lays a hand on my arm as we settle on the couch next to the playing children. "Children have an incredible ability to compartmentalize, and rationalize. She'll heal, probably faster than you. You should let her take the lead."

I wipe tears off my cheeks. "No, it won't," I say dully. "Nothing will ever be all right. There's always going to be something new. A new disaster. I can't live like this. What if this happens again? What if someone else wants to hurt her?"

"Kerry." Carmen's voice is sharp. "Don't bury yourself in 'what ifs'. Live your life, savor what's given to you and don't mourn what you don't have. You have something beautiful," she nods toward Cecilia, "there, and you have a man who will quite literally kill to keep you safe."

I flinch.

"That's all he is," I whisper. "A killer."

"No, that's not all he is, and you know it. Stop it now. Take your girl, and go rest. I'll show you to a room."

I glance down at Cecilia, who is leaning against my legs, her little body warm and her moves sluggish. "Come baby." I pull her up in my lap and then rise to follow Carmen through the house.

We're shown to a large room with a king-sized bed, neatly made.

"Go rest, Kerry. Don't think too much. It's not good for you. Sometimes you have to play the cards you're given." She begins to pull the door shut behind her.

"Carmen," I blurt out. "Thank you!"

She smiles beautifully, displaying an even row of white teeth, her dark eyes flashing.

Cecilia sleeps. I pull the comforter over the both of us and hug her tight to me, my mind spinning with feelings and images. I'm too tired for words to form.

I fall asleep with one vision burned into my retinae. A wild-looking Christian, carrying our child, coming toward me, beautiful, lethal. Mine.

Christian

We reunite with Ivan, Johnny, and Adrian in Salvatore's office.

"Linden," I say. "Evan Thomas."

Johnny nods and taps on the laptop that's standing with its back to me on the desk. Lots, and lots of shady business has taken place in here, lots of decisions that have destroyed people, and even empires, decisions that have made the Russo clan climb to the top.

My uncle is an evil genius, as is his sister Bianca, the woman who birthed me.

We have everything, and still *one* single weasel of a man came so close to destroying us today. My lips curl in fury as I think of Kerry's fucking ex-husband.

"Christiano, are you all right?" Salvatore lays a hand on my shoulder in a rare display of something akin to affection. The only time Salvatore seems to touch someone is when he fucks them or when he beats them.

I pull myself out of my reverie. "Yeah," I grit out. "Let's go do this."

Salvatore pats my back. "Atta boy. We'll pass The Milane, you and I, while our boys here track down Linden."

FRANCESCO SITS WITH HIS FEET ON A TABLE WITH A BEER IN front of him. Opposite him sits a nervous girl who twines her hands in her lap.

"Staff started arriving. Not sure what to do with her." He jerks his head in her direction as he jumps to his feet with surprising ease despite his size. "Heard you got the little one back all right!"

Salvatore walks up to the girl who stares at him with wide eyes. "Sugar, why don't you take a fifteen-minute walk around the block? Hm?"

She darts to her feet. "Okay, Mr. Salvatore. Of course."

We watch her back as she hurries out of the venue. Francesco grins when he turns back to us. "Cute girl."

"Mind out of the gutter, boy." Salvatore slaps him on his back. "Is he tender yet, our dear Rusty?"

We walk through the dimly lit restaurant. In a couple of hours this place will be bustling with people. Right now it's silent, almost ghostly with its empty chairs and tables.

"His face had an interesting color last time I checked."

Pulling open the door to the small room, we all stop and cock our heads, taking in the sight of Rusty's swollen blue face.

"Rust—" begins Salvatore, then he shrugs and pulls out his gun from under his suit jacket. "Never mind."

Rusty's body jerks when Salvatore plants five bullets in his chest. The young man never regains consciousness.

"Cut him down and clean this shit up. I'll come around to the back with the car."

Salvatore disappears as Francesco and I look at each other and then at the blood that's pooling on the floor, then we spring into action and do what we've done so many times before in our lives.

I pant way too heavily when we throw Rusty's limp, plastic-wrapped body in the trunk, and I'm drenched in sweat. Fuck! If I can't do this, I don't know what to do with myself. I don't know anything else for fuck's sake.

Salvatore side-eyes me as I hop in next to him in the front, but he doesn't say anything. He doesn't need to. I know what he's thinking. He's said it before. This isn't the life for me anymore.

"Mr. Linden is home alone. Johnny and Adrian are making sure he isn't leaving."

"Good," I growl. "Let's get to it."

"Are you up for it, Christiano?"

I give my uncle a dark glare. Even if it's the last thing I do, I'll make sure to annihilate the one who threatened my woman. Even if it means she doesn't want to see me again.

As the car speeds through the darkening streets, the thought gives me pause. Images of Kerry's pale, determined face flash by before my eyes.

Don't kill him.

Why the fuck not? I don't understand. I'm not jealous. I know she's not romantically interested in the little shit. Someone wrongs you, you end him. That's what you do. That's how I grew up. Revenge. Blood. Hate.

We come to an abrupt stop outside an apartment complex in one of the shadier parts of the city. Johnny and Adrian join us and the five of us travel in silence the thirteen floors up to the home of Evan Thomas Linden.

Cecilia's innocent face haunts me. Kerry's agony twists my guts. I kick the door open with ease and raise my gun.

"Evan!" I roar.

Two remain by the door as the rest of us advance through the dank two-bedroom apartment. The sound from a TV guides us toward the living room. It's a mess. Beer cans everywhere, cartons from fast food covering the table, clothes strewn across every surface.

It's more a sixth sense than an actual sound, or movement. I kick the couch, making it slide several feet to the side, and behind it crouches the fucker who hurt Kerry more than I ever did. Who hurt *my* offspring. My daughter.

I raise my gun. "Evan Linden."

He screams, high-pitched, and holds his hands over his head. "Don't shoot! Who— What is this? Who are you?"

I kick his chest. He falls on his back, gasping, clutching his side. "Dude!"

Putting a foot over his throat, I press until his eyes bulge. He flails, and tries to escape. I lean in and put the gun to his forehead, making him go completely still.

"You made the single biggest mistake of your life today, Evan, when you fucked Kerry over, when you let Richter's men take her little baby. You see, you were right. She *did* fuck a Russo. Me. Cecilia is my daughter, and a Russo. You don't hurt a Russo without consequences and I'm *not* the forgiving type."

His eyes widen. "Please," he hollers, saliva spraying from his mouth as tears begin to fall along his cheeks. "I had no choice. Please!"

"There's always a choice," I roar and press the gun harder into his flesh as his face contorts in pain.

My own words give me a stab of a flashback to what will soon be three years ago. *There's always a choice.* I didn't give Kerry a choice.

Kerry's words ring in my ears as I stare down at the pathetic existence under my boot. A dark haze washes over me. Pure hate, today's agony, Kerry from three years ago, Kerry fighting for her life in my hands, Kerry the mother of my child whom she had to birth alone in a foreign city, Kerry pleading for me to change. I glance over my shoulder, at my uncle who stands passive, watching the scene, then I remove the gun and slam my fist into Evan's face. Blood sprays as I hit him again and again. I crush his nose, split his lips. His thick blond beard is soon streaked with red. When he stops screaming and his head lolls to the side, I force myself to stand, my knuckles sore, painted with his blood.

"Call. The. Cops," I manage to grit out, still fighting the urge to beat him until he stops breathing.

"Christiano?" Salvatore sounds surprised.

"Don't!" I snarl. "Ivan. Just do it." I turn to the two men. "This is my call, and this is how it's gonna be. We'll make sure he never sets foot outside prison again. Pin the deaths of Richter's men on him, whatever."

Salvatore studies me a few more moments, then he nods at Ivan. "Do it."

As I wash off my hands in a dirty little bathroom, my uncle regards me, leaning against the doorframe, his arms crossed over his chest. "You must really love her."

His words find their way straight into the deepest recesses of my heart. I do. I really do love her.

TWENTY-FOUR

Kerry

I wake and have no idea where I am or what time it is. Cecilia is sleeping, snuggled up between my arm and my chest, and seeing her it all comes rushing back. From somewhere comes voices, hushed but upset. I free myself of Cecilia and pat the sideboard to find my phone.

1:03 a.m.

I stand and tiptoe to the door that's slightly ajar. A sliver of light comes through the opening and I push the door a little more open to hear better.

"You shouldn't be here, Christian." Carmen's voice is both pleading and upset.

"I can't stay away."

Christian's low growl, the despair in his voice, sends a shiver running down my back.

"You're drunk. Go home."

"I've done... things. I can't... She'll never forgive me."

"*Ay Dios mio*! *Hombres!* You're impossible! Sleep it off. Stop wallowing in what has been and look forward instead. Kerry is confused and hurt, and it will take her some time to come around. Give her that time. Now shoo, get out of here."

There's a rustle, a shuffle of feet.

"Christian, I can't move you. It's like trying to lift a *montaña*. Do you want me to call Ivan?"

"No, fuck." He groans.

More shuffling.

A door slams. Silence.

I lay awake for a long time, hugging Cecilia to me, reliving the moment over and over when they took her from me. I don't know if I care what they did to Evan anymore. I hold her little body and I can't help thinking that it really *was* him, and him alone, who did this to us. I hope he rots, wherever he is.

I DON'T SEE CHRISTIAN THE NEXT DAY. LUCAS DRIVES US home.

"Did you work for Salvatore, Lucas?"

The tall man, sporting a giant beard, and a thick mane of blond hair tied back in a ponytail gives me a quick glance. "That was a long time ago."

"What was it like? What's *he* like? Did you work with Christian?"

Lucas sighs. "Look, Kerry, I understand that you wanna know, but I have put that behind me, and I'm never opening that lid again." He's silent for a while, then he adds, "I did work with Christian. He was one of the worst."

It hits me hard, like a punch to my chest.

He was one of the worst.

I fight to breathe, fight to hold back the tears.

Lucas shoots me a glance again, and doesn't speak until we pull up outside my house. As he closes the car door after Cecilia and I have climbed out, he looks at me with such a serious expression that my gut clenches. "These are dangerous people, Kerry. Take care of yourself. Take a stance, try to stay away. For her." He nods at Cecilia, then he raises his hand, hops in the car and leaves us on the sidewalk, my heart shattered.

Stay away.

I don't have the luxury of a choice.

I know I should, but I don't know if I have the strength to even try.

I SPEND THE DAY AT MOM'S. I'LL NEVER TELL HER WHAT happened. There's no need to worry her. I have secrets that have piled up for years. This is just another one. I end up spending the night too, twisting and turning on her sofa bed, unable to sleep, wondering if Christian has come by my house and found it empty.

The next day I read in the paper about Evan Linden arrested on a no bail warrant for involvement in seven murders in what appears to be a war between criminals. I quickly push the newspaper into the garbage bin, hoping Mom will never learn of it. Christian *didn't* kill him! A shudder runs through me. Has he really changed?

Then I remember Chloe.

He can change, but some things can't be undone.

With my heart in my throat, I text him.

> Thank you.

I stare at the screen as it sends, is delivered, and read. I hold my breath as I watch the little dots indicating that an answer is being written. It takes forever. Typing. Then nothing. Typing. Finally:

> I'll stay away. It's for the best. Take care of yourself.

My stomach plummets as I stare at the message. *No.*

I'm just about to answer, I don't know what – something, when Lucas' words ring in my ears.

He was one of the worst.

My knuckles whiten as I clutch the phone. This is for the best. I recognize the gift he's giving me after all the pain and drama. He just wants us to live and be happy. And happy for me has to be without him.

Right?

I END UP STAYING WITH MOM TWO MORE DAYS. I CAN'T attend my classes at the university. I can't let Cece out of my sight. I just can't.

My house feels so empty. At night I keep listening for a knock, and Christian's absence follows me into my dreams. There's a hole where my heart should be, as if he's taken it.

After a week, I come to the realization that I need to work if we're gonna eat, I need to attend school if I'm ever going to get my exam, and one sleepless night I come up with the perfect solution. The next day, I call Carmen.

Carmen's response has me crying with relief. Of course she'll look after Cece.

The only place on earth that would feel safer would be with her locked up in Salvatore's mansion and in Christian's care. But that's not happening.

One afternoon when I come to pick up my daughter Carmen looks different, stiff, her jaw clenched. She tosses back her long curly hair and gestures for me to follow.

"There's someone here who wants to see you."

My heart leaps to my throat. Christian?

In the living room, with Cecilia by his feet and David next to him sits Salvatore. I take in the scene. It's surreal seeing this dark and dangerous man surrounded by children in the bright afternoon sun that shines in through impeccably cleaned windows. He belongs in the shadows, not here.

When he sees me, he stands and spreads his arms. "Kerry Jackson, my favorite person on earth."

I curl my lips as I cross my arms over my chest. "What do you want?"

He tsks. "Can't I just come by on a friendly visit?"

"No," say both Carmen and I at the same time.

Salvatore rolls his eyes and throws up his hands. "What have I done to deserve these women in my life? Anyway. Business, then. This little treasure," he strokes Cecilia's head, "will be having her second birthday on Friday, and you're invited to my house for a birthday party."

I stiffen. I was going to my Mom's. "That's... very kind, but no thanks." I swallow nervously, someone once told me that you don't say no to Salvatore.

His eyes darken a shade. "I wasn't asking. Four p.m. Good day." He nods to Carmen, gives David a quick kiss on the head and whispers in his ear, then he brushes past me and leaves.

Carmen and I stand in silence until we hear the front door slam closed. I spin around, about to ask her what to do.

"You go," she says before I have a chance to get a word out. "You don't say no to Salvatore."

Fuck.

THE DAYS PASS TOO FAST. CECILIA IS GETTING increasingly excited about gifts, about cake and balloons. I'm also getting increasingly excited, or rather, terrified.

Friday, 3:55 p.m. finds me standing on the gravel, clutching a bouncing Cecilia's hand, more for my sake than hers. The parking area to the side is half-filled with exclusive cars but not a sound is heard except for birds chirping.

The doorbell clings softly when I push it, and the door opens almost immediately. Before me stands a tall, broad blond man, his face neutral as he nods for us to come inside. Ivan, if I recall correctly.

"Happy birthday, little one," he says and goes down on one knee to be level with her.

"Thank you, sir," says my little daughter to my great surprise. Sir? Wow. Who taught her that?

Ivan stands and a ghost of a smile passes his lips. "You've raised her well. This way."

My legs are heavy with trepidation as I follow the giant through the house. The sound of people talking, of laughter and music increases. Suddenly I feel so alone, and I surprise myself by wishing I had Christian by my side, holding me tight.

We enter a large bright room with a whole wall of sliding glass doors pushed to the side, a large patio outside, people everywhere and children running around the legs of the adults. Cecilia bounces and pulls my hand as she sees the balloons, the serpentines, and the table with beautifully wrapped gifts.

Everyone turns as we enter. I hold my breath, my eyes darting over the crowd. There's only one person I want to see, and by God, I really do want to see him. It's been weeks. Salvatore spreads his arms as he walks up to us, grabs my shoulders and kisses my cheeks. Then he crouches and does the same with Cecilia.

"The young lady of the hour!" He sweeps her up in his strong arms, and spins around. My cheeks burn hot from his surprisingly gentle greeting. "Everybody, let me present young Cecilia Russo!"

I widen my eyes. "Jackson," I hiss in his ear.

He laughs. "Jackson. For now." He smacks Cecilia's butt. "Now go play. There are kids everywhere." He puts her down and she runs toward the garden, toward the colorful flags and begins to chase a stray balloon.

I inhale to protest.

"And a whole slew of people looking after them," he tells me. "She's safe."

A tingling sensation of being watched makes me spin on my heels. To the far right stands Christian, his face guarded, tall, beautiful, dressed in a dark gray suit that fits like it was sewn directly on his body. He looks more buff than when I saw him the last time. My eyes look to his powerful hands, his thighs, and my body reacts with no connection to my brain whatsoever. I forget Salvatore, the people around me, whether it's day or night, as I take a step toward him. He seems to hesitate a moment, then he moves too, and we meet halfway.

"Hey," we say with one mouth.

"How've you been?" he asks.

"Okay," I say.

"I heard Cecilia is with Carmen. That was a clever move."

"Did you visit her?"

He shakes his head.

"Why?"

"I told you I'd stay away."

"But you're here."

"I'm not very good at keeping my promises," he says darkly.

My eyes dart between his. "You confuse me so much, Christian."

He licks his lips and I can't help that my gaze is drawn to his tongue. "Is that a good or a bad thing?" he asks.

The air between us thickens, ignites. I stagger back. "We should—"

He swallows audibly. "Yeah, let's go— The party." Sliding up next to me he puts a palm to the small of my back, electrifying my whole body, then he removes it. "Sorry," he mumbles.

Don't be, I want to say. But I don't.

We walk up to a group of people. A woman in her sixties with steel gray hair, neatly curled in an old-fashioned look, turns and regards me, giving me a once-over, then she lifts an eyebrow and turns to Christian.

"Bianca," he says to her. "I want you to meet Kerry Jackson, the mother of Cecilia. Kerry, this is my mother, Bianca Russo."

I give her my hand. A few moments pass when she doesn't take it, awkwardness mounting, the whole conversation around us dying.

"Miss Jackson," she finally says and gives me a too-hard handshake. "I have heard a lot about you."

It doesn't sound one bit like she has heard good things about me. Do they blame me for Christian nearly dying? I realize I also almost killed him once before. I have to force my legs not to tremble under her scrutiny.

"Mrs. Russo. So nice to meet you."

Her black eyes pierce mine, and it's easy to see the similarities between her and her brother Salvatore, both in looks as well as manner. "I have a grandchild I have yet to see." She turns to Christian, while still holding my hand.

"Bianca," he says, his voice cold and hard.

She narrows her eyes, then she lets go and blood returns to my hand. I'm suddenly extremely self-conscious about being here. My eyes move to the other men and women around me. Do they all hate me? Does everyone here know about Christian and me? How much exactly do they know?

In rapid succession I'm introduced to Matteo, Luca, Eric, Anna, Nathan, and Sydney. It's less tense. There are smiles, and greetings, and congratulations on Cecilia's behalf, and a lot of 'we can't wait to meet her'. I'm trying to remember all the names. It's overwhelming. The two women greet me a little more heartily. Nathan is polite, but I sense an underlying tension. Eric radiates danger. Much like Christian does when he turns dark. I shrink back and glance at the woman by his side, Anna. She looks so timid, but she's gotta have balls of steel if she's chosen to be with him.

Or did she get to choose?

You're mine. Christian's words come back to me. Was it the same for her?

We eat. There's an overabundance of cake, and Italian delicacies that I fail to remember the names of as soon as they've been introduced to me. There are games. Lots of laughter. Cecilia is finally properly introduced to her large extended family and finds a little soulmate in Ava, Nathan and Sydney's little beauty of a daughter.

Christian doesn't leave my side the whole afternoon. I'm tingling from his presence, constantly aware of him, his scent, his low rumbling voice.

I'm stunned by the change in demeanor in the Russos as the hours pass by. I've seen nothing but cruelty, possessiveness, force, but Salvatore seems genuinely fond of the children. I miss David, but I know that with his autism he'd find this crowd too much, so it's probably the right choice to let him stay at his mom's. Nathan and Eric don't leave their women's sides the whole evening and are constantly attentive to their needs, as if they worship the ground they walk on.

I glance at Christian with a sucking feeling in my chest. Is that how it could be? Would he care that much about me? Our days in the cabin come back to me. He can be tender. He can be beautifully tender and caring.

What am I doing? Why am I fighting this?

Something makes me turn and look behind me. In the doorway in the far end of the room stands a woman with long strawberry blonde hair, cascading down her shoulders, wearing a demure, white dress and white ballerina shoes. My heart stops as our eyes lock.

Chloe.

Chloe!

I rush through the room and throw my arms around her. "Chloe!"

"Kerry?" she gasps and pushes away, taking me in. "Kerry! Oh my God! What are you doing here?"

"*Me?* What are *you* doing here? Where have you been? I've missed you so much! Your parents! Do they know you're back? Where have you *been?*"

"That's... a very long story. Kerry... are you and Christian..." She chews on her lip and a worried expression crosses her face as she glances over my shoulder. I follow her gaze and see that Christian is studying our interaction, his eyes dark and unreadable.

I beat her up.

Oh no. I look back to Chloe. "*No!* No, we're not," I say quickly.

She looks relieved and my chest clenches. We're not, but my whole soul yearns for him. How could I betray my friend? I can't.

"I heard what he did," I say quietly. "I'm so sorry."

"That's a long time ago."

I regard her, my best friend, and realize that I don't quite recognize her anymore. There's a harder streak in her, she seems taller somehow, mature. My happy-go-lucky girl has a new darkness in her.

"What happened to you?" I ask. "Where have you been?"

"Here. And away," she says, avoiding my gaze, glancing over my shoulder again. I follow her gaze and find Salvatore right behind me, towering over me, locking me between him and Chloe. Tension crackles, surrounding us, and then it dawns on me. He knew where she was, all this time. Salvatore *knew* where my friend was, and he didn't tell me. A black cloud of rage rises in me.

"You fucking bastard," I yell and slam my fist right in his face. "How—" I scream as I'm pushed face first into the wall, and then he snatches me with him into the next room. My face hurts and my hand throbs with pain.

All hell breaks loose, Chloe pleads, Christian tears Salvatore off me, and the two men face off, their fists tightened. Everyone comes rushing, yelling. People step in between Salvatore and Christian. I cry as I cradle my hand.

"You're quite the little troublemaker, aren't you?" says a cold voice behind me. I spin around and stare right into Bianca's hard gaze.

Anna steps in between us. "She didn't choose this, ma'am." Her voice is just as stern as the older woman's. "I'll take it from here." She lays her arm around my shoulder and pulls me with her.

"Cecilia," I gasp and look around me.

"The kids are on the upper floor, watching a movie."

"Oh *God*," I whimper. "What have I done?"

"That man needs a good punch. Too few dare. Good on you."

"He's gonna kill me!"

Anna pulls me down on a leather couch in the next room, away from the ruckus. "Christian won't allow that to happen."

"But without him?"

"You'd be pretty fucked."

"Everyone hates me!"

"No, they don't, Kerry. Stop it. You've had shit luck. I kinda recognize myself in you."

I look up at her. "Yeah?"

She smiles warmly, her large, brown doe-eyes twinkling. "Yeah, but it turned out really well in the end."

"It's really fucked up... Between Christian and me."

"Kerry. I don't know enough about it. What I do know is that you have one hell of a man who wants nothing but to take care of you and your beautiful child."

I swallow and glance toward the other room, where things seem to have calmed down. Everyone keeps telling me that. It's what my heart has told me for a long time, while my brain keeps telling me to run.

TWENTY-FIVE

Kerry

I fight to keep up the charade of everything being normal as I leave the mansion. Salvatore has been unreadable at best, charming with Cecilia, less charming with me, his cheek a little red below the left eye, where I hit him.

His parting words to me have chilled me to my core: 'You and I are gonna talk.'

My fist hurts and I regret hitting him with a vengeance. Anna and I have exchanged phone numbers. Chloe has promised to call me. She looked guarded, though, and I just can't shake the feeling that she'll disappear on me again.

Cecilia rushes to Christian who follows us out, hugs his legs. "Kis! Don't leave."

He crouches before her. "It's you who's leaving, honey." He glances up at me and a stab of uncertainty shoots through me. They need each other.

"Do you want to come by? Some day? See her?"

Christian stands and his lips pull into a smile. "Yeah. I'd want that."

I raise my hand in an awkward goodbye. "Okay... See you."

Then I flee. I feel his gaze as a tingling in my back until I've passed the gates.

I don't know how to maneuver this new world I've been thrown into. Christian's less than friendly family, his outright hostile mother, and Salvatore, who had murder in his eyes when I'd punched him. I hope Anna can help me. I hope Chloe wants to see me. I still need to unravel the mystery with her disappearance and now reappearance. I'm relieved to know that Christian was honest. He actually didn't know.

Cecilia is exhilarated, full of sugar and happiness. She talks about Ava, and some other kids, and with a twinge in my heart I realize I live pretty isolated. I meet with Mom, Gayle and Rebecca, but I don't know any other families, or people with kids. At least she's with Carmen's children during the days. That's gotta make up for it. Right?

My head spins as I drive home. The afternoon, turned early evening, was tumultuous, but there's one single thing that stands out, and that's Christian's expression of joy as I invited him.

Christian

I sit outside her house and wait. For what? I don't know. I should get out of the car and go to her, but I'm frozen from the shock of realizing how much I depend on these two people.

It's been five days since the disastrous birthday party. Salvatore is furious, but so am I. He deserved that punch, and he should own up to what he did instead of blaming Kerry for being unstable. What the fuck was he doing hiding away Chloe Becker? All this time? Did he keep her locked up somewhere? He's gotta fucking talk to me. Kerry thought I had something to do with the girl's disappearance, and at least that's out of the way.

I've also had a serious talk with Bianca. It hadn't occurred to me that my family would hold a grudge against Kerry. None of this shit is her fault and they gotta back the fuck off and accept my choices.

Kerry. I know she's home, alone with Cecilia. I've circled the neighborhood twice. I just don't fucking know how to hang with normal people and be what... chatty? What do we even talk about? Weather? Last night's TV?

I don't fucking know, but I'll learn. Maybe.

Kerry

Cecilia jumps on the couch in front of the TV, transfixed by cartoons. I am putting plates in the dishwasher and almost fly through the roof when the doorbell rings. It's six fifteen Wednesday evening. Christian hasn't called, or texted, or made even a peep and I've become increasingly worried that he won't come.

When I walk up to my front door with a palm over my slamming heart, I swear to God that I *will* install a peep hole, because opening this door, never knowing who's outside, with the life I live, is frying my nerves. Filled with trepidation I unlock and pull open the door.

Christian's imposing presence fills the doorway. Neither of us speak, we just stare at each other as the space between us suddenly crackles with energy.

"Can I come in?"

I twitch to life, coming back to myself. "Yeah, sure." I take a step to the side and gesture for him to enter.

"I think this is the first time you've actually invited me here," he says as I close the door. "Voluntarily."

"Maybe." I feel him in the house all the time. Every square inch of this house is inundated with his being, or the absence thereof. "Cece is in front of the TV." I nod toward the deeper recesses of the living room.

He glances at me and an expression I can't interpret passes his features. "Okay."

As he moves toward the couch where our daughter sits I flee back into the kitchen. My body is on fire. His appearance makes me breathless. This won't work!

I keep listening to them chatting, playing something. Cecilia's light voice. Christian's grave murmur.

After I've put everything away, wiped every surface, and my kitchen is squeaky clean, I don't know what to do, so I pour myself a glass of white wine, and then I just sit there by my kitchen table, paralyzed.

"Kerry."

I almost tip the glass over from the surprise. "Hi. Yeah!"

"She's sleepy. I should—" He glances over his shoulder, and then back at me, his eyes unreadable. "—be on my way."

In my mind I grab him and beg him not to go. In the real world, I force a smile. "Okay. I'll follow you to the door." I veer off to pick up Cecilia on my way, hitching her up on my hip. "Wanna say bye to daddy?"

"Daddy," she says and reaches for him.

Christian takes her hand, but his eyes are trained on mine. My heart speeds up as the air thickens. Yeah, this is *not* gonna go well.

"Ker," he licks his lips and my eyes follow his tongue. His gaze falls to my mouth, and then back up to meet my eyes again. He clears his throat. "Thank you." He takes a step back.

"Wanna come again?" I blurt out.

His skewed smile makes my heart skip a beat. "I plan to."

When he has left, I put Cecilia to bed, and then I pour a second glass of wine. And a third. I'm shaking.

SLIGHTLY HUNGOVER THE NEXT MORNING, WHILE BOILING water for tea, I get a text message.

> We should talk. Call me.

It's from Salvatore. My heart rate skyrockets and my mouth turns desert dry in an instant. The memory I've tried to suppress, his black eyes, the glare with a promise of pain, after I hit him, comes back with full force. It knocks the wind out of me, and I stumble back until the back of my knees hit a kitchen chair and I sit. My hands shake.

Fuck.

Suddenly I want Christian, but I can't use him as a shield between me and everything that isn't right in my life. In many ways he's part of the problem.

I text back, autocorrect messing up everything I write, but finally I manage a few words.

> Can't now. Later.

It delivers. Is read. A message is being written, interrupted, then the phone rings. My gut clenches hard. Salvatore.

"Yes," I gasp, out of breath as if I've been running a marathon."

"Miss Jackson. I'm not used to people telling me no."

"Then maybe you should learn some patience." *Fuck no!* "I mean—"

"You are to arrive at my place in one hour. One of my men will pick you up."

"I—"

The line is dead. My body goes slack with raw fear. He's not beyond hurting a woman. Luciano Salvatore isn't beyond anything. Every instinct screams at me to call Christian, but at the same time I have such a vivid feeling that I need to face this. It's my actions that put me here and I have to grow some balls and just do this. I'm not waiting, though. I refuse to just sit idle until some goon comes by and pulls me with him.

I stand and dart out into the living room. "Ce, we're going to Grandma."

She perks up and stands. "Gramma!"

I run up the stairs and put on jeans instead of my soft pants.

In the car I call Mom, making sure she's home. She hears something is off, but what can I say? Nothing. As usual.

"What's going on, hon?"

"I just need to do something. I'll be at your place in ten, and I won't be gone long."

I hope I won't be long. I hope I'll come back in one piece.

After having left Cecilia with my mom, her worried face full of questions, I hit the freeway toward the more affluent suburbs on the hills. It's a twenty-minute drive, and it messes fundamentally with my mind. When I finally arrive at the gates by his mansion, I have conjured up images of corporal punishments, of torture and agony.

One of the guards, a man I saw a few days ago at the party, leans in as I roll down the window. "I need to speak with Salvatore," I blurt out before he even opens his mouth.

He narrows his eyes, stands and turns half to the side, speaking into his radio. Turning back, he nods and the gates slide open. "Good luck with that."

I swallow hard and stare at him, then I press my lips together and rev the engine. Fuck them all!

The always-present Ivan opens the door and gives me a curt nod. I want to ask him if he ever does anything else other than stand there.

"He's in the dining room," he says and tilts his head toward the double glass doors at the far end, between the two wide, curved stairs that lead to the upper floor.

I nod. "I know the way."

I walk with heavy steps, my legs barely obeying me. At the far end of the large dining table sits Salvatore with an espresso cup and a laptop in front of him. He looks up when I enter, raising an eyebrow.

"You're a woman of many surprises."

"Yes," I say, my lips numb, my mind blank. "I'm sorry," I blurt out.

"You look like a frightened little bunny." He stands and walks toward me, his steps measured. My mouth goes dry as he rounds my corner of the table and comes up behind me. "I like it."

I swallow hard, the instinct to run immense. Fingers touching the skin on my nape, pushing my hair to the side make me jerk, but I force myself to stand still. He leans in, his breath fans my ear.

"You're real trouble, Miss Jackson. I lose face when I get fucking slapped in my own house. By a girl, no less."

"I—I'm sorry, Mr. Salvatore. I didn't think."

I scream when he suddenly grabs the hair at the back of my neck and forces me face first down on the table.

Salvatore leans in, his body pressed against the whole backside of mine. "You know, I can do what I want with you. I can fuck you. I can have you thrown in chains and beat you to within an inch of death. I can kill you. There's no one who can challenge me. Your beloved Christian will bitch about it, your dear friend will pout, but there's nothing anyone can do. You do best remembering that."

I fight the tears, but it's no use, they fall anyway. His hold on my hair is vice-like and my scalp screams in pain, but it's nothing to the chill that spreads through my body. I don't want to plead. I refuse to plead. I can't imagine for a second that Luciano Salvatore would listen to sniveling and tear-filled excuses.

"What do you want from me?" I finally ask, squeezing my eyes shut.

"I want your absolute obedience. I don't want to hear no fucking 'later' if I tell you to come here. I don't want stubborn glares and silent disliking. You're in my world now, Kerry Jackson."

"You really don't know me, do you?" I say, my voice hoarse.

He rips me up by my hair, making me cry out and clutch for his hand, then he throws me into the wall, following suit, his hand grabbing my chin. He leans in, pressing his body against mine, his nose traveling along the side of my neck until his mouth is by my ear. A scent of expensive cologne wafts up.

"Sweetheart. I've tamed more stubborn women than you in my days. Sooner or later everyone breaks. Is that really where you want to go?"

"No," I whisper. "I'm sorry. It's just... my friend."

He straightens and looks me over, then his hand comes up before my face. I flinch, but all he does is trace my hairline with the tips of his fingers. Our eyes are locked. I stare into his dark gaze that softens slightly as he tucks a lock behind my ear.

"There were reasons. It's her story to tell one day, when she's ready. I suggest you leave her alone until then."

Salvatore takes a step back and I sag, gripping the cupboard next to me for support. "Is that you telling me?"

He grins. "You're learning."

"What now?"

"Go home, Kerry Jackson. Go home and take care of that beautiful little daughter of yours. Until next time."

I don't go straight to my Mom's. I have to get the shaking under control. I've cried all the way here. My cheek is red and slightly swollen from when I was slammed to the table. Gayle takes one look at my face, then she drags me through her shop and pushes me down on a couch in the backroom of her bookstore and makes me a large cup of herbal tea.

"What happened?"

"I can't talk about it." I pull up my legs and hug my knees. "I did something stupid."

"Something with... them?" She chews on her lip as she studies me.

"Yeah," I say on an exhale, "but I think it's sorted. It's just... it's never gonna be all right. There's always gonna be something."

"I'm so sorry this happened to you."

I think of Christian, of Cecilia, see their faces before me. Warmth, passion, a love larger than life.

"I don't know what I feel, Gayle. Nothing is ever easy, is it?"

She grimaces and shakes her head, sighing. "It's life."

THE WEEKS PASS. IT'S LIFE. MY LIFE.

No one is after me. No one wants to murder me. Life is not terrible anymore, only really weird. Why can't I just leave it at that?

The sun is setting, dropping fast. It should be a peaceful moment, but I itch with frustration. Over the last couple of months, as autumn has turned to winter, I've come to expect his visits, once, twice, sometimes three times a week.

He is great with Cece, makes her laugh, but I'm getting increasingly skittish. I hate the unpredictability, the unplanned visits, the sudden knock on the door. What if I have a visitor already? What if someone sees him? How would I explain? What if he felt threatened? Would he become violent? I don't know what he does when he's not with me. Is he killing again? Working for Luciano Salvatore? I don't know anything, and I don't know how much longer I can stand it.

I hate that he doesn't make a move on me. Apart from that first visit, he hasn't hinted at there being something between us. Is there someone else? I can't stop thinking about him, and the cooler he seems, the hotter I get. I don't want to be pathetic and make an absolute fool out of myself, so I don't ask.

Time passes. We nod and smile, we're polite with each other, but it's clear that we walk in circles.

He leans back against my table, crosses his arms over his chest and glances at the orange tinged sky over the ocean. "I think she's sleeping. I should be on my way."

"What are you doing, Christian?"

"I'm... leaving?" He gives me a weird look. "What do you mean?" Rubbing his forehead, he sinks down on a chair. Small beads of sweat pearl at his temples and make his hair curl slightly from the damp. From the sound of it they ran through the upper hallway, back and forth, for a long time before she settled down.

"When you're not here, Christian Russo. What do you do when you're not with us?" It's not what I want to ask. I want to ask what happened between us. But I can't.

He looks uncomfortable and my frustration turns to anger as he doesn't answer.

"Are you back to killing people? To the mob business? Do you work for that asshole Salvatore?"

"What the fuck? You shouldn't be asking about that."

"I think I have a right to know. I see you more than any other person, including Mom, my best friends, anyone. Cecilia adores you and asks about you when you're not here—"

"She does?" He lights up.

"So I think I have a fucking right to know. And yeah, she does." I slam down on a chair opposite him. "Talk to me. Whatever it is. No matter how brutal, tell me the truth. Please. I know too much already. I'm the worst liability both you and your uncle can have, but here I am. When did I ever betray any of you? Have some faith."

Christian pinches the bridge of his nose and sighs. "Do you believe me if I say I haven't killed a single person since back when we saved Cecilia? Do you believe me when I say I don't work for Salvatore anymore?"

I gape. "What do you do, then?"

He looks at his hands. "I don't do much, to be honest. I'm still trying to figure out how to live. I've been visiting my family, hung with Nate, Syd and Angela in New York. I'm fucking lost, Kerry."

My heart pounds. "I'm sorry, I—"

"Don't be. It'll be all right."

"Christian," I lay a hand over one of his, and pull it back when I realize what I just did. He looks at his hand, and then scans my face. "Can you let me know when you wanna come by? It's driving me insane never knowing if you'll suddenly show up. Call me, text me, whatever."

"Sure," he says. Just like that. All this time, all I had to do was to ask.

"Maybe we should talk a little more often?" I say. "People do that. Or so I hear."

He laughs his warm, rich laugh, his eyes twinkling. "I had no idea. I never knew any normal people."

"What about your family? You never talk about them. Your sister, your brothers?"

"Oh, they're not normal."

"Are they also in... the business?" His silence tells me everything. I shake my head. "You never stood a chance, did you?"

"My sister isn't," he says. "She stays away. Look, I made a choice. Every person makes a choice and you gotta own up to who you are. I'm not gonna put the blame on anyone else."

"That sounds... very mature."

Christian laughs. "I'm forty fucking years old. I hope I've learned some shit along the way."

"I'll be thirty next year. Time flies, doesn't it?"

"Yeah. What do you wanna do for your big three oh?"

"I have no idea. It's a little early, don't you think? What did you do when you turned forty?"

"I was here, putting our daughter to bed."

I stare at him. "You're kidding. Why didn't you say something?"

"I never imagined it mattered to you."

I'm stunned. Why would he think that? Does he think I hate him? Is that why he's been so cold?

I say it quick, before I change my mind.

"Wanna come by Friday? I'll cook something for us? We can watch a movie with Cece?"

My heart leaps to my throat. Did I just invite Christian back in? For real? Like to not only hang with Cece but... with me?

It's as if time stands still. Something shifts. The world goes absolutely silent.

"Friday it is," he says.

As he stands to leave, I suddenly find it hard to look at him. I usher him out of the door. "Yep. See ya."

After he's gone, I fall back against the wall, my mind spinning, my heart slamming in my chest. All I wanted to do was to grab him, hold him, and never let him leave again.

TWENTY-SIX

Christian

I feel like a fumbling, sweaty teenager when I stand with my hand raised to push her doorbell. A new person has awoken in me that I never knew was there. Inside is a man with hope, with a sliver of light and dreams for the future. I clutch a pot with fresh herbs, noticing yet again how she never seems to have that at home. This is essential for good cooking, everyone knows that. Hanging on a finger on the same hand is a bag with a gift for Cece, a stuffed unicorn, because right now they are apparently the best there is.

Pushing the button, listening to the soft chiming, I hold my breath. From inside comes sounds of everyday life, someone's muffled talking, music, rapid steps approaching.

I take in Kerry as if I see her for the first time. She's got on a white blouse with embroidery that shows hints of skin on her shoulders. It's tucked into skinny jeans that hang low on her hips. Her flaming auburn-red hair hangs loose, reaching her shoulders. Her heart-shaped pale face, and her hazel-green eyes are filled with a shadow of still-there trepidation every time I see her. It disappears after a few minutes, but it's still as if she always expects the worst. It's been a little over three years since that fateful week when we met and everything went to hell. I can't imagine those wounds are still so deep, but she did live in fear for two whole years after that, and maybe that will take some time to heal.

I have nothing but time. When I want something, I get it. I didn't know I could be so patient, though, but maybe I have changed?

Her eyes dart to mine, slide across my chest, then land on the pot. "This feels familiar."

"I come in peace," I say and hold the pot up between us, well aware of the last time I brought her herbs, and when my intentions weren't so pretty. If they ever are.

Kerry bursts out in a laugh. "Come in."

Cecilia comes rushing. "Daddy!"

I hand Kerry the pot and scoop Cecilia up on my arm. "Little one!"

"Present! For me?"

I show her the contents and her eyes go wide. "Unicorn!" She slithers out of my arms, grabs the bag and runs back to her play corner, pulling the stuffed animal out of the bag and begins to introduce it to her other toys.

"Cecilia!" half-shouts Kerry. "What do you say?"

"Thank you!"

"Good girl." Kerry turns to me. "That was a hit. Totally. You know her well."

I trail after Kerry to the kitchen, and can't help taking in her mouthwatering butt, snugly fit in the jeans, embroidered red roses on the back pockets. They look a little like that rose tattoo on her belly and my cock suddenly twitches to life, thinking of her naked under me. She seems so innocent, but when I tie her up and spank her to tears, there's a sinful heat in her that even she can't deny.

"You want a glass of wine?"

I pull myself out of the images of her naked. "Sure. What've you got?"

"Red." Kerry holds up a bottle. "I'm... no wine person. I mean, I like it, but brands... grapes. It's—it's Italian at least. I don't know..."

"It's perfect, and yes please."

Kerry smiles, an expression of relief crossing her face, and pours us half a glass each, handing me one. "I'm only half done. I'm making pasta Bolognese. I was thinking it'd be all right with an Italian." Kerry suddenly looks aghast. "Or maybe that was super stupid. Damn. You're probably used to your mom's amazing cooking."

"Bianca?" I sputter, "she never cooked. Dad did, and then us kids."

Her face falls a little and her mouth forms into the cutest O. Fuck I want to catch those lips and just take her.

"Is that why you're good at cooking?"

I shrug. "I like good food. Can't always eat out. I like it. It makes me think of something else for a while. Makes me focus."

"Something other than...? Never mind," she adds quickly. "Know what? I'll put out plates. You be in charge of the sauce."

"And the pasta," I add.

"You don't trust me?"

"I'll do it better." I poke the packet of dried spaghetti. "And at my place I'd have made this fresh."

Kerry throws out her hands. "You do the pasta. Can I do anything?"

I smack her butt. "Make us a salad, woman."

She gives out a little squeal and jumps, her cheeks turning red. Her pulse thuds visibly on the sides of her throat and tension crackles between us, syrupy, heady. Kerry spins on her heels, mumbles something I can't hear and then literally flees out into the living room. I'm left breathless, and with a cock that hardened in a second. Clearing my throat, I get to work, rummaging around her kitchen until I have everything neatly arranged before me, losing myself in the art of cooking, making good use of the herbs.

Kerry comes back after a while, her eyes a little glossy, as if she has been crying, on her arm Cece whom she sets down at the kitchen table.

"Wanna do the salad, hon?"

Kerry throws me a shy gaze, then she busies herself with our daughter and their task. I grin. One day she'll be ready, and that day isn't that far away anymore.

Dinner is light and friendly, and we chat about mundane things. Kerry can talk about her work at the daycare for hours. I like listening to her. I don't have a lot to say myself, but I do tell her about how Manhattan has transformed for Christmas, and that I suspect there might be another baby on the way in the Russo-Lewis household even though they haven't confirmed it.

Cecilia eats with her whole body, and in a three feet radius. After I wash her face and hands and Kerry finds her some new clothes, the three of us watch Cinderella. Our daughter sits between us, blissfully unaware of her mother's flushed cheeks, and her father's pounding heart.

When there's nothing more to be said or done, movie is over, plates are in the dishwasher, and the table is wiped, I put Cece to bed, she is asleep the moment her head hits the pillow. When I come back down, Kerry has folded the throw blankets, and restored Cecilia's play corner. Standing by the large windows, she clutches a cup of tea. When I walk up to her, she flinches slightly, making me take a step back.

"She's sleeping."

Kerry swallows audibly. "Okay, good."

She makes no move to close the distance between us.

"I should go." I don't want to go.

"Okay."

I can't read her.

"Thanks for dinner."

Kerry gives out a little laugh. "It was you who made it."

"Joint effort."

"That's... very generous of you."

I grin and shove a hand through my hair as I let my gaze wander from her eyes to her mouth, to her soft perfect handful of breasts, to her jeans-clad hips. Then I back yet another step. "Okay. See you." A shudder runs through me as I turn toward the door. I don't know how much longer I can hold back. But I want more than sex. I want her whole being. I want her to *want* to be with me. I'm used to taking what I want, but that's not going to work with Kerry. She needs to come to me, or this will never happen.

As I pull open the door, I hear her quick steps behind me. "Christian!"

I turn. "Yeah?"

"Happy belated birthday."

Leaning in, I give her a quick kiss on the cheek. Her sweet strawberry scent nearly does me in. "Thanks."

I leave while I'm still in control of my urges.

The whole way home, I curse. I feel the ghost of her shape in my arms, her scent lingers. My steps echo in my abandoned house as I walk straight into the kitchen and pour a whiskey. There's nothing here for me. Everything I need exists in a little townhouse forty minutes away, downtown. I down the smoky liquid, lift the bottle to pour a second glass when I set both bottle and glass down on the counter with a sharp slam and spin on my heels.

Fuck it.

I can't stay away.

Pounding my fist against her front door, I wait, listen. I raise my arm to pound again when I hear quick, light steps.

The door opens a sliver and a fresh-faced makeup free, pajama-clad Kerry peeks out. "Chr—"

"Shut up." I push open the door and then slam it closed behind me. "I'm done with these games," I growl and grab her hips, pushing her in front of me until I have her up against the wall.

She inhales to speak, her eyes widening, but I catch her lips and crash my mouth to hers as my hand finds her breast, kneading it none too gently. Kerry moans and her nipple turns into a delicious little peak that I pinch hard enough for her to try to squirm free. I grab her arms and push them up over her head, flush against the wall. We stare at each other, the closeness overwhelming, then my primal side takes over and roars in me to claim my woman.

"Not a sound," I whisper, then I catch her nipple through the fabric of her T-shirt, rolling it between my teeth. Kerry arches and whimpers. "If I have to keep telling you to shut up, then I'll punish you, girl," I growl.

She stares at me, her eyes ablaze, chewing on her lower lip, then she slams her mouth shut and it's all the consent I need. I lift her and carry her into the little office, locking the door behind us, then I put her down and grab the hem of her shirt, pulling it over her head.

"Beautiful," I moan, taking in her perky breasts and dark, mouth-watering nipples.

"I—"

I put a hand over her mouth. "Did I tell you to speak?"

Wide-eyed, she shakes her head.

"Turn around and pull down your pants."

"Don't wake up Cecilia."

I sigh and spin her around. "You're absolutely hopeless at obeying."

"No, I'm—" Snapping her lips shut, she turns, a visible tremor running through her. I grin. I like her afraid. I like her not knowing what's about to happen. I like her completely at my mercy.

Kerry hooks her thumbs into the waistband of her pajama pants and begins to push them past her hips, her panties along with them, revealing a soft round ass, the sight making my cock grow even harder. Good, good girl.

When her pants fall down past her knees and she takes a step out of them, I kick her legs wider apart. "Bend over."

She throws me a glance over her shoulder, eyes huge and dark, a look that shoots straight to my gut, then she obeys.

"Stay."

I walk up to the desk and pull out the drawers, one after the other. I can't help the smirk that spreads at the sight of a plastic ruler. Girl, this might sting a bit. When I turn, my choice of punishment in my hand, my choice of foreplay, Kerry darts up.

"No," she whispers. "Red!"

I scoff and grip around her waist, pushing her toward the couch. "You want this on your boobs or on your butt?"

A gasp escapes her. Her eyes turn a little glossy and her lips part. Then she turns, supporting her hands against the armrest of the couch.

I lean in, whispering in her ear: "And babe. You can safeword. But have some faith. Don't fucking safeword before I've even started. Now, don't move."

I caress her butt cheek, letting a thumb slide along the crack, down, up again, teasing, making goosebumps erupt on her skin. Then I raise my arm and let the ruler come down on her left cheek. Not too hard, a light slap that shouldn't do more than sting briefly. A gasp escapes her, but she remains still. I kiss the skin where I smacked down, then I lift my arm again. Harder, faster. Kerry groans and her toes curl. I correct my cock, fuck I'm hard. In rapid succession, I let the ruler fall on her left side, her right side, her upper thighs, making her dance from side to side, but no safeword. I bend over and kiss the pain, blow at the swellings, at the angry red welts. Sliding my hand in between her thighs, I caress my way up to her wet pussy. Kerry moans and pushes back. I move along her slit, parting her lips, circle her clit. It grows under the tip of my fingers and Kerry begins to make little mewling sounds.

"You missed me," I whisper as I unzip and pull out my cock, stroking it in my other hand.

She shakes her head which makes me laugh. "Yes, you did."

"No. Whenever I'm with you it hurts."

I grab the ruler and slap her again, five times on each side, making sure to hit where she's sore the most. She groans, but still no safeword.

"Touch yourself," I say. Put your hand between your legs, push your fingers inside your pussy and spread your lips for me. Let me see you."

I ache to take her. It fucking hurts. It's been such a long time and all I've had, after all my visits here, has been my right hand.

I stroke my rock-hard cock as I watch her obey me. The thought that I can do everything I want with her is mind-blowing. I can take her, tie her up, gag her, use all her holes, until she cries and begs. Something dark in me *wants* to hurt her, use her, and I have to keep that part at bay. At least for now.

Her long slender fingers move in her pussy, spreading her lips. I groan as I watch the pink folds, glistening with her juices, open. Lining up my cock to her opening, I push away her hand and slam inside her in one rough thrust, making her squeal and jerk forward. I grab her hips to ground her to me, waiting just a little to let her catch her breath before I thrust again, and again. Kerry pants and writhes. I stop for a moment and pull off my shirt, tossing it to the floor, then I begin to pound in her in earnest. When Kerry pushes at me, trying to ease the pressure, I lean in and catch her arms, pushing them tight against her lower back, holding both in one of my hands. That leaves her with no leverage, and completely at my mercy. I find my way to her clit and rub it, pinch it, making her shake. Small sobs escape her and at the same time she pushes back on me, rocks with me.

Falling forward, she buries her face in the cushion, her cries muffled, as her inner walls convulse around my cock.

I am so fucking close to coming when I realize that I have no clue if she's on birth control. Still. I pull out and grab her arm.

"On your knees."

Kerry has no resistance, no will of her own, as she numbly lets me spin her around. I grab her hair and push my cock deep into her throat. She gags, and her hands slam up, pushing at my thighs. I'm so close and she isn't going anywhere.

I come hard, clenching my teeth to muffle the wild roar that wants to erupt from my throat. Kerry hits my thighs, and then she finally breaks free as I release my hold. She darts to her feet, wipes come off her chin and slaps my chest.

"You piece of shit!"

I laugh and grab her hands, pushing her down on her back on the couch. "Let me make it up to you." Nudging her thighs apart I hold her gaze as I lick along the inside of her thigh, all the way up to where her legs meet, to where she's swollen, tender and deliciously wet.

Our eyes are locked as I let my tongue lick a path from her ass all the way up to her clit, then her eyelids fall closed and she raises her hips to meet me. I push two fingers inside her slick channel, finding that ridged spot in the front wall, rubbing it, making sobs erupt from her throat. Kerry bites down on her forearm to keep from screaming as she comes, shaking and shuddering. Kissing my way over her little patch of red hair, veering past the rose tattoo in my track across her belly, I then climb higher and pull her to me, a thigh over her legs, my arms around her chest, locking her in. I don't want to let go. Ever.

"You're not right in the head," she finally whispers.

"I think we've established that."

I'm drenched in sweat, spent, but I'm also so fucking relaxed.

"I don't think we should be doing this."

My heart skips a beat. "Why?"

"It's... I— I don't know, Christian. It's just too much."

I rise on my elbow and study her. "But you like this?"

Kerry pulls back, struggles to get up, and I let her as something grows colder inside. She finds her clothes that are spread around the room and puts them on, one by one. As she turns her back on me my cock stirs again at the mottled skin and the sweet red welts on her butt. It's as if she reads my mind, because she tentatively puts her hand on her ass and lets out a hiss.

"Tender?"

She pulls up her pants, holding out the waistband as she passes the bruised skin, then she spins around.

"You never give me a choice, Christian. I never get to make a decision. It's always about you, and your needs. You never ask what I want."

I narrow my eyes as I stand and move toward her. Kerry, brave little Kerry, doesn't move. "I take what I want, and you're loving it. I know it."

Kerry has to tilt her head to meet my gaze. The heat grows in the almost non-existent distance between us. "This won't work, Christian. You're an awesome dad, but I never know when you'll... turn on me."

"This isn't me turning on you," I snarl.

Kerry throws up her hands. "You're doing it again!"

I groan and take a step back. Picking up my jeans and pulling them back on, I look at the determined little woman before me. She hugs her chest that rises and falls rapidly. Her hands tremble slightly. I know she isn't unaffected. I know she wants me. I just don't know how to make her see it.

You never ask what I want.

"Christian." She lays a hand on my arm. "Let's just be her parents. It's enough, isn't it?"

I pull her hand to me and kiss the tips of her fingers, one after the other. "No, love. It's not enough. It will never be enough for me."

"You can't just take me."

"I won't," I say and unlock the door, stepping out into the dark living room. "Let's just be Mom and Dad, then, Kerry." The words taste wrong. That's not what we are, and I know she knows it. I see it in her eyes, feel it in the energy between us. She wants me just as much as I want her, she just has to come around and acknowledge it.

I put my hand on the front door handle.

"Christian."

I inhale and turn. Meeting her gaze, I wait.

"Sunday? In the park?" She sounds so unsure, as if she's afraid I'll reject her. She still doesn't understand. She's mine. I'm hers. That will never happen.

"Sure," I say, clenching my jaw, then I leave while I still can.

Twenty-Seven

Kerry

I look at us as others must see us. We're picture perfect. We look like any other couple in the park, the mother sitting on a bench, enjoying the sun, the father playing on the playground with their two-year old daughter.

If they only knew.

No one but me knows of the darkness in him, of the longing in his eyes he doesn't know that I see. No one knows of my long, lonely nights when I wish we *were* that normal couple, when I put a hand between my legs and conjure up the memories of our latest meeting, fantasizing of it happening again, fantasizing of his possessiveness, the fright that turns to heat, of his complete domination over me.

It's as if he hears my thoughts. His dark eyes dart up and meet mine for a brief moment, making my heart stutter.

We share so many secrets, and then there's the one we never share: where we stand with each other.

He's the only man I want, but I can't function when I'm with him. He devours my whole being. We're just not meant to be. So why do I long for him every moment of my life?

I close the journal and put the pen down. I brought it because I figured I could catch up while we're here, but I have nothing to say. I glance again at father and daughter. He is good with her, really good. He's good *for* her.

Does time heal all wounds? I don't know. At least it makes it harder to remember why they hurt in the first place. He sacrificed himself for our daughter. He's her father, a hero, and a real person, a real man. No matter who he is, and what he has done in the past, it doesn't matter anymore.

PART THREE
BLESSINGS

TWENTY-EIGHT

Kerry

Christian has an amazing house. An old mansion built in the forties, part brick, part wooden panel. Back then it was probably pretty much the only house on the hill. Now a whole community of more modern, and larger houses surrounds it, but they lack the charm of this older building. It's got pillars on either side of the front door, two floors and a mysterious attic window, nooks and crannies, a balcony on the backside with my favorite view in life, and a large, old swimming pool with blue mosaic in the pattern of a dolphin on the bottom.

It's also almost empty of furniture. It's like he sleeps here, but I wonder where he lives.

I got the tour when I left off Cecilia the first time, but after that I've only stood in the hallway. I don't want to intrude on their time together. It's like this place has become theirs. Father's and daughter's.

A light chair on his patio has flipped over and flaps in the wind, rattling against the hard surface. It bangs and slams like an out-of-control child. I look out into the darkness where the streetlights are dancing a funny dance and then I glance behind me. He should secure the outdoor furniture and wrap up the newer plants. It's getting colder. Why hasn't he already?

He's reading to Cecilia and the wind has increased dramatically just in the last twenty minutes. Maybe he isn't even aware of the severity of the situation.

A storm is well on its way and I need to get her back home before it gets too bad. I press my nose against the window. The rage outside translates through the soulless surface and makes me quiver. Where are they? I spin around and walk with determined steps across the room only to meet Christian in the doorway. "I wondered where you were." I can barely hide the irritation in my voice. "It's getting windy. You should put your patio furniture in the garage."

He looks uncomfortable. I frown. "Trust me," I add. "You don't want to leave them loose. If something comes flying through the air, your windows will crack like eggshells if this thing keeps up with its promise."

He pushes his fingers through his hair and sighs. "I know. I'm not sure I can do it alone."

That is the least likely of all answers I would have thought possible. "Why?"

"Can you please help me?"

And there's that word again. Please. It'll never cease to amaze me, hearing it from his lips. "Oookay. Where's Cece?"

His features lighten. "Sleeping. After the walk she was exhausted."

"Sleeping? But... we need to get going. Real soon."

He steps into a pair of boots. "Are we doing this?"

I frown and reach for my sweater. "Sure."

We almost have to double over as we fight against the gusts and I curse him more than once for not having done this earlier this afternoon. When it was still bright. When it wasn't so cold. Together we carry furniture across the dark patio and Christian struggles with canvas and rope to tie around the plants, saving them from the rage and the possible frost. I think of my bed, my TV, of a warm cup of tea and my cozy pajamas. Why am I here again? I frown as I look at Christian who seems to be more holding onto a large terracotta pot than wrapping it.

"Hur—" The wind steals my words, almost before they even leave my lips, and I realize I can scream as much as I want to and he won't hear it anyway, not over the wind. I struggle across the lawn and shudder. The temperature has dropped several degrees in just the last couple of hours. He jerks when I tap his shoulder. "You need to—" Even in the dark I see how pale he is. He looks exhausted. "Just leave it!" I shout. "Come on!"

The wind comes from behind us now and shoves us forward, almost lifts us back. Once inside, the door slams shut behind us and we're thrown into silence, our hearing temporarily stunned by the alarm we've just fought our way through. I gasp and lean back against the nearest wall. Christian's chest heaves and he's sweaty.

I frown. "What's wrong?"

"Noth—ing's wrong," he hitches.

I leave my spot by the wall, taking a few steps closer, studying him. "You look absolutely exhausted, Christian. Are you ill?" Putting my hand to his forehead, I feel if he has a fever. He's sweaty and warm, but not hot. At least not feverish hot.

"Funny," he gasps, his eyes following the track of my hand as I let it drop. "Isn't it quite the déjà vu? The wind, the cold."

"Not the isolation, though," I say quickly.

"Not the isolation. Hell, I don't ever wanna see a forest again in my life." He sighs deeply and kicks off his boots. "You should stay, you know."

"No. We have to go!" Sleeping in the same house as him... bad, bad idea. Memories of ropes and belts, of pain and half-panic run through my mind, making my blood run hotter through my veins.

"You don't *have* to go, Ker. I have like... six guest rooms or something." He sighs. "Just... be reasonable for once. I won't touch you. I know what you said."

"No, we can't—" Why the fuck does *that* hurt? I should be pleased. *He's* reasonable for once. Then I take a closer look. "What's wrong, Christian?" He suddenly worries me. He looks as if he would fall into a heap if I poked him.

"I'll tell you in front of the fireplace. After you've made yourself a bed."

"No! I—" A loud crack outside has us both jumping. I glance out the window but see nothing but my own reflection. "It's— I. Well—" I realize I can't justify endangering Cece and myself by going out into the blustery night. It's not impossible, not like in Canada, it's not like we're trapped, it would just be really stupid. And she is already asleep. I want to fight it, I want to find a way, but there is none that is reasonable, and I nod reluctantly. "Where do you keep your spare sheets?"

"In the closet."

"Where?"

"In whichever room you pick."

"I'll take the one closest to Cece."

"Okay." He turns his back on me and starts toward the living room. "You realize it's also the one closest to mine?"

I groan. I can easily picture the smug look on his face.

Cece's door is open. She snores lightly. Maybe I could sleep in there? Awkward doesn't quite cover how it feels to actually be making a bed in his house, and the little thrills that run through me have got nothing to do with his closeness. Nothing at all. Staying is practical, that's all there is to it.

When I'm done, I plan to quietly slip between the sheets and forget I'm even here, but I realize I have nothing to sleep in, and no toothbrush. My palms get sweaty just from the thought of going back down to him. I think of skipping the toothbrush, sleeping in my clothes and... somehow it doesn't seem very mature.

I tiptoe down the stairs. He sits with his back to me in one of the two leather chairs that stand in front of the fireplace. A few strands of hair peek up from over the back of the chair and a foot dangles from a leg slung over the armrest. I know these chairs are new, and still they look old and worn. I wonder how much that cost. Everything has a price.

I wonder what it will cost me to get a toothbrush.

Everything has a price.

I won't touch you.

A shiver runs through me.

I'm not very good at keeping my promises.

"Hey," I say. "I wonder—"

"Sit. Please. Just for a few minutes." His voice is soft, and still I sense the underlying need and it makes my stomach clench again. He leans back, his eyes on me. In front of him, on a little sideboard with a smoky glass surface, stand two glasses filled with a creamy, yellowish content.

I clear my throat. "I was just wondering if you have a toothbrush I could use."

"Sit with me and I'll give you everything you need."

"Just a little while then, it's late and I should—"

"It's eight thirty, Ker."

My cheeks heat up. I hate when he sees right through me. The fire is crackling peacefully, though, and the warmth is nice. There's a throw blanket on the arm rest. Grabbing it, I hang it over my shoulders before I sit down next to him and gesture to the glasses. "What's this?"

"Eggnog. It's warm. It's really good."

"I've never tasted it."

"Then what are you waiting for?"

I enjoy the feel of the warm heavy glass in my hand before I sip on the sweet creamy contents. The bourbon in it makes my taste buds bounce with surprise. But I like the aftertaste. "It's nice," I say.

"Aw, come on. It's more than 'nice'. This is an art form."

"The art of making eggnog?"

"The perfect eggnog. And not only that, but the fire, the blanket, the weather. Perfect conditions."

I eye him suspiciously. "For what?"

"For a moment of real peace."

I'm quiet. I'm bad at that. At taking it easy. I rush from this to that, avoiding time for thought, time for reflection. It's a habit I've perfected over the years. I had no idea he did things like this. I wonder what he and Cece do when they're alone. Suddenly, I'm jealous. They have something I don't take part in. I take a larger sip and enjoy how it warms my chest. This *is* nice.

"Are you all right now, Christian?"

He glances at me and smiles. "Sure I am."

"What happened out there? You were exhausted. I've never seen you like that."

"I was."

"Why? What had you been doing?"

"Nothing."

"You said—"

"Nothing now. It happened a year ago to be precise."

Canada. "I think you need to explain that."

He drinks from his glass and licks his lips before he continues. I force myself not to get lost in the sight of the wet trail on his lips.

"After I'd been in the river, I developed a pneumonia that almost killed me. I was slipping in and out of consciousness. I don't remember much of it, just... that I couldn't get enough air."

"I had pneumonia too."

"Yeah, but you were treated in a hospital, with antibiotics." He doesn't care to hide the bitterness in his voice.

"So..."

"When I finally got care a lot of the damage had already been done. I live at half capacity at most. My lungs are badly scarred. I'll never run a marathon again."

"You've run a marathon?"

He is quiet.

"Are you ever gonna tell me more about yourself?"

"I just did," he answers softly.

"Did you run a marathon?"

He smiles and suddenly the heat from the fire seems hotter on my cheeks than a moment ago. "Yes."

"Wow," I say as I wave my hand in front of my face, trying to cool myself off. "That's impressive."

"Yeah, it is. It was exhausting. But fun."

I sit and contemplate that for a few moments, taking another sip from the creamy yellow liquid. I've never thought he had an actual life outside of the killing business, and it hits me hard how little I know about him. How is it that I feel like I know him so well? I know how he reacts to things, what makes him smile and—God, yes—what makes him angry, what triggers him, his preferences in bed... I have no idea, though, what has shaped him, what made him into the Christian I met a little more than three years ago. For the first time I realize I want to know.

"Huh," I say, and take another swallow. The bourbon burns in my chest and makes my heart beat faster. I sink deeper into the chair and close my eyes, listening to the wind that pulls and tears at the old house. I jerk as he suddenly speaks.

"What? A little more information than you wished for?"

I open one eye and peek at him, finding him grinning. "Oh, no, no. I'm sorry. I got lost in thought."

"You want pajamas to go with that toothbrush?"

"Yes, please."

"Sure. I'll get you something. If you tell me what you were thinking."

I regard him. "How very you. There're always terms."

He spreads his hands. "I'd be helpless without them."

TWENTY-NINE

Christian

S he inhales deeply, on a little shudder, then lets it out in a heavy sigh. "I was thinking that I don't know that much about you."

I tilt back my head, leaning it against the backrest, and study her. "You'd be surprised, Ker. You know more about me than anyone else."

"That's not saying much."

"Maybe."

She raises the glass toward me, her index finger pointing at my chest. "You know a lot about me."

"In a way, yes. It was my job. And then... it spiraled a bit out of control." I grimace. More than a bit.

She looks down and fiddles with a loose thread at the edge of the checkered throw blanket. My whole being reaches toward her. I want to take that little hand and hold it tight until she knows she is safe with me.

"Are we enemies, Kerry?"

She goes absolutely still, then she slowly raises her head and meets my gaze, the fire making her eyes gleam. "No... I don't think so," she whispers.

"Good."

Silence mounts between us and it gets increasingly harder to breathe.

"So, uhm... you went for a walk today?" Kerry's eyes dart to the fire and then back to mine.

I laugh. "That was an awkward moment just then, wasn't it?"

Kerry hugs the blanket tighter around her and stares into the fire, shifts, shifts again.

I glance at her occasionally and finally our eyes meet. "I'd almost given up hope on that," I say.

"On what?"

"On being non-enemies."

"I don't think we've been enemies for a long time," she says slowly, her voice huskier.

"But that's not the same as being friends, is it?"

She shakes her head.

"Are we friends?" I ask.

She's silent a few moments. "I'd say we're friendly."

My heart jolts. "That's a start."

"Yes."

"All right." I slap the armrest and stand. "Let's go get you those pajamas and a toothbrush. I'm a man of my word."

"I thought you were bad at keeping your promises," she blurts out.

I spin around. Her eyes widen, as if she realized what she just said. Oh, yes, I am. With her I fucking am. This gentleman thing is getting old. Clearing my throat, I take the half-stair in three long strides and pull open the closet in the corridor opposite one of the bathrooms, pulling out a pile of what she needs. As I turn, I find her close. Too close. Her sweet scent reaches my nostrils and something primal in me awakens. A couple of steps away there's a bedroom with a door we can lock, Cece's asleep, and my cock suddenly screams for her touch.

"It's nice to have the both of you here. Good night." I push the items into her arms and dart toward my room without waiting for an answer. I'm trying to keep my promises. I really am.

I lie and listen to the whining and cracking for what feels like hours, tossing and turning, repeating the moments in front of the fireplace over and over. She's here. In my house. They both are, breathing life into it. For the first time in the ten years I've owned it, it feels like a home and not just a house with my bed in it.

PREPARING A LAVISH BREAKFAST, I THEN GO AND WAKE MY sleepyhead of a daughter. She widens her big brown eyes as she sees me.

"Daddy? Daddy's house?" She looks around her. "My room!"

"Yes, sweetie, now go see if Mommy's awake and tell her there's breakfast."

Cecilia darts out of bed and follows me into the corridor. I point to the almost closed door next to us. "She's in there," I whisper. "Go hop on her bed."

My daughter swings open the door with full force and bounces into the room. I'm quick to get out of sight

"Mommy! Slept at Daddy!" Cecilia squeals.

I smile. I had no idea it would mean so much to her, if I had known I'd have gotten her to sleep here much sooner.

"Bwekfast!" There are bounces and steps. Kerry groans. "Mommy come," shouts the little one, and then: "Mommy's in pajamas, Daddy!"

Slicing the last of the avocado, I can't help feeling a bit smug, thinking about the robe I hung on a chair in her room a little earlier. I wonder how pissed she'll get.

Pitter-patter of little feet, and soft steps of slipper-clad adult feet make me turn. Kerry has a little blush on her cheeks, and she pinches the robe as she raises an eyebrow.

"You couldn't resist sneaking in, could you?"

"Did you mind?"

She purses her lips before she scoffs and turns toward the table. "Oh my goodness! Who's going to eat all this?" she gasps.

"Me," says Cecilia and jumps up on a chair, reaching for the avocado. Her little fingers manage to grab hold of a good chunk of the slices before Kerry grabs her. "Yum! Cado!"

"Let her," I say. "There's more where that came from."

Breakfast is a little awkward. Cecilia is chatty and chirpy. Kerry keeps stealing glances my way when she thinks I'm not looking. She devours toast, her black coffee, avocado, tomato, and cucumber, with cottage cheese. There's also prosciutto, poached eggs, and three different marmalades.

"More coffee?" I hold up the pot.

Kerry darts up, wiping her mouth, and then begins the process of getting crumbs of egg off Cecilia. "We should be going. Be right back." She takes Cecilia's hand and pulls her with her. When she comes back, our daughter is clean, and Kerry has dressed.

I stretch out my legs and put my hands behind my head, studying her. She's got my favorite jeans on. The flowery ones. The ones that fit so snugly around her ass. I wonder if my gaze burns her as much as the sight of her scorches my gut. She agreed to celebrate Christmas here. I caught her in a weak moment right after her mom had told her she'd be going away to the Bahamas for a week with a man.

Wondering if she regrets it, I take a bite out of a lovely piece of toast, butter half melted, slices of avocado and some grains of salt on top. It tastes wonderful, full of sin, just like her. Reluctantly, I follow her to the hallway. I don't want them to leave.

She grabs her jacket and bag, hiking Cecilia higher up on her arm. "Well... we're off."

I lift my chin in acknowledgement. "See you guys on the twenty-fourth."

Kerry nods and then stiffens. "We said Christmas Day."

I move in on her and put my mouth to her ear, whispering: "You don't have a fireplace, a chimney, anything. Let her have the whole package, the full experience. And who knows, maybe Santa *is* coming this year." I take a step back and wink.

Kerry looks a little dazed, then her lips tighten as her eyes darken a shade. She crossed a line by sleeping in my house. She knows it. I know it. Something went down last night, in front of the fireplace. Something innocent, seemingly insignificant, but there's a shift happening between us, and she's just as aware of it as I am.

"Sure."

She grabs the bag tighter and shoulders open the door, almost stomping down the stairs. I can't help the grin that spreads on my face.

Christmas will be interesting.

THIRTY

Kerry

The week is intense. We make Christmas decorations with the kids at the daycare and throw a pre-holiday party for the children and the parents one evening. We comfort the ones who panic at the thought of Christmas, and gifts, and meeting relatives.

Cecilia and I celebrate an early Christmas with Mom the day before she leaves. I'm curious about this man who is suddenly more important than Cecilia and me, and she promises to introduce him later. I'm not sure I'm *that* curious to be honest.

I barely have time to think and all of a sudden, I wake one morning from Cece jumping on me and not from the clock's annoying buzzing. I pull her down under my blanket for a few seconds of enjoying her warm, soft skin. It's the twenty-fourth. Everything stills for a moment. I've promised to spend the night with Christian. Well, in his house. But that's quite enough. Cecilia squirms out of my bed.

"Go Daddy? Santa come?"

I moan. "Yes, sweetie. We're going to Daddy's today and we get to *sleep* there too. Again."

A few hours later find us standing outside the gates to Christian's house. Outside the greatness of Christian's house, now decorated with blinking white lights. He greets us with a wide smile and scoops up Cece before I even have time to catch my breath. They disappear into the house while he shouts back to me. "Make yourself at home. There's some white wine in the fridge if you'd like."

I look around me as I stroll after them through the hallway. He hasn't done as much decorating as I figured. There are three Christmas stockings hanging above the fireplace, and a large number of candles in a wide variety of holders, wood, brass, concrete, real stone which are spread all over the living room. It has a romantic feel I don't quite associate with Christian Russo.

My heart suddenly speeds up. Right, where was that wine?

Christian plays with Cece in the garden, tossing a ball to her and trying to get her to catch. In the simple game I see some of what probably makes him him: he never seems to lose patience, never gives up. I'm sure he is good at whatever he sets his mind to.

I study him while I take another sip from the glass. He doesn't move around a lot, and when he has to catch the ball, again and again, he walks instead of running. He really seems to have told me the truth about his condition. I wonder what it means for all of us, the fact he is somewhat disabled. Is it chronic? Will it progress? Should I worry?

Why should I worry?

When Cece shows signs of finally tiring of the games, I've downed my glass of perfectly chilled white wine, slouching in one of Christian's expensive patio chairs that he has put back in place after the storm subsided. Two heaters make the semi-enclosed space comfortable. He's panting soundly when he comes up to me, sweaty and grinning from ear to ear.

"You okay?" I ask.

"Yeah, yeah," he pants happily. "Did you see her catch it? She's a future Dan Marino, I tell you."

I laugh. "Dan Russo." Then I realize the mistake. "Ehm... Jackson. But Dan was more famous for passing anyway. She'd be more like Jerry Rice or Terrell Owens."

Christian looks amused. "Really? Shows what I know of sports." Then he winks at me and turns toward the house. "Time for dinner."

In the kitchen he hands me and Cece one dish after the other and we put them on the counter next to us. Bread, ham, cheese, a Christmas cake, and pudding. Then comes plates, forks, knives, he hesitates for a moment before handing me the bundle of knives and I scoff. Very funny. There's more: cranberry sauce, smoked salmon, gravy, salami, mortadella, parma ham.

"Who's going to eat all this?"

"We are," he grins. "I've had bad experiences from being under the same roof as you and I figured a little excess wouldn't hurt."

I almost choke. "You've had bad experiences—"

"And the remains I'll give to the Red Cross charity down at Lawson."

I stare at him. I don't know this man anymore. He opens the fridge again and backs away with something heavy. Turkey.

"You made a turkey? Did you make all this?" The doubt must be obvious on my face because Christian bursts into a laugh and pats Cece who looks up at him.

"Nah. I made the turkey and the cabbage, the rest isn't that much really. I just bought it."

He hands me a bowl of a greenish substance. I sniff it suspiciously.

"What's this? It smells like weeds. Like boiled weeds."

"Green cabbage sautéed with spices and with the drippings from the turkey and then cooked with lots of cream. Put it next to the stove with the turkey, we're heating it."

"Cabbage? You made cabbage for Christmas? What are you, vegan?"

Christian actually looks slightly hurt. "I'm not a fucking—" He gives Cece a quick glance, "vegan!" He leans closer and whispers in my ear, making me shiver all over. "She said fuck the other day. I'm gonna have to watch my fucking mouth." He leans away and grimaces and I can't help but giggle.

"Okay, I'll try your cooked weeds."

We work surprisingly well together and soon everything that needs to be heated is in its right places and we've set the table beautifully with lit candles reflecting in the silverware. An egg clock starts beeping from the kitchen, but we stand a moment longer together, admiring the beauty we've created.

"I didn't know you owned stuff like this," I say.

"What? The antiques?"

I nod.

"I'm interested in all things pretty." He nudges my shoulder with his.

I don't look at him. My cheeks heat up and it isn't from anger, or from all the candles. Or, possibly, it may be from the candles and I decide to blame them. I clear my throat. "Let's eat."

We find Cecilia – on the floor – with the cake.

"Ce!" I holler.

The cake is in molecules and what isn't smeared on her lies all over the kitchen floor. I take a long step and pull her up.

"Oh, Christian, I'm so sorry! Ce, what have you done?"

"Don't yell at her. There're disasters and then there are disasters. Just clean her up and put on some new clothes and I'll fix the rest here. When you come down, we'll eat. If someone's still hungry." He winks at her as she happily sucks at her fingers, completely oblivious to the mess she's caused.

"Cake! Yum."

"Yes, yum," I mutter and drag her off to clean up the little hooligan. I'm sure this is from his heritage, not mine.

When we come back down from the bathroom, Frank Sinatra is singing a soft slow melody. We talk about non-threatening things: with Cece, about Cece, about the food, about the almost-wintery day we had last week. I taste the cabbage on the edge of my fork. Cece ignores it completely.

"It's... spicy. It's funny... it doesn't quite taste like a vegetable, more like meat, or a mix maybe."

"You like it?"

"It isn't as bad as I thought it would be."

"Did you think I would eat anything that tasted less than fantastic?"

I frown and study him. "I don't know if I know enough about you to judge"

He winks and smiles. "Sure you do. You just refuse to acknowledge it."

"No, I don't."

He purses his lips as he wipes off Cece's face. Then he glances up at me. "We're gonna have to do something about that one of these days, aren't we?"

My heart lurches from his gaze. I scoot back my chair and catch Cece before she touches anything. "Honey. A fork is a good tool for eating, you should try it." I escape Christian's presence for a few relieving moments while washing her hands, then I put her in front of Disney. Cute Disney. Christmas Disney.

"When Santa come?"

I caress her cheek. "Tomorrow. You're gonna have to look out for him so he doesn't get stuck in the chimney."

"Tomorrow," she concludes, and then she's absorbed by Donald and Mickey, and some new characters I don't recognize.

When I come back to the table Christian has lit more candles and has already put away most of the dirty plates. I find him in the kitchen where he's stirring a small pot.

"Do you want me to do anything?"

"Mmm, I can think of many things... But I'd be glad if you helped me get the last off the table."

I grunt and flee out of the kitchen, happy to occupy my hands with anything so I don't strangle him. I work quickly and as soon as I've finished, I sink into one of the chairs in front of the fireplace, nurturing what's left of my wine. I've taken a couple of sips when I hear him behind me.

"I'm gonna have to take that away from you."

I follow his moves as he settles in the other chair. He's holding two cups with steaming contents in his hands.

"What's that?" I ask apprehensively.

"Always so suspicious of my intentions."

I stare at him for a moment and then I realize he's right. It's as if I always suspect he's trying something. And he never is. He's been completely honest and straightforward with me since... well, maybe always. Almost. "Oh, God, Christian I'm sorry. I really am! Can I try again?"

"Sure."

"What's that?" I blush at how false I sound and he laughs.

"Fuck, Ker, that was awful. Just be yourself. This is Glühwein. It's kinda like with the cabbage, you take one thing and turn it into something else with the help of some cinnamon, ginger and a few secret spices."

I sniff the contents. "It smells nice. Like gingerbread."

He nods. "Many of the spices are the same. It's sweetened."

I take a sip and realize everything he gives me is good. "Will I die?" I ask.

He nods, looking dead serious. "Yes, you will. But not from drinking this."

I can't help but smile and when he smiles too, I burst out in a laugh. I drink another sip and enjoy the warmth seeping through my chest. My head is buzzing, and I lean back against the chair. This is nice. It was right to come here. Last time was nice too. It's always nice. *He* is nice. A version of '*Hallelujah*' is playing on the radio and the beautifully sad lyrics go straight to my heart.

"This is a very good song."

"Jeff Buckley," he says. "It's one of the best songs he ever produced. He died much too young."

"I didn't know he was dead."

"Drowned, some twenty years ago. He was one of few who had gotten out."

I lift my head and give him a glance. "What do you mean?"

"Raised himself up out of his shitty childhood. It's a fuckin' shame."

"Oh." I'm not sure how to respond so I keep quiet. We sit and listen to the words. "They could be about us," I say after a while.

"That sad?"

"I don't know."

Jeff sings about hurting the ones who show weakness, the ones who show they care. I wince at the harsh words. It's just a song.

"Do you love me, Christian?" I ask with a pounding heart, shocked at the words that flew out of my mouth on their own accord, as if my brain had no say in the matter.

"Yes. I do."

My heart stutters. "How long—"

"A very long time."

THIRTY-ONE

Christian

A little voice behind us makes us both flinch. "Mommy, I peeded."

"Oh, no. Where, baby?" Kerry stands and takes Cecilia's little hand.

I dart up. "I'll get some towels."

On the radio they play *"Santa Baby"*. The little incident along with the music changes the mood in the room, lightening the heady atmosphere.

When we have finished wiping the couch and the carpet, we pull out some blankets and sit with Cece between us, snacking from a tray on her lap that's filled with plates of chocolate, figs, raisins, tangerines, roasted chestnuts, slices of pineapple and more. Disney is still celebrating Christmas and I wonder in how many ways it can be done, how many versions there are. This is most certainly one. Ours. Outside it has gone completely dark and I see lights in the distance, a ship in dark water. Like me. I wonder if I'm the light or the ship. Or the darkness.

"It's getting late for her," says Kerry. "You think we should eat some more before I put her to... or if you want to put her to bed that's fine, I mean... I didn't mean."

She stutters and blushes. Things are changing between us, almost by the minute, and I need to find my place, where I stand, and she clearly feels the same.

"I don't know. You hungry Ce?" I ask.

"Choc'late." She grins.

"I guess not," I say and shrug as I turn to Kerry.

We remain sitting a little while longer, quietly watching the flickering TV screen and the cartoons' adventures. Finally, Kerry kisses our daughter goodnight and hugs her until she starts squirming. I feel her eyes on my back when we leave the room.

Tucking in Cecilia, I tell her that she needs to sleep really fast if Santa's gonna make it. Her eyes go wide, then she nods and squeezes her eyes shut.

When I come back down, Kerry seems to have lost herself in an old black and white movie.

"Classics?"

"Sister Benedict struggles to save her church in "*The Bells of St. Mary's*", she puts a finger to her lips. "Shh."

I take a detour past the kitchen and pour us some wine. Handing her a glass I then sit next to her. When the end credits start rolling, she turns to me. "That one was amazing. I hadn't seen it before. How did it go?"

I frown.

"With Cecilia," she adds.

"Oh, that was easy. I told her she had to go to sleep quickly because Santa only comes when children are sleeping."

She smiles. "That true?"

I shrug. "Fire's still burning. You wanna watch TV some more or—"

She stands. "Fire sounds nice." We cross the large, mostly empty, living room and head for the two comfortable chairs. In hers I've placed a small box wrapped in silvery paper. Kerry gasps. "I didn't bring you anything!"

I nod at the gift. "Open it. Please."

She carefully peels off the paper and lifts the lid. A beam of brilliant beauty hits my eyes. I take in its beauty, still amazed at my catch. The necklace is made of platinum, Art Deco style, with small diamonds, emeralds and one hanging pearl in an intricate pattern creating a small heart shape.

"I can't accept this," she gasps. "It must've cost a fortune."

"Do you like it?"

"It's— it's so beautiful. But I can't—" She clutches it, looking as if she'll never let it go, her eyes wide as she takes it in. "I can't let you give me this."

"Why not? It's not like I have anyone else to buy gifts for except the two of you."

"You could save the money and give it to charity," she whispers. I look at her, deadpanned. She sighs. "I love it. Can I try it on?"

"It's what it's meant for," I say, my voice suddenly thicker, the joy over her surprise overwhelming me. I motion for her to turn around, then I push her hair to the side, the tips of my fingers stroking the soft skin on her nape. Goosebumps rise under my touch, and it's not the only thing that rises. I hang the necklace around her neck, snapping it into place. Her hand flies up to touch it as she turns, her fingers tracing the outline of the heart.

"Let me see," I say and push her hair back over her shoulder. It hangs perfectly, heavy around her slender pale neck, as if it had been created with her in mind. "Beautiful."

"Can I see?" she asks. I smile wider and she almost jumps out of the chair and heads for the nearest mirror, the large one in the hallway.

When she comes back, she has a goofy grin on her face.

"It belongs around your neck," I say, almost breathless from her beauty.

"I didn't bring you anything, Christian."

"Yeah, you did."

She shakes her head. "No."

"You're here. You and Cecilia. You have no idea what that means to me."

She frowns and throws her arms around her chest, looking aghast.

I put a hand on her shoulder, and to my surprise she doesn't freeze up. "What's wrong?"

"Nothing. Everything! I can't believe how you've changed. It's like you're two different people."

"I know."

"You really are trying, aren't you? I've just refused to accept it. I've just kept judging you for... how you were, a long, long time ago."

"I've—"

"No, let me talk. I've never given you a second chance. Not for real."

"You haven't had any reason to... I haven't—"

"I know you haven't asked for it, and I've been wondering about that for a long time. Why you haven't... Who—"

"Yes?"

"Who are you, really? I mean, the Christian I met first was so sweet, listened to my sniveling, whining... and then you turned into the most awful man. And now you've been..." Kerry throws out her hands.

"Been?"

"Which one of them *are* you?"

Who am I? I've been many men. I've been who I needed to be, what circumstances forced on me. I was a boy who turned into a man way too early, too abruptly. I was wounded, traumatized and still I had to be a rock for my younger siblings, including a newborn. I was raised by an emotionless woman who bathed me in steel, poured acid and hate into my veins until I became the merciless killing machine she needed. I met Kerry and found a human inside the beast, became a father and tamed the demon. He'll always be there, the other Christian, the ruthless creature, and I can never promise that he is gone, but for her I want to be more. I will be more.

How do I explain all this?

I am all of them.

"You were really nothing but a hit, a job, until you turned around that night, in that bar, and looked at me with the most expressive eyes I had ever seen."

Kerry looks like she's about to object and I raise a hand to silence her.

"I didn't follow you home to be cruel. I couldn't pull myself away. I needed more of you, I wanted to know what it was about you that suddenly made me hesitate."

"You tried to kill me. You didn't hesitate."

"I wasn't given a choice."

"Salvatore?"

"He threatened my sister."

"*God*, I wish I had punched him harder!"

I laugh and stroke her cheek. "I was born into this. I was taught not to question an order, was taught to obey."

"Where did you grow up?"

I hesitate. I'm not used to talking this much about myself, and it makes me uneasy. She tightens her lips and I realize I have to open up, or she'll never trust me.

"Chicago. I was born and raised in Chicago."

She stares at me. "I moved there, trying to get away from you. I'm such a loser."

"No, you're not. You couldn't have known it was my turf."

"What was your family like?"

"Us kids had to look after each other. Dad died young. He left Mom with five kids between the ages of fifteen to newborn."

"That's terrible!"

I grin. "It is, isn't it?"

"You don't look too upset."

I shrug. "It got Mom off our backs. She took over the business. On paper one of her cousins ran the business, but in reality, it was her. She's a ruthless bitch. Everyone's afraid of her."

"She doesn't like me," she mumbles.

"She'll come around."

"They all blame me for you almost dying. Twice."

"We look after our own. You're with me, no matter what. They'll have to suck it up and deal with it." She shudders and looks away, wiping furiously at her eyes. I lay a hand on her shoulder. "Kerry?"

She doesn't shy away, and when she leans in, ever so slightly, I pull her to me. She rises from her chair and falls into my lap. My heart stops for a moment, then I lay my arms around her and hold her tightly to my chest. We sit in silence. I listen to her breathing as we watch the fire eat its way through the last log until there's nothing but a large pile of intensely glowing charcoal.

"I always felt something for you," she whispers.

"Ditto." I squeeze my eyes shut, forcing myself not to hope for anything as I wish for everything.

"In all this time, Christian Russo, you've never asked me to forgive you. You've said you're sorry a thousand times but you've never asked me for forgiveness."

I fight to draw the next breath. "I've never dared to assume you were ready."

"I want you to ask me."

My head spins and a shudder runs through me as I hold her gaze, drowning in her beautiful dark green eyes. "Kerry, will you please forgive me for—" I swallow so hard it hurts. "—taking without asking, for cheating you into believing I was someone I was not, for drugging you, hurting you, scaring you, stalking you and assuming I could make you mine without even making an effort, for taking you for granted, and for believing you were weak and moldable." He's silent for a moment. "Kerry. I am so, so sorry. Please, forgive me."

"Yes," she whispers and my world tilts. "Christian."

"Yes?".

"Please put your hands on me."

THIRTY-TWO

Kerry

I feel like I'll faint when he cups his hand around the back of my head and pulls me to him. His breath is hot on my lips as he hovers near without closing the distance. I groan and lean in, pressing my lips against his, opening my mouth fully to his exploring tongue.

"Oh God, Kerry," he moans, the sound rumbling through his chest. "What do you want?"

I sit with my body twisted awkwardly and, breaking the kiss, I shuffle around until I straddle his lap. He looks up at me, searchingly, questioningly and when I sink down, pushing the apex of my thighs against his rock-hard bulge, his eyes roll back. I smile. I can give him pleasure. I want to give him pleasure.

"I want you to sit absolutely still." Giving this man any kind of order is terrifying, but I have to try this.

Christian's eyes flash dark and dangerous, making my stomach lurch. What am I doing? I'm already hot and needy. He has to feel how electrified my pussy is, tingling desperately for him to touch me, to fill me. I rock my hips, making him gasp. Glancing over his shoulder, toward the dark entrance to the corridor to the bedrooms, I make sure we're alone, then I lean back and undo the first button on his dark gray shirt.

"You're walking a dangerous path," he whispers.

"Oh yeah?" I lean in and kiss the little patch of warm skin that I've freed, right below his Adam's apple. It moves as he swallows. I savor the warm scent of sandalwood with a hint of leather as I flick open the next button, and the next, pushing the shirt aside, widening the gap. His chest hair rasps delicately against my chin as I move my lips down the sliver of bared, caramel colored skin.

"Oh yes," groans Christian. "You're a breath away from me ripping your panties apart and taking you right here and now."

"Restrain yourself. You're such a caveman."

He grips my chin and tilts my head up, catching my eyes. "Caveman? Really?"

I grind my very damp pussy against his cock, making him exhale on a shudder. "Yeah. Pull your woman to the bed by her hair-caveman."

He scoffs. "I'll indulge you. A little while."

A thrill runs through me at the hint of a threat. The right kind of threat. I want him. I want him when he takes, and when he gives. I want him so fucking much to push me down and ravage me, but I want to know, just once, that he'll really see me, and hear me. That he'll respect my wishes.

I undo the rest of the buttons, freeing his chest and his amazing six-pack of a stomach. I poke him, then I trail the ridges with the tip of my index finger, down to the waistband of his pants. "You've done some serious working out."

Christian rocks up his hips, pushing against me. "I've been frustrated," he mutters.

Opening the clasp to the belt, I then pull it off him, loop after loop, slowly gathering more and more around my fist. When it's free I wiggle it in front of him as I raise an eyebrow.

"You want it?" he asks.

"I was thinking I'd try it on you."

He barks out a loud laugh. "I'd flip you over in a second, love. I'd like to see you try."

I purse my lips, then I drop it on the floor. "Guess not," I mutter.

"Good girl."

I stick my tongue out at him and in a flash, he grabs my head and pulls me to him, claiming my mouth. Moaning, I push at his chest. "I'm not done," I mumble into his mouth.

Letting me go, he then puts his hands behind his neck. "All right. Give me what you've got."

Sliding out of his lap, I hold his gaze as I unzip his pants, and stroke the hot hard length through the fabric of his briefs.

He moans, a low almost-growl that shoots straight between my legs. Then I stop abruptly. "Cecilia. I... don't want her sneaking up on us."

Christian groans, then he stands. "Hold that exact thought." Darting up the few stairs to the corridor at the far end of the room, he soon comes back with a little device he fiddles with and then places out of sight behind the back of the chair. "Baby monitor. No sneaking now." He plops down in the chair again. "Now, where were we?"

"Oh you clever boy."

Grinning, he nods toward his crotch and I'm more than happy to oblige. I kiss along the trail of hair that disappears under his briefs, then I begin to pull them down, a little at a time, as I hold his gaze.

"You fucking tease," he moans.

I pull the rest of the way, freeing his magnificent cock. My pussy clenches at the sight, but I'm caught up in the seduction, in the illusion of control, and I want to play a little longer. I know it won't last. Sooner or later Christian will take over, and I know what happens next. I both fear it and long for it. There's pain, and there's heat, there's intense closeness, and emotions I never knew existed before I met him.

Licking a path from the base of his cock up to the tip, I then take it in my hand and wrap my lips around it and begin to move. Before, I never knew what a turn-on it is to kneel before a man and pleasure him, seeing and hearing him lose himself in what I give. The submissive stance is mine to give, not his to take. I don't even know why I know this, but instinctively I do, I feel it with my whole being. I am his, because I give it, because I'll let him take me.

There's liberation in the thought and when I stop pleasuring him, my eyes watering from gagging, having taken him as deep as I possibly can, I only move my hand up and down and meet his hooded gaze. I know I'm ready.

"I want you to take me, Christian."

His eyes turn nearly black as his nostrils flare. "How?"

"I— I want you to take me hard. I want you to hurt me, and scare me. I want to give myself to you."

He sits up straighter and inhales sharply. "I got the impression I've been too rough with you."

"Well... you've never asked, have you?"

"That's what bugged you?"

I nod.

"Oh, baby. Get the fuck over here then. Stand up."

Darting to my feet, my heart leaps to my throat. What did I just start?

His hand slides in between my thighs and move up under my dress, up to my drenched panties. Pushing them to the side, he slides his thumb along my slit, back and forth, spreading the juices, teasing my clit until my legs tremble, electrifying my whole body, my whole being.

"Oh, you're wet," he growls as he grabs my panties and pulls them down until they fall to my feet and I step out of them. "Spread your legs wide."

My dress covers my naked pussy, but he doesn't lift it, instead his hand finds its way back up to where my legs meet and then he pushes his fingers inside me in one rough move. I grit my teeth against the brutal handling of my sensitive flesh, but at the same time heat spreads from his fingers, through my belly, along my thighs, making me writhe as he thrusts his fingers in me, spreading me open. He pulls out and suddenly pinches my clit. I jerk back on pure instinct.

"Don't move," he growls as his cock twitches, mouthwatering hard and thick.

I take a hesitant step toward him, his legs between mine, straddling him, but still standing, wide open, vulnerable.

His.

"You have a very hard time obeying, don't you?"

He grabs my butt cheeks and pulls me even closer, a finger, slick from my juices, finding my rear entrance, pushing inside. I jerk, but remain where I am. He's been there twice, but we never got very far as I clenched up and begged him to stop. He did other things then... tied me up, used his belt, pushed the limits for pain beyond what felt good, until after, when everything was good, when he caressed me and made me come, again and again, until I lost my notion of pain and pleasure and it all mingled into one.

He pushes further in, adding a second finger, his other hand finding its way to my pussy again, pinching my clit, hard. I twitch and moan from the lance of pain that spears through me but that soon turns into a furnace of desperate need.

"I'm going here," he says and thrusts in my ass, deep, rough. "And tonight we're not stopping until I've buried my cock to the hilt and claimed every little bit of your delicious body, Kerry."

A shiver runs through me. I've given myself to him, and he's going to take everything. He won't hurt me, not for real. I know it, and I trust him with my whole heart. It's a shocking realization, but I really do.

"I'm yours," I whisper, holding his gaze.

His dark eyes flash and my stomach lurches at the heat and raw savageness in them. "Sit on me."

I move up on the chair, kneeling on the cushion on either side of his hips, bunching up my dress in one hand as I support myself on his shoulder with the other.

"Get in position. Put my cock to your pussy, and then stay."

My heart pounds wildly in my chest as I let the head of his massive cock rest against my slick hole. The temptation to slide down on it and let him fill me is almost impossible to resist.

"Good girl." He holds my gaze as he starts caressing my clit, rubbing it, back and forth, circling, making it tingle and ache, making it pulsate. My thighs tremble and I can't control the whimpers that erupt from my throat as the laser sharp focus of a pending explosion gathers there. I can barely breathe, on the edge of losing myself when he grabs my hips and slams me down on him, all the way to the hilt. I come completely undone in convulsions that make me thrash in his hold. Burying my face against his chest, I grit my teeth to not scream as he begins to move in me, slamming me down on him over and over again and a new orgasm claims my body.

"Fuck, Kerry!" he groans. "Fuck!"

"It's—good," I gasp, limp in his tight hold as he keeps thrusting.

"Of course it's good. You fit me like a fucking glove. I've never—" He suddenly lifts me off him and stands, pulling up his pants. I wobble and he steadies me with an arm around my waist. "Come." Dragging me toward our bedrooms, he snatches up the baby monitor and belt and hauls me along with him to a room at the far end of the corridor. It's got a large bed with four bedposts, and then nothing else. No other furniture. The room is not wall to wall to our daughter's room and I have a strong feeling that's very much on purpose.

He gives me a push. "Get in there."

I stumble forward and turn in time to see him lock the door. Christian turns and stalks toward me, like a predator approaching his prey.

"I like seeing you like this."

"Like how," I whisper, my heart fluttering.

"At my mercy. Helpless. Afraid."

"I trust you."

Christian smiles, and my breath hitches from the beautiful sight. "Good. Get out of that fucking dress."

I finger the heavy necklace, the metal now warm and comfortable, then I turn and present the zipper to him. Goosebumps race along my spine as his warm fingers touch my skin. The air cools me as my dress falls open and I give a little shrug so it falls off my shoulders and sails to the floor. With a flick of his fingers, the clasp of my bra opens and I let it fall off me with yet another shrug.

"Raise your arms straight out and spread your legs."

Naked, my back against him, and trembling slightly, I do as he tells me. There's silence, then I flinch as I feel his chest to my back.

"Close your eyes. Don't move."

My arms shake slightly from holding them straight out. A soft, silky material touches my forehead, then he puts it over my eyes and ties it around my head. On instinct I break the stance and touch the fabric. His tie. Christian tsks and grabs both my arms, putting them on my back, holding them tight with one hand as he steers me forward.

"What are you doing?" I whisper, stumbling in the dark.

"Whatever I want."

"What do you want to do, then?"

"You ask too many questions. Bend over." He pushes me forward and I fall face first on the bed, my feet still on the floor, my ass presented to him. I tense, bracing myself for everything and anything. "Are you afraid yet?" His mouth is right by my ear, his breath hot.

"No," I say, but my voice quavers slightly.

"Yeah?"

Christian gets off the bed, letting me go, and for one brief moment nothing happens, then the first blow lands on my butt, full force. I'm rocked forward and my hips dig into the bed frame. I throw out my arms and grab the bedspread in my clenched fists, biting down on the whimper that wants to escape me. A second blow on the other ass cheek makes my skin explode, or so it feels.

"No," I gasp and wriggle to get free from his hand that pushes me down on the bed.

"You're mine, Kerry."

Smack!

"Mine to do with as I please."

Smack, and *smack* again. I gasp from the pain and tears spring to my eyes.

"I've been so fucking patient. Waited and waited for you to come around. You've no idea what you've unleashed tonight."

Suddenly a much more distinct, sharper pain hits my upper legs. Once, twice. I scream, pushing my face into the bed, forcing myself not to be loud. Is that the belt? Fucking hell! I shudder with need, with deep longing, as he drags his fingers gently across the pulsating tender skin, kissing the pain, mumbling words I can't hear.

I realize I really don't know what I've unleashed. We never discussed any limits, not anything. I cling on to the hope that this beast of a man behind me will listen if I safeword. A shiver runs through me at the thought that he won't, that he'll take and take and take, and then the same thought turns chill to scorching heat. Something inside me feeds off that same insecurity. I want him rough. I want him dangerous. I want Christian just as the man I met.

THIRTY-THREE

Kerry

"Tell me you want me."

"I want you," I say.

"Tell me you need me."

"I need you."

"Tell me you're mine."

"You're one fucking needy bastard."

His hand slides soothingly over my butt, slides in between my legs, finding my slick core. I squirm, wanting so much more. He grabs hold of my wrists, forcing my arms up on my back again, and with the blindfold every other sensation intensifies, multiplies.

The slap comes unexpected, hitting my pussy. I scream into the mattress.

"You are one fucking mouthy woman. Tell me you're mine." He slaps me again. But this time, the impact pushes me forward and then he yanks me back, pressing his hard bulge against my desperate flesh.

"I'm yours," I gasp.

Another blow sends spikes of agony and intense heat shooting all the way up to my scalp. "You always were, Kerry," he whispers, his mouth to my ear, the sudden closeness making me flinch.

"I need you," I whimper.

Christian pushes his fingers inside me, thrusting, stretching me open. My heart pounds so hard that all I hear is my pulse roaring in my ears when I feel his cock at my entrance and his fingers slide to my clit. Oh, yes, please!

"I know you do," he says, his voice a low rumbling, as he slowly, torturously slowly pushes inside, little by little filling me. "Oh, you're so tight," he groans and then he thrusts the rest of the way, stretching me to the exquisite limit.

I moan, pushing my hips back, like a bitch in heat. I feel like I'm losing my humanity, parts of what made up Kerry. I knew this would happen. Christian devours, and I've been so afraid, but I'm so alone and lost without him, and I'm ready to take the risk, because I love what comes with it.

His answer is to pull back and then slam inside again. Ruthlessly hard. He releases my arms and grips my hips as he ravages not only my pussy, but my everything. I feel like I'm dissolving in his hands. Something warm and wet falls on my rear entrance and he begins to push a finger inside. Deep. Deeper. Adding a second. One hand keeps caressing my clit as he moves in me, and the three sensations begin to build, liquify my core, making my legs tremble. I tense up as he adds yet another finger.

"Relax, baby. Push back on my hand."

I can barely control my breathing, my release so close, so cruelly close. In the darkness I have no control. It's both frightening and relieving.

He pulls out. "Climb up on the bed."

I fumble and stumble as I obey, and yelp when he grabs my hips and pulls me toward him. My ass is spread open and my heart pounds with apprehension. I know where this is going, and he's not gonna stop tonight. The thought shoots a bolt of heat right between my legs and makes my insides pulsate. I'm his. I never knew it could feel so right to give in and put myself in his hands. I force myself to relax when his thick cock pushes against my tiny hole.

"Be careful," I whisper.

Christian leans in and cups one breast, molding it in his hand. "I've told you. I'll never hurt you. Not really hurt you." He keeps pushing, rolling my nipple between his fingers and I gasp as that first resistance is breached. "Good girl," he pants. "You—" He pushes deeper, impossibly thick. "Are—" Deeper. My belly clenches as I'm spread wide, as my ass ignites in a pinching, stinging fire. "Fucking—" He lets go of my breast, and I haven't really felt anything but the scorching heat in my rear entrance for the last few moments. "Fantastic!" He stops. His hips connected with my ass cheeks. "You still with me?"

"Mm-hmm," I whimper.

He slides his large, warm palm over my ass, up along my back, to between my shoulder blades, then he grips my nape and pushes me down, hard, as he begins to move in me. I'm blindfolded, locked in place, and beautifully helpless in his hands as he thrusts, taking my last piece of resistance. Still immobilizing me, he finds my clit with his other hand and caresses it, in the exact right way, just like he always does. I clench up, harder and harder, until I can barely breathe.

"I'm gonna come," I mewl, not recognizing my own voice. Staggering on the edge of my release, I want him with me, I don't want to come alone. "I— Can't get—" I fight to hold back, which only makes it so much harder. "Pregnant there!"

Christian intensifies his thrusts and I think I'm gonna die soon. My heart can't take more, and neither can my ass. "You still not on birth control?" he pants.

"I am. I can't—" I scream into the mattress as my body takes over, overriding my mind and my will. I don't feel Christian, I don't feel his hands or the bed. It's as if I soar, blackness surrounding me, creeping inside me, filling me. I'm pulled right back, my insides still spasming as he roars and falls on top of me, clinging to me as if I'm a lifeboat and he is drowning.

"God!" He bites my neck, my shoulder, my ear, still moving in me, but slower.

"Ow."

Christian chuckles. "Where."

"Everywhere."

He laughs. "I doubt that." Nuzzling my neck, kissing the stinging marks from where he bit, he whispers, "Thank you."

"You're big," I mutter, coming down from my high, still tingly all over, and all the way deep into my heart.

"Did I hurt you?"

"Mmno..."

"Not good enough."

"Hey!"

"Just kidding, Ker." He moves, pulls out and rises. "Don't move."

"I couldn't if I wanted to," I mumble, my face almost buried in the mattress.

His warm, strong hand cradles my nape, then he slips off the tie. I turn my head and take him in, gut-clenchingly beautiful in the soft light that still manages to make my eyes ache.

"Right back, hon." He disappears into an adjacent bathroom that I hadn't even noticed, water flushes, and then he comes back with a towel that he carefully presses between my legs. I follow him with my gaze. I can't stop looking at him, admiring his toned body, his strong hips and thighs. He grins at me and falls down beside me. Sweat beads on his forehead and his chest heaves, but he looks happy. Happier than I've ever seen him.

He pulls out the comforter from under us and tucks us in, warm, tight and secure. The sheets smell clean and fresh. We don't. The sensuous weight of the necklace, the metal pleasantly warm, reminds me of his gifts. Not only the jewelry, but Cecilia, love, passion, strength and protection. I have just about curled up on Christian's arm when he gasps.

"Fuck!"

"What?"

"It's Christmas Day."

"So?"

"Her gifts. I gotta stuff the stockings."

"I'll help you."

We wrap ourselves in new towels and tiptoe past Cece's room. Luckily, she's still a heavy sleeper. After having accomplished our goal, he steers me to his room, moving me in front of him, steering me to his own bed. My skin already longs for more of his touch and he doesn't disappoint.

This time there's no hurt. There is tongue and lips, and soft, careful lovemaking.

After, he pulls me into his arms again, but I push him away and motion for him to turn around. Then I wrap my arms around his waist and spoon up behind him, reveling in the warmth he radiates.

"Merry Christmas," he mumbles.

"Mm," I mutter, already drifting.

When Cecilia barges into the room I feel like I haven't slept at all. I rub my dry eyes and make sure the sheet covers us properly. It must be early. It's still black outside.

"Mommy, Mommy, Santa was here!" She waves with a small box. Then she stares at us. "Mommy slepted Daddy!"

"Mm." I wonder how we're going to explain this, but our daughter doesn't crave explanations. She wedges her little body between ours, on top of the sheet, and starts unwrapping the gift. Christian's eyes meet with mine over her head and warmth spreads in my chest from the way he looks at me. Cecilia triumphantly waves with a small pink and golden jewelry box before she drops it on the bed and slithers away to find more gifts from Santa.

I lift the sheet. "We should go to her." I tingle all over when a warm, strong arm wraps around my waist and pulls me back down.

"Soon," he whispers and presses against me, capturing my mouth with his. I cling to him as if for dear life and wrap my legs around his, ensnaring him. His dark eyes are filled with warmth and we lie in silence, listening to the sounds from the living room of paper tearing.

"We're gonna have to visit the Salvatore household tonight, hon."

My heart makes an unhealthy leap and a groan escapes my throat.

"There's no getting away from that. There'll be a gigantic Christmas party, like every year, and my uncle doesn't take no for an answer."

"Who'll be there?"

"Everyone."

I groan again and bury my face in the sheets.

"Christmas is the time for forgiveness," he says and lets the tips of his fingers trace the hairline on my nape. "If you could forgive me, then anything is possible." I inhale deeply and let the air out on a shudder. He pulls me to him harder. "I'll take care of you, Kerry. Now and always."

There's no getting away from meeting his family. Not today, not in the future. I've chosen this man and with him comes his baggage, a mob family, ice cold, dangerous men and women. I've stood up for myself before. I can do it again.

I kiss him on the earlobe, then graze it with my teeth. "I trust you. I'm with you, I'll stay with you. I've chosen you, and it means I've chosen the rest too."

He lifts his chin in silent acknowledgement. "Do you love me?" he asks, echoing what I asked him last night when everything changed, when our worlds finally melted together.

"Christian," I catch his hand, twining my fingers with his. "I have loved you for a long time. Thank you. Thank you for her, for tonight. Thank you for being you."

The look he gives me shatters my heart. I have never seen someone so naked, so happy, and so afraid.

"It'll be all right, you know," I say with a profound feeling I'm holding his heart in my hand. I could crush him with a flick of my wrist, but he is my whole world too.

"Marry me," he says.

My heart leaps, but I tsk and he widens his eyes.

"I want you on your knees, with a ring."

A sly smile spreads on his face, his gaze devouring me. "Yes, ma'am. Your word is my law, will always be."

"Always?"

"Except in bed."

I laugh. "I can live with that."

Till death do us part.

EPILOGUE

Kerry

"Y ou look absolutely stunning, honey!"

Mom flutters around me, correcting invisible wrinkles. I haven't had any of the champagne I was offered, I just brought the glass to my mouth and pretended. The new life I carry inside doesn't yet show, and it will be my and Christian's secret for a little while longer.

Staring at my image in the mirror, I'm amazed at how this all came to be.

"Isn't she pretty?" Mom turns to Bianca Russo who, with her perfect hairdo, and extravagant makeup, I've come to realize, is way too similar to my mom. They're both women who fight for what they want, carry themselves with pride and plow through life, determined to bend everyone to their will. They're also both deeply involved in making me the prettiest bride in history.

Bianca fiddles with bobby pins, even though my hair already looks fantastic, red with newly added highlights, most of it high up on the back of my head, but letting little curly tresses fall along my nape. There are diamonds in my ears, and a thin platinum chain around my wrist. I have Christian's necklace around my neck, and I chose the simple, creme-colored, bare-shouldered dress to go with the beautiful jewelry, rather than choose jewelry after my dress.

My whole soul reaches for him. I haven't seen him since yesterday.

On a couch in the far end of the room sits Chloe, feeding little pieces of bread to Cecilia. Our gazes meet and Chloe smiles shyly. We still haven't talked. I know she was away. I know things happened to her that changed my happy-go-lucky friend and hardened her, but we're slowly finding our way back to each other, and the rest will come. I hope.

The door slams open. Gayle and Rebecca storm in, their cheeks a little rosy. Just like Chloe and Cecilia, they have pale pink dresses, all in different styles. I made no one maid of honor. How could I choose? They're all equally important to me, all in their own right. Rebecca stands for light-hearted fun. Gayle has known me the longest and centers me. She knew my father. She can hold her own against my mother. Chloe knows all my darkest, dirtiest secrets. I don't have to pretend anything with her.

"Girl! It's time," says Rebecca.

"The fricking church is full, Kerry, you wouldn't believe it. Who *are* all these people?!" Gayle spreads her arms wide.

My gaze flickers to Mom and Bianca. "I think they're relatives to Christian."

"The Italian side of the family decided to join," says Bianca, and that's clearly all the information we get.

"Kerry, you're so beautiful," says Gayle. "Cecilia, doesn't Mom look like a princess?"

"No. She should have worn pink," says my soon-to-be three-year-old, "and the skirt isn't fluffy."

Chloe laughs and puts the sandwich back in the box. "*You* look like a real princess, hon."

"America doesn't have princesses."

Bianca spins around and crouches before Cecilia. "They do now."

Cecilia squirms, a shy smile on her face, then she throws her arms around Bianca, who stiffens visibly.

"You're the best gramma ever!"

My mom looks from me to Bianca and Cecilia, then back to me. "I can't win, can I?"

"Mom," I whisper, "it's not a contest."

Her eyes narrow as she glances at Bianca again and I sigh. The contest is clearly on.

"Wanna see Mommy marry Daddy, then?" Chloe puts a stray lock of hair back behind Cecilia's ear.

Bianca pulls it right back out, letting it fall in a corkscrew curl along her temple and Chloe throws out her hands, looking at me, rolling her eyes.

We all straighten when the bells start ringing and my pulse skyrockets. St. Patrick's Church is gigantic, and it's filled with people I don't know, and a few that I do know. There'll be a choir, a boy soprano singing solo, the ceremony will be part in English and part in Latin. Suddenly I want to escape out the window, jump from the second floor and just run. Chloe must sense my panic because she comes right up to me and grabs my arm.

"It'll be all right, hon. Christian loves you, you love him. That, and your baby, it's all that matters. The rest... you'll get the hang of it. Just, you know—" she bumps her hip to mine, nudging me, "grab'em by the balls. They like you more than you think."

Bianca claps her hands and opens the door. The bells are still chiming, the sound louder now, echoing in the stone corridor. We move as one unit. Rebecca holds up the back of my dress. Chloe clutches my clammy hand. We all seem to hold our breath, standing outside the giant double doors that lead into the chapel, and when the organist starts playing Mendelssohn, I choke up. The custodian swings open the doors and I take in the massive chapel, the people, the flowers, my knees going weak. Chloe squeezes my hand reassuringly, then she starts walking down the aisle with Rebecca and Gayle. The moms go next, together, no partners by their sides. Two proud women who I think will find each other eventually. My eyes fall on Salvatore. He's standing to the right, impeccably suited up, calmly waiting for me and Cecilia.

I swallow and give him a nod. He winks and I step up to his side. He's giving me away. He didn't ask.

I give him my arm and whisper to Cecilia, "It's time, baby."

A female custodian gives her a little basket with flower petals. Everyone turns to look at us as we make our way down the aisle. In front of the altar stands my man, my soon-to-be husband, my tall, intoxicatingly beautiful partner, and right then and there, calm washes over me and everything in the world is all right again.

He's mine.

I'm his.

It was always us. It just took us a little while to understand it.

Are you ready for more?

I have a **BONUS CHAPTER** for you.
Type BookHip.com/VZXMNWA in a browser
or scan

Next up: the Russo Saga finale.
Christian finally got his Kerry and all is good.
Except there's one more dark mystery to crack. What happened to
Chloe? How did she end up with Salvatore?
**Read the pitch black, depraved, steaming hot madness that is the
Russo Saga finale in CAPO.**

BEWARE of darkness. You might have realized that Salvatore doesn't do cuddly.
The last book is about Chloe and Luciano.

(Flip the page for a preview)

CAPO - THE RUSSO SAGA FINALE

BOOK 6

Chloe

"I don't know," I moan as they wheel me past my broken front door. I heard them knock. I couldn't even scream. I've never felt so helpless in my life. I kept whispering to the dispatcher that I was here, that they had to break in, that I couldn't move. Finally, after a loud crash, cops and EMTs seemed to be everywhere.

"Who did this to you?"

"I don't know," I slur hoarsely.

What else can I say? Tell on the mob and die.

In the elevator, things begin to get weird. The ceiling spins, the walls expand. Their voices seem to come from farther away. I feel weightless.

"What'd you give—," I try to wet my lips, "me."

"A shot of morphine, hon—"

She keeps talking, but I float off. Being in not-so-much pain is amazing.

"I don't know." That's my mantra the next couple of days. I don't know. I don't remember. It was dark. No, he didn't speak. No, I don't know anyone who'd want to hurt me.

I cry when I look at myself in a mirror for the first time. My face is blue and swollen beyond recognition. My right arm is wrapped in a thick, warm, itchy cast and sits in a sling. My broken nose has been straightened out and I've got bandages both across it as well as in the nostrils. Not being able to breathe through my nose is more panic inducing than I'd have ever thought. My mouth dries up and I feel like I'm choking. It doesn't help that I have several broken ribs. Standing is hell. Lying down is hell. Sitting is a nightmare.

My emotions are all over the place, my mind a cacophony of images, voices, happy times, horrible times. One moment I long to talk to Kerry. She knows. She'd understand. The next minute I loathe her existence. It's not a pretty feeling, the darkness that creeps into my heart when I think about my former best friend. It's not her fault, but my rational side has given way to primal fear, and in that void she's the root of this evil.

I don't sleep. I feel his hands on me, hear his low voice in my ear, his promise that he won't give up. I don't know why I'm alive. Does he still think I know where Kerry is? Is it even safe to go back home? The realization chills me to my core. It isn't. Of course I can't go home. Oh my God. I can't talk to anyone about this. I don't have *anyone*.

If it hadn't hurt so fucking much I would have curled up and cried. I cry anyway, flat on my back, the tears wetting my temples in floods before they soak the pillow.

I have a minor brain hemorrhage and they want to make sure it disappears. 'Only' a small amount on the surface of my brain, apparently. My arm will heal, my bruises and swellings will subside as time goes by. The body is an amazing organism. If I'd have been a car, they'd have just dumped me in a scrap yard and dismantled me. I don't know if I wish I'd have been a dead thing, or if I really want to be alive. I beg them for sleeping pills, but I still wake up around two a.m. from my own whimpering until I realize I'm not at home, and that I'm not being beaten.

One day they release me. I'm not ready. The hospital bed, the staff outside my room, they've become my safety blanket. I don't want to go out there! Kerry was stupid. She went home. I can't go home.

I call a cab, giving him directions to a hotel downtown, fighting the panic that's clawing in my chest. There are too many people on the streets. My enemies can be anywhere. I need to plan how to proceed from here. I think of my friend, of her fear. She must have felt exactly like this. Or worse. That man, that monster that came after me in the dark night, in my own home – he befriended her first, he fucked her, he made her believe there was something going on between them. Then he tried to *murder* her. The only person I could have talked to about all this has disappeared because of him. I live in terror every minute because of him.

No, not him.

Salvatore. Luciano Salvatore.

As I sit in the taxi that drives fast through the streets, a wave of hate suddenly surges through me. My whole fucked up life flashes before my eyes. I've had a few good years, and now it's all gone to shit. I fled once, I'll be fucking damned if I do it again.

I tap the window that separates me from the driver. "Hey, we're going somewhere else." Giving him the address of the center for autistic children, my heart begins to pound harder. This is really fucking stupid, but I need to tell that creep Salvatore exactly what I think of him. He's robbed me of everything.

The staff look horrified when they see me. I say bike accident and that I forgot something when I quit, that I just want to try to find again. Two minutes alone with our archives give me an address to little David's father. Young, shy David, who loved Kerry. He must be about nine now. Salvatore took that away too when he had David removed from our care. It crushed my friend. He walks over everyone, destroys everything.

Even more determined, I hop into the taxi again and give the guy the new address. It's a fancy neighborhood, a world away from my home address, and the shabby street where we stand right now. He gives me a once-over before he shrugs and starts rolling.

It's not hard to see that it's the right place because Salvatore surrounds himself with security. Three men in black suits pace the gravel outside a wide barred iron gate. The taxi driver meets my gaze in the rear-view mirror. He looks as nervous as I feel. I'm sweating and my mouth is desert dry.

I lean forward, feeling the eyes of the guards on me. "Can you come with me? Please?"

His eyes widen. "No, ma'am. That's definitely not in my work description."

My heart sinks. "Can you at least wait here, please?"

His gaze flickers between me and the guards, then he licks his lips and nods. "I'll wait a little to the side. Meter will be running."

I take a deep, shaky breath. I have to do this before I change my mind. "Okay, fair enough. I won't be long."

He looks skeptical, and I don't like it at all. What the fuck am I doing? I jump out of the car, give him one last glance, then I close the door and put my palm on the roof as the car immediately starts rolling. With a heavily pounding heart, I turn toward the gate and the serious men who stand there. They have lined up, and somehow they look taller and wider than they did a few seconds ago. A gun, catching a ray of sun, glints in the belt under a suit jacket, and almost changes my mind. My legs want to take a sharp turn to the left, to where the taxi waits. No! I need to settle this. I lick my swollen lips. My face is still strained and tender. My arm doesn't really hurt anymore, safe in its cast, but my head aches and every breath I take is a bitch on my broken ribs. I ran once. I made myself a new life. My friend fled for her life. This is for Kerry as much as for myself.

Fuck Luciano Salvatore!

My legs feel as if they're filled with lead as I walk up to the one who looks like he's in charge. "I need to speak to Salvatore." Every cell in my body tells me to run but my mind forces me to stay put. I think of Kerry as I left her at my cousin's house, her posture stiff and unnaturally straight. I wonder if that's how I come off too.

They look at each other and two of them bark out a laugh. One of them doesn't move a muscle, he just keeps staring in a very discouraging way.

"Now why would we let you do that?"

I'm at a loss for words. "Please."

The man in the middle, the one who spoke, pulls out a gun and gestures with it toward the road. "Trot along, little girl."

I freeze up. The blue-black metal of the handgun glints. It's not aimed at me, but a slew of memories assault me from the sight. My parents shot to death in their car. One of my brothers assembling weapons as I walked in on him a few years later. I knew then it was all going to shit. Next time I saw him, my worst fears had come true as he had been thrown in county jail. My aunt and uncle weren't having it anymore. My other brother had already moved out. I was nineteen and I fled from everything. I'm not fucking doing it again.

"I know where Kerry Jackson is!"

Well, I don't, but I'll sort that later.

"Is that supposed to mean anything? Get lost, lady."

I gape as my cheeks heat up. I don't know why I thought that was important. Maybe because I was beaten black and blue because of it?

"Well, check with your boss," I spit.

I lose the staring contest as my eyes flicker between them. Of course, I do. I'm fucking scared out of my mind. But I'm pissed and I won't budge. I raise an eyebrow, as does he, then he puts his hand to his collar and turns away. I hear him speak, but I can't make out the words.

The other two stand with their arms crossed over their broad chests as they look me over, their lips curled in distaste. I'm suddenly uncomfortably self-conscious about the absolute mess I am. My insides squirm, but I force myself to stay still.

I jerk when the gate starts moving and the man who spoke comes up to me, grabbing my good arm. I wince. 'Good' is relative. It's also been beaten and he's squeezing my bruises.

"Ow."

"Move," he growls.

I stumble next to him as he strides up the driveway, toward a beautiful white mansion. To the far right stand several exclusive cars, BMW, Mercedes, Tesla. The lawn is perfectly trimmed and emerald green, the bushes cut in shapes of balls, and cylinders. Birds sing and it all seems both very unthreatening and completely lethal at the same time.

He can't be all bad, can he? He's a father. There's got to be a streak of humanity in him.

A rough man in the dark in my apartment. Merciless beating. My friend scared witless. No. He has no redeeming qualities. As we walk up a long set of granite stairs the loathing in me grows. I'm gonna fucking tell him what he needs to hear.

When the door opens I jerk back, instinct telling me to run, but the fingers around my arm hold it in a vice grip, and all I do is hurt myself. The man who has escorted me pushes me toward a blond giant with a crooked nose. He looks me over, stone-faced, but I still see a hint of curiosity when he takes in my swollen face and the cast.

"I'll take it from here," he murmurs, a slight, undefinable accent to his voice. "Come."

My legs shake as I walk toward him, across the threshold. My stomach is in knots and I fight to keep my breathing under control. I keep the vision of Kerry before me, broken beyond recognition, heart, body, and soul. My own pain is still vividly present with every breath I take.

I have to do this.

The hallway is stunningly beautiful, but I only register it in the periphery of my mind. I have tunnel vision as my gaze closes in on an oak door on the far right, toward which we're clearly heading.

I jump as the man next to me knocks on the door, and then opens it. I see a bit of hardwood floor and an oriental carpet, then I'm pushed inside and the door closes behind us. He's standing too close behind me and I stumble forward a step, my back crawling from his presence.

In the middle of the room stands a giant desk, an old-fashioned, dark wooden desk. On it an ashtray, a laptop and a few sheets of documents. Next to it stands a man, tall, dark hair, impeccably dressed in a gray suit. Luciano Salvatore. He doesn't move as he looks me over from head to toe, and then back up to my face before he slowly removes his suit jacket and hangs it over the back of his chair. He takes his time, and it seems as if the clocks have stopped. I stare, transfixed, as he rolls up the sleeves of his white shirt, showing off well defined muscles beneath the rich dark hair on his forearms.

Then he walks toward me. I glance over my shoulder, at the man behind me. It's not a comforting sight. His light gray eyes meet mine, his face expressionless. I look back at the man I'm here to see, my heart slamming so hard in my chest that I can barely breathe.

His eyes are slightly hooded and pitch black, his Roman nose and his sharp jawline make his face both rough and awe-inducingly attractive. There are vertical lines on his forehead and frown lines between his thick dark eyebrows. He has some years on him, looks to be in his forties.

"I was told you wanted to speak to me, Miss—?"

Read **CAPO** - the sexy, dark conclusion to the Russo Saga.

Also by Nicolina Martin

NICOLINA MARTIN lives with her daughters, her kitties, (and her dust bunnies...) in a little house on the Swedish west coast. She escapes the long, dark winter nights by writing naughty romance with morally gray heroes, strong heroines, and all the feels.

IF YOU LOVE THE SMELL OF PAPER:

I'm all for it

linktr.ee/martinpaperbacks

If you need to read *now* - get your instant dose of sexy e-books WITH an exclusive **discount**.

Visit nicolinamartin.com/collections/all

Apply promo code **Absolution10** for an instant 10% of off all ebooks.

West Coast Doms series:

- **Punishing Penelope**
- **Commanding Casey**
- **Saving Sandra**
- **Restraining Reeba**

Russo Saga:

- **Heat**
- **Ruin**
- **Shame**
- **Redemption**
- **Absolution**
- **Capo**

Standalones:

- **Mortem**
- **I Am Eve**
- **Sugar Princess**
- **Break My Chains**
- **Anomaly**
- **Her Vampire Hero**

Pure filth...

- **Honey Trap**
- **Firefighter's Pet**
- **Demon Lust**

For everything Nicolina
BOOKS, SOCIALS, ETC
linktr.ee/nicolinamartin

ACKNOWLEDGMENTS

Dedication

To my daughters, and my cats, for sharing Mom with her passion for the words.

Acknowledgements

Beta readers - who have read parts of, or the full manuscript, throughout its many shapes, thank you all!

My tribe - my wonderful group of readers who have come together in my Facebook group Martin's Misfits. You rock!

Sandra Havro for editing, and Deranged Doctor for the awesome cover.

Reader - thank you! What would I be without you?

Made in the USA
Monee, IL
30 November 2023

47839993R00180